THE
FINAL
OPTION
(Bahamas)

{Book 1 of the Final Option Trilogy}

AN
ADVENTURE
NOVEL

JOHN
ANDERSEN

THIS BOOK IS A WORK OF FICTION.

EXCEPT FOR ACTUAL HISTORICAL EVENTS,
PLACES AND CHARACTERS, WHICH ARE USED
FICTICIOUSLY, NAMES, CHARACTERS, PLACES
AND EVENTS IN THIS NOVEL ARE THE PRODUCT
OF THE AUTHOR'S IMAGINATION.

ANY RESEMBLANCE TO ANY PERSON,
LIVING OR DEAD,
ANY LOCATION,
OR ANY SITUATION
IS ENTIRELY COINCIDENTAL.

Copyright © 2016 by John Andersen

This book is dedicated to my wife, Suzanne,
and also to several good friends, who for reasons of their own, wish to remain anonymous.
Thank you for the help, expertise and encouragement you gave me,
keeping me on track throughout this project.
My wife, as usual, did a superb job in keeping the facts straight
and the story flowing during her proofreading of the drafts of this book.
That being said, any mistakes the reader may find, I acknowledge are mine
and mine alone.

Any comments, encouragement or criticisms can be left on the author's page
at goodreads.com
I check it on a regular basis.

Prologue

September 6th, 1622.

El Capitan Juan Ramon de Castillo, stripped of his uniform and his pride, clung desperately to the stump of the mizzenmast for dear life and threw heartfelt curses against his God heavenward, even as his ship disintegrated around him. He knew his blasphemous excesses would deny him what he thought to be his rightful place in the hereafter but he was beyond caring. After months of valiant effort by himself and his crew to bring the ship safely to its destination, this final challenge, this accursed hurricane, had defeated him. He cried bitter tears of regret at the thought of his failure to bring the treasure he carried in the hold of his command to adorn the palace of his benefactor, the King of Spain.

His old but still sturdy vessel, the Spanish caravel, *Nuesta Senora de la Navarre,* had left the sanctuary of the port of Cartagena sixty two days ago and should, if all had gone as planned, have been sailing more than halfway across the Atlantic Ocean by now in company with the rest of the ships of the yearly Spanish Silver Fleet. Unfortunately, because of an interminable delay in loading the fabulous treasure he now carried, caused by the sudden appearance of English ships at the entrance of the port, he had found to his annoyance that he was days behind in his schedule when he finally left and therefore he and he alone had made the fateful and unfortunate decision to bypass the rendezvous with the fleet in Havana. Instead of being carried by the swift, reliable current of the Gulfstream east of La Florida, he had been determined to attempt to sail the shortcut across the Navidad banks, sail east of the Baja Mar Islands and rendezvous with the main body of the fleet somewhere to the north of those islands which sprouted like clumps of weeds throughout the shallow sea. As he found out, much to his dismay, the best laid plans of men and mice often go astray, and although his plan was sound, nature didn't cooperate in the normally expected way.

He had barely committed himself to the winding, twisted and narrow channels between the ever present sandbars, numerous coral heads and shallow reefs directly across the deep water passage to the north of Hispaniola when, inexplicably, during the season of the most reliable sailing weather, he had been becalmed. For weeks on end the ship drifted aimlessly, at the mercy of the tides. From horizon to horizon in all directions lay an unbroken sheet of salt water, which was normally a sailor's delight. But they all knew that in most places except for the channels, that the sheet of water was only a foot or two deep. At times the Captain had been forced to send members of the crew into the longboats and tow the heavily laden ship away from sandbars. It had been an arduous ordeal. At all times the sailors had to take extra care of themselves because of the menace of the many sharks in the area. Those ominous black triangles stood clear of the water to amazing heights and all of the crew knew the dire consequences of falling overboard to share the water with those man eating machines.

Due to their gallant efforts, they actually grounded only twice, both times fortunately without damage, although once they had to wait for high tide to refloat the ship. The mainmast fairly bristled with the knives of the crew in a vain attempt to bring the winds that they needed to move the ship out of its predicament. The fresh water grew scarce, and they knew that they would have to replenish their supply before venturing across the wide Atlantic. Maybe even a provisioning call at Fort Matanzas in Saint Augustine in the far northern reaches of La Florida would be called for before they committed themselves to the crossing. Of course, by that time, the rest of the Silver Fleet would be well on their way and they would have to make the crossing alone.

Only after weeks of struggling were they able to break clear of the northern limits of the shallow banks which had held them prisoner for so long. The early days in the open, deep water before the winds came were like heaven to them, for there was rest for the weary men who had literally towed their ship across the sandbanks. Although the ship was moving very slowly, it was at least moving in deep water, and only the normal watches were being stood. This allowed the off watch to get some much needed sleep.

When the winds did come, gentle at first but continually increasing in strength, it was seen as a sign from heaven that God was watching over them. Soon, however, the men learned to curse at the wind, ever increasing in velocity, as the waves grew in size and power to pin their small ship on its leeward rail. Even the men who admonished the Gods with their requests for more wind by leaving their knives in the mainmast were cursed. The relatively small ship, which only a few days ago had seemed such a huge burden to move against the tides, suddenly seemed tiny in comparison to the size of the waves bearing down them.

Surprisingly, the mainmast was the first to go, sheared off without warning ten feet above the deck by a combination of a tremendous roller at the stern of the ship which slewed her to port and a terrifying rush of wind which twisted the vessel around and sent the sails in an uncontrolled gybe from one side to the other. The mast, which comprised the main motive power of this small caravel, toppled seemingly slowly, but carried with it the yards, sails, pennants, rigging, and the unfortunate sailors who had been aloft shortening sail. Only two of those unlucky enough to be thrown so rudely into the water made it back on board through that savage sea, the others succumbing to the wild water and their inability to keep up with the hard driven ship.

With axes and swords, the mainmast was quickly cut away, there being no question of attempting to salvage any part of it, for the shattered base of the mast, tethered at an acute angle alongside by the tangled rigging, was already trying to beat a hole in the hull. As it finally floated clear of the vessel, the screams of those unfortunate souls caught up in the lines or otherwise unable to swim to the ship, could be heard clearly above the incessant roar of the storm. Before such wind and waves, any attempt at rescue would have been foolhardy and both those in the water and those in the boat knew that the chances of survival in those conditions were slim to none. As the mainmast bearing its human cargo was left astern, many prayers were directed heavenward, both for the soon to drown and for the survivors.

At the Captain's order, all the remaining sails were quickly furled and the men allowed to come down from the masts and to go belowdecks to ensure their safety while the ship, with its tiller tied down fore and aft, was left to its own devices, to allow it to find its way the best it could through the tumultuous seas. But even this desperate plan failed to achieve its intended purpose of keeping the ship afloat. An hour later the foremast was torn from the keel of the wooden vessel like a rotten tooth, taking some of the outer hull planking with it. The warm salt water flooded in and the ship began to founder. Panic finally set in as the crew realized their vulnerability in remaining down below, and the surge for the gangway was instantaneous. Their timing was unfortunate, however, for at that moment another tremendous wave swept clear across the ship, taking with it half the crew who were emerging from the flooding hull. This wave also caused the mizzenmast to snap like a twig a few feet above the deck and it joined its brethren, floating free in the vast ocean.

As the next wave in line swept across the suddenly unobstructed deck, Juan Ramon felt himself being picked up by the unyielding force of the water, which was attempting to wash him overboard to join his crew. But he was determined to stay with his command until the end. As he slithered across the deck he managed to catch hold of the stump of the mizzenmast and through sheer determination hung on until the wave had dispersed its fury on the other objects on the poopdeck.

Suddenly, above the maniacal shrieking of the storm, his ears picked up another sound. Despite being immersed in warm tropical water, this sound sent an icy dagger through his heart. He had heard the deep, hollow booming of large, wind driven waves breaking on a reef only once before, when he had been shipwrecked in the Philippines during a typhoon some years earlier, but it was a sound that he would never forget.

He turned to face the direction in which the ship was traveling and the sight which met his eyes made him cry out in terror. The gray cliff, which met his salt encrusted gaze, was at least fifty feet above his head. The bow of the boat, burdened by the water in its belly, could not raise its head above the rebounded wall of water from the cliff, and was aiming itself towards the bottom of the ocean. As the water swept over him for the last time, he wept at the thought of never seeing his sweet Constanza again, knowing that his wife of just two years would be waiting alone for him at Cadiz forever.

He felt the strong suction of the warm water close over his head as he and his ship left the surface for the last time and with a sudden calmness, knowing that he could do nothing more to save the situation, noticed the lack of motion down below. His last conscious thought was of his father, Sebastian, the Count of Navarre, and presently the Governor of Cuba. He wondered idly about which his father would regret loosing the most; his youngest son or this fabulous treasure, which was now bound for the bottom of the cruel sea.

November 3rd, 1944.

Korvettenkapitan Ernst-Jurgen Schmidt braced himself awkwardly against the coaming on the conning tower of his command, the Unterseeboot U-362 as, once again, another huge wave slammed into the side of the boat. Its force sent tons of salt water skyward in sheets into the darkness to augment the driving fresh water coming from the storm which was roaring at him and his crew out of the east. The semi-submerged sleek black hull of the U-boat shuddered violently and heeled over again with this fresh assault on its forward progress and strained to right itself against the incredible fury of the hurricane which had beset them. The constant roar of the powerful diesel engines was consistently muffled by the shrieking and howling of the wind as the powerplants continued valiantly to do their assigned job of recharging the depleted battery banks of the boat, even as they attempted the immense task of pushing the boat forward against the out of control elements.

Schmidt, clad in foul weather gear over his uniform, let out a string of curses under his breath, bracing himself further into the more protected weather corner of the bridge in a vain attempt to stay dry whilst still maintaining his footing on the slippery and half-flooded bridgedeck. It was actually a futile exercise to try to preserve any semblance of comfort under the conditions they were experiencing. The wind, gusting at times to one hundred miles an hour, roared and moaned and whistled about the superstructure of the exposed bridge like demons from Hell. The water from the storm and from the ocean, dumped unceremoniously on all flat surfaces, cascaded in torrents from the decks of the writhing boat. Since it was four in the morning, visibility was almost zero, but even if it had been daylight, nothing of their surroundings could have been seen.

"At least, I'm a little more protected here than those poor souls," he thought to himself as he glanced backward and up, sensing rather than seeing the two lookouts braced in their cages on the Wintergarten, that part of the conning tower which was abaft the attack periscope and perhaps only fifteen or twenty feet behind him. The conditions that they were facing were well nigh impossible. He thought briefly about ordering them below but decided that, even though they probably couldn't see anything, and probably weren't looking, someone needed to be there and it might as well be them. As he turned and looked forward through the driving deluge, he could distinguish the bow of his boat only by the iridescent sheen given off by the almost continuous spray of foam which was thrown up as the sharply pointed U-boat plunged into yet another huge roller. The solid green water sped along the deck, totally burying the 88 M.M. deck gun, which was their primary defense whilst on the surface, before crashing into and half swamping the high conning tower where he huddled.

"This is a thoroughly miserable night to be on the surface at sea," he thought, and with great difficulty, studied intently his waterproof watch, slowly calculated the time remaining to fully recharge his boat's batteries.

The U-boat was finally settling into a kind of abrupt and abbreviated rhythm now, for while the confused waves appeared to be coming at them from seemingly all directions, the throttleman below played with the power settings of his engines and the helmsman, who was inside feeling the pattern of the waves against the pressure hull, attempted to steer courses which somewhat smoothed out the U-boat's wild gyrations.

"Only another four hours of this," Schmidt thought, taking notice of the slightly easier motion, which was due entirely to the efforts of the crew in the bowels of the boat, "then we can submerge to the relative calm of the water under the surface for the final run to our rendezvous."

As the storm raged on, Schmidt's mind performed one of those tricks for which the human computer is renowned. It shut out the prevailing conditions and wandered, away from the current situation and its discomforts to the circumstances that had led them into the dilemma which they now faced.

It had been a long but relatively uneventful voyage up until this storm had hit them 100 or so miles short of their destination in the Bahamas. Their departure from the often bombed by the Allies but still serviceable U-boat pens in the port of Brest in Occupied France, slipping out of the mouth of the Loire River and into the Bay of Biscay under cover of darkness, had been, as far as they knew, unobserved. At the very least it had been unimpeded, for they had sighted no vessels, and observed no aircraft, friendly or hostile, and the underwater journey to Dingle Bay in Free Ireland, after surfacing only twice to recharge their batteries, had not produced any causes for alarm.

Easing the U-boat toward the wild, rock strewn coast of the Dingle Peninsula by the light of a waning moon, guided only by a few temporary leading lights on shore which were held by men of the IRA, and watching the depth sounder carefully, the actual navigation to the first rendezvous had thankfully turned out to be much easier than he had imagined. There had not been even a sense of urgency or danger in this most important voyage of his long career. It seemed almost like a training cruise. He could not afford to let his guard down, however, for this was probably the most important voyage he had undertaken for the Fatherland. Perhaps the outcome of the war, even the Third Reich itself, depended on the successful completion of this mission.

As the seldom used rough stone and concrete landing became visible out of the gloom, their slow speed was reduced to barely crawling, and suddenly there appeared shadowy men on the dock to catch the heaving lines as they went ashore. Once the boat was secured, and with armed men standing guard, Schmidt stepped onto the dock to be greeted somewhat hesitantly by a short, stocky man who immediately started organizing the scores of men who appeared like ghosts out of the darkness. An engine started somewhere in the distance and shortly thereafter a large but very dilapidated truck backed slowly onto the pier and stopped opposite the loading hatch in the front of the U-boat, which had by now been opened by some of the sailors on board. A line of men was quickly formed between the truck and the hatch and soon a large number of small but stoutly nailed, heavy wooden crates were being loaded aboard the submarine, under the close supervision of Schmidt and the stocky man.

After 30 minutes of intense, backbreaking work, the truck was finally emptied and all of the men piled gratefully aboard it before the engine was started and it was driven back into the darkness. The two leaders walked together to the seaward end of the pier and stood for a while smoking cigarettes and talking quietly.

"I counted 297 crates altogether," said Schmidt, "so they are all accounted for."

"Yes, I counted them as they went aboard and got 297, too. Not that I would have expected anything else, these men are all good, honest and reliable. I wish we had more of them in my country."

Looking back down the pier and satisfying himself that they were still alone, Schmidt asked, "So, where do you go from here? Or am I not allowed to know?"

The stout man smiled ruefully before answering, "It doesn't really matter as long as you don't know the details. I am going back to the States to get a bunch of documents together so I can meet you at the rendezvous point at Eleuthera in the Bahamas on November the 4th. The details are here in this pouch. I should be back in the States before you get to the Azores." He handed Schmidt a thin leather pouch and, as if he had been dismissed, started to walk back down the pier toward the U-boat and the shore beyond it.

"How about a drink before you leave, while the gold is being stowed?" suggested Schmidt.

The stout man hesitated before answering. "Sounds like a hell of an idea to me. It is rather cold tonight."

They stepped off the pier and onto the deck of the submarine, entered a hatch in the side of the conning tower and descended into the cramped bowels of the U-boat. Weaving their way amongst the men and machinery which filled the confined space inside the pressure hull, they made their way to the captain's cabin, a cramped 8x10 cubicle, where Schmidt produced a bottle of Johnny Walker Black Label Scotch Whiskey and two glasses which he proceeded to fill.

"How the hell did you manage to get a bottle of this good Scotch? Even in America I haven't seen one of these since before the war started."

Schmidt smiled and said, "You'd be surprised what we can come up with when the need arises."

"In that case, it's a pity it ain't bourbon."

Small talk and several rounds of drinks helped disguise the smells of diesel fuel and body odor and the atmosphere was comfortably relaxed before the reverie was shattered by the appearance of another man who suddenly stepped into the compartment, produced a 35 M.M. Leica camera and snapped several pictures of the two men before they could react.

"What the hell do you think you're doing?" The stout man shouted, getting to his feet and starting towards the man. Before he could reach him, however, Schmidt grabbed his arm and stopped him.

"Allow me introduce you to OberGruppenFuehrer Hans Kessler," he hesitated for emphasis, "of the Gestapo. The man likes to record everything with that little camera of his," he explained before turning to Kessler.

"What can I do for you now?" Schmidt asked, struggling to but not quite succeeding in keeping the contempt out of his voice.

Kessler smirked, challenging both the captain and the visitor with his cold gray eyes to argue with his authority. Finding no resistance, he went through an elaborate pantomime of carefully putting his camera away in his coat pocket, and sneered, "I just wanted to let you know, mein Kapitan, that the boat is secured for sea and we can leave any time your visitor chooses to go ashore." Then with a smug expression on his face, and ignoring protocol, he turned without another word and left.

The stout man was seething with anger as he turned back to Schmidt. "Damn it all!!!" he swore under his breath, "I don't suppose that you could get those negatives and destroy them?" he asked.

"I doubt it." Schmidt shrugged. "He has pictures of everything. His masters seem to think that his behavior is acceptable. I might be able to get you a print, though." he said.

"I don't want a damned print! I want those negs destroyed!" He paused for a moment to gather himself, drew a deep breath and added, "I guess it won't matter as long as you make the rendezvous in the Bahamas."

"God willing, I'll be there."

"You'd better be! I have received word that some of my comrades have been able to secure some very important plans which you need to deliver to the Generals at their base in Argentina and, believe it or not, it is something which could yet win us the war!"

"Really? And what would that be?" Schmidt's expression and tone of voice showed that he was somewhat skeptical at the thought of the war being won by the Axis powers at this late stage of the game.

"They are plans for a new kind of bomb being developed in a place called Los Alamos in New Mexico. A much more powerful bomb. One which could change the outcome of the war. From the encoded signal I received from my operative yesterday, he has been able to smuggle out the entire plans package of the bomb and will have it for me in Boston when I return."

The stout man rose slowly from the table, suddenly weary, and the two of them left the cabin and retraced their route back to the hatch and out onto the deck of the U-boat. They shook hands and wished each other a safe journey and the stout man walked onto the pier while Schmidt re-entered the hatch, closed and dogged it down, and climbed to the bridge at the top of the conning tower. The diesel engines were started, the lines cast off and the remaining men scurried below and secured the last hatch.

The stout man walked off the pier and disappeared into the woods, where he turned and watched as the U-boat left the dock and slowly disappeared into the darkness of Dingle Bay.

"And I'll make sure you get yours, Mister Bloody OberGruppenFuehrer Hans Kessler." he muttered, clenching his fists, his eyes showing that his fury had barely abated.

The U-boat in which they traveled was a Type VIIC built in 1942, and although barely two years old it was already considered obsolete due to the high attrition rate amongst German submarines of late. Even though it was capable of 17 knots on the surface, all too often they were forced to submerge and rely on their electric motors for forward progress due to the presence of the enemy, and that was slow going at best. They could only achieve a maximum speed of 7.6 knots for 1 hour before having to surface to recharge their batteries, a process which could take as long as 7 hours. Maximum submerged range was 130 nautical miles but at only 2 knots, involving 65 long, cold hours of dreary boredom. With a maximum range of 8850 miles at the most efficient speed and on the surface, in order to reach the Rio de la Plata after a detour to the Bahamas, a mid point refueling stop was necessary and the Azores had been chosen because of their success in establishing a hidden fuel dump in that half-forgotten backwater of the war.

Several hours later and with daylight dawning, the batteries had finally been fully recharged and with the last smudge of land being barely visible astern, the boat submerged and the crew settled down for the long run to the Azores.

Eight days later, under cover of darkness, they crept slowly into a small, almost land-locked bay on the island of Faial in the Azores to refuel from that previously positioned fuel dump and allow the crew liberty. They would need every drop of fuel to get all the way to Argentina. In the harbor on the other side of the island, at a base leased to the Allies by the King of Portugal, an

American destroyer-escort was also refueling. The U-boat had barely finished securing her lines before Kessler, dressed in civilian clothes, leapt ashore and, commandeering a car, disappeared in the direction of the main business district. A heavily armed guard unit was assigned to protect the U-boat from intruders and saboteurs while the business of refueling was completed. Half the crew was given liberty, while the other half operated the hand pumps to replenish the sub's fuel supply.

Unfortunately, during this time, the U-boat was spotted by a man who, since Kessler had taken his car, had to walk to the harbor to report them. Several hours passed without incident before the first half returned and the other half of the crew were relieved from duty to partake of their liberty. Although the few hours ashore was not enough time to go anywhere, for this crew as for most submariners, just walking on solid ground, smelling and inhaling fresh air and seeing green things growing, was like almost heaven itself. Most of the sailors agreed with the more cynical members of the crew who asserted that if it really was heaven, they would have all been getting laid.

Kessler returned to the boat about midway through the second liberty, whistling and smiling as he walked back from his commandeered car, seemingly at peace with the world and all its citizens, and carrying a small package under his arm. As he boarded the boat, he ran into Schmidt coming up the stairway.

"Ah, mein Kapitan, I have something here which might interest you," he indicated the package he was carrying. "Do you have a few minutes?" he hesitated, smiling, but the smile didn't touch his eyes. Those cold, hard, gray eyes of a killer riveted Schmidt in place. "In your cabin. Now." He didn't wait for an answer, but brushed past Schmidt and started downward, knowing with certainty that the older man would follow him, despite any hard feelings between them.

When they were both in the Captain's cabin, Kessler ignored the annoyed, exasperated look on Schmidt's face, spent several minutes unwrapping, removing from the package and sorting through a number of small photographic prints which he, smiling, handed to the Kapitan. As Schmidt glanced at them quickly, aware of their implications, Kessler sneered, "These photos will be most valuable to us if your friend tries to get out of line, don't you think? Be sure to lock them in the ship's safe. I'm certain that the Amerikan government would be more than interested in learning who is smuggling their gold and secrets to their enemies."

Schmidt looked more closely at the photos that had been handed to him. Both faces were plainly visible and both had a somewhat startled expression on them. The setting in the Captain's cabin of a Nazi U-boat and Schmidt's uniform would show quite clearly the guilt of the American spy to anyone who saw them.

"Keep those for posterity, I have others. And, I have the negatives," Kessler said, laughing openly.

"One day, Kessler, you'll go too far!" Schmidt was very much annoyed at this man's arrogance.

Kessler's gray eyes suddenly narrowed to slits and his face hardened as he moved very close and hissed into Schmidt's face. "Is that a threat I hear, mein Kapitan?"

Schmidt blanched visibly, knowing full well the power his position in the Gestapo gave the younger man. "Not a threat, Herr Kessler, merely an observation." he said.

Kessler continued to stare into Schmidt's eyes intently, until finally under that withering glare, the captain looked down. "Just as well." he said triumphantly, and grabbing the package with the rest of the photos and the negatives, stalked confidently out of the cabin.

Schmidt sat wearily down on the bunk and looked at the photos more closely. He slowly placed the photographs in the top pocket of his uniform jacket, and then, without thinking, he grabbed the bottle of Johnny Walker, uncorked it and upended it into his mouth. After several swallows, he started to feel somewhat better, but he knew it was only temporary. He knew that sooner or later he would have to do something about Kessler and his arrogance.

Soon after the confrontation, the second liberty crew returned and, the refueling having been completed, the U-boat was once again prepared for sea.

They left that evening on their 10 day leg to Eleuthera in the Bahamas. The actual exit from the bay was an eloquently executed dance, for the American destroyer-escort, having been told of their presence by the observer, had left the harbor and was charging around the top of the island intent on capturing or sinking them. It was only by several judicious and well-timed course changes, following a crash dive in the still shallow waters of the outer parts of the bay that allowed Schmidt to bring his command and its crew back out to sea without damage. For six long hours they hugged the bottom around that volcanic island before the destroyer's captain, in utter frustration, decided to hunt the U-boat to the north of their actual position, while Schmidt crept south at one knot. Throughout the attack, the gold bullion, secure in its many stout wooden crates, remained evenly distributed throughout the boat, in nooks

21

and crannies and taking up space which normally was occupied by other crewmen and used for other purposes.

For this trip, they carried only two torpedoes, both already mounted inside their tubes, while the racks for the other torpedoes normally carried were taken up with crates of gold. The hand picked crew for this trip was far short of the usual complement so that under and in the bunks of absent crewmen the securely fastened, innocuous but valuable crates resided.

After their escape from Faial, the trip proved to be remarkably smooth, the water being flat and calm and the routine boring but normal, with crew members relaxing and sunbathing on deck in this little-traveled part of the North Atlantic, right up until two days ago when a deep low in the tropics far to the south of them decided to strengthen and a tropical storm was born. Since then it had been pure hell on the surface, at those times that recharging the batteries had been essential. The submarine's journey below the surface was smoother, but also slower and still extremely uncomfortable. The crew had had little rest in the past few days, for with the constant wild motion of the boat, even staying in one's bunk was an ordeal.

Something indefinable suddenly snapped Schmidt out of his reverie. A fresh and more powerful onslaught of wind and rain had hit the bridge and heeled the boat, sending Schmidt's body slamming into his corner, but as unpleasant as that was, that wasn't what had caught his attention. The motion of the water around him had somehow changed, and it seemed that the waves were higher and steeper and shorter in scope. But it was more of a feeling rather than something visual. Much of the time the spray from the bow's plunging descents obscured the surroundings and enclosed the viewer in a wet, windy cocoon of his own. He stiffened and listened intently, concentrating for anything out of the ordinary, trying to shake off the roaring of the wind as it assailed his senses, but he had been temporarily deafened by its constant assault.

Then came a different sound, a dull metallic thud deep within the steel structure below him, no louder or stronger than the crashes of sound that reached his ears from the storm, but it was a sound that reached him from his feet and not his head; it was felt rather than heard. It was instinct that caused Schmidt to quickly glance around and begin to assess the situation which he knew with certainty was wrong. It is the true mark of a blue water sailor who has spent his entire life at sea, to know when something is terribly amiss when all appears to be constant, and Schmidt was such a sailor.

Unbeknownst to the captain and his navigator, the storm which raged around them, pushing them steadily further to the west of their planned course, had combined with a strong westward flowing current which had set the boat much closer to the rock-strewn, sandbar-infested east coast of Eleuthera Island than they had realized. Since they had been unable due to the storm to get an accurate fix for the last two days, their dead reckoning plot showed them to be 50 miles east of their actual location. At their actual position in relation to the Bahamas banks, the depth of the water goes from 2,440 fathoms, literally off the scale of most depthsounders of the day, to less than 1 fathom or 6 feet in depth in less than 2 miles. Everything considered, it was indeed unfortunate that, having stared at a non-reading on the fathometer for 10 days straight, the sonarman chose precisely this moment to lurch back to the mess for a cup of coffee, and due to the reduced complement of the U-boat, left only an empty seat to witness the impending doom of U-362. The instrument faithfully informed the empty room of the seafloor's rise from 2000 to 1000 to 100 to 0 fathoms. When he finally returned from the mess, he stared unbelievingly at the indicator for a split second, dropped his mug of coffee and dove for the voicepipe to the bridge.

That same voicepipe in the corner of the bridge blared suddenly, startling Schmidt, "Achtung, Kapitan, this is sonar! We have no water under our keel!!!!" it yelled, the intensity and urgency in the voice cutting through the tumultuous noise of the storm.

"What!!!!" Schmidt yelled back, rooted to the spot, his feelings of misgiving suddenly realized.

"According to my instruments, Kapitan, we are aground!" the incredulous voice screeched.

Before he could react to this announcement, he felt a huge breaker pick up the stern of the U-boat and accelerate it toward the unseen shore. The sub had, in a split second, been transformed from a deadly ship of war to a 770 ton surfboard, attempting to ride the crest of the wave. Higher and higher the stern rose as the water became progressively shallower and, as the stern rose further, the sharp bow of the sleek vessel grazed and then buried itself in the sandbank, shuddering violently and coming to an almost complete stop. A furrow one hundred yards long and gradually deepening was created by the bow of the boat as the breaker, now towering higher than the bridge, continued to lift the stern. Schmidt knew it could not last and he was right. The boat slewed sideways and the breaker, in triumph, rolled the sub onto its back. Schmidt felt her going, leaning further and further to starboard until he knew that she would not return.

"At least that schweinhund Kessler will not survive this, either," Schmidt thought as he felt the deck tilting beneath him.

Down below, some of the crates of gold broke loose and, falling to the low side of the boat, added to the carnage, breaking bodies on their descent, and increasing the impetus the wave had created. The conning tower struck the hard packed sand and buckled, causing numerous high pressure leaks which immediately started to flood the boat.

Schmidt had been hanging on to the voicepipe and clawing for the coaming when, it seemed to him, the whole sub came down on top of him and the world went black.

The conning tower, being wedged in the hard packed sand, suddenly broke off entirely as the U-boat continued its death roll and it was thrown aside to be deposited in a cleft in the reef. The remainder of the sub, now filled with salt water, screaming and kicking, writhing in agony and hurting grievously at the cuts and abrasions of the coral reef, finally gave up its fight to remain a vessel floating free on the surface of the ocean, and became instead a tomb.

His first feeling was a weariness that went to the bone. His throat hurt, his muscles ached and he felt sticky and gritty all over. His eyes, although closed, hurt from the brightness, and he felt unable to move. His body was racked with pain and when he tried to open his eyes, the brightness and the pain got worse. He passed out again.

Hours later, he again struggled into semi-consciousness, and this time, although the pain and brightness were still there, he did feel stronger. He was about to attempt again to open his eyes when he felt a hand on his shoulder and heard the soft voice in his ear, "You jest lay still now, and don't you worry. I be lookin' out for you, mon."

He relaxed finally, knowing that, despite the odds, he had made it ashore.

Chapter 1

Present Day

The alarm clock radio announced its presence with a soft click. Enya's melodious voice came through the speakers singing 'Caribbean Blue' very low at first but gradually increasing in volume. Jack came awake and lay in bed, just listening. For him, everything else in the world stopped while an Enya song was playing. Although it was only 5 a.m., he rolled over and, when the song was done, got out of bed. There was only a slight movement of the boat as he drew back the curtain on the porthole and looked onto the pre-dawn gloaming and saw the beginning of another hot, glorious Florida day. He threw on a robe to cover his naked, six foot one inch frame, opened the door of his midship stateroom and walked the few steps down the companionway and up the stairway to the galley. One of the pleasures of living aboard his seventy foot Neptunus yacht was that everything was close at hand; rarely more than a dozen steps away.

He switched on the coffee pot, which he had prepared the night before, and opening the fridge, got out a carton of orange juice. While waiting for the coffee to brew, he drank a glass of the pure sunshine and walked over to his computer. Checking his email, he was quite surprised to see that he had no messages, apart from the usual spam. Invariably, one of the few clients he had left was up at 3 in the morning and would email him a query.

He switched on the TV, muted the sound and tuned into the Weather Channel, then went and poured himself the day's first cup of coffee while watching today's forecast, which as normal was for hot and sunny. He added two spoonfuls of sugar and milk to the coffee, because he liked things sweet, and walked the three steps up to the pilothouse where he sat down at the dinette table, sipping his coffee and watching the world sleep around him.

He liked mornings, especially when everything was still.

After a short while, having finished his coffee, he rose from the table, walked down to the saloon and turned off the TV. He went below, where he changed into shorts, a T-shirt and running shoes. Not being a slave to fashion or conspicuous consumption, his running shoes were not expensive Name Brand shoes, but value priced, generic trainers from the local K-Mart. He went through too many pairs of shoes during his training regimen to justify the extra expense of name brand shoes, which weren't any better than the ones he used.

He left the boat, carefully locking it up behind him, and stepped onto Pier B at the Hyatt Regency Pier 66 Marina, where the boat he lived on was berthed. As he walked down the pier, he stretched his leg muscles on the concrete utility posts occasionally and when he reached the parking lot, he broke into an easy jog. Taking his usual route, he passed under the finally rebuilt 17th Street Causeway Bridge, which took road traffic across the Intracoastal Waterway, and through the Harbor View Shopping Center, now much more run down and decrepit than it used to be, and into the old but still affluent community of Harbor Beach, where older homes commanded astronomical prices simply because of the value of the land upon which they sat.

He ran with a relaxed stride, only occasionally exerting himself by picking up the pace. As he passed the Point of Americas towers which guarded the entrance to Port Everglades, he took the beach accessway onto Fort Lauderdale Beach. Now the going got much more demanding, running in shifting sand being a great deal more difficult than on solid ground. As he ran he edged toward the hard packed sand at the water's edge, and as the sun rose out of the water to the east, his attention was drawn to a wonderful sight. An old, wooden schooner around 80 feet long was just leaving Port Everglades, bound for who knows where. The magic of the vision was the crew setting the sails, silhouetted in the rising sun. He wished he had brought his camera, and vowed once again to always carry it with him.

Born Jackson Elliott, Junior in Chicago, Illinois, he had moved with his parents to Broward County, Florida, when he was 10 years old. He'd had various identities over the years, JJ to his childhood and school friends, Jack to his present friends, Junior to his father, and Mr. Elliott to the majority of his clients, those who he didn't consider his friends. His father, Jackson, Senior, had soon become a top corporate attorney in Broward County and his mother, Anne, was still one of the best known society gadflies in the county. His parents still lived in the modest home on the canal in Victoria Park near downtown Fort Lauderdale that they had bought when they had moved down from Chicago. He still saw them occasionally, although less often than normal since his divorce three years ago. It seemed to him that his parents were more fond of his ex-wife, who was there every weekend, than they were of their only son.

Although his marriage had lasted for over a decade, she having been his parent's choice for an ideal wife, being the daughter of a close family friend, and they had manipulated and cajoled him until, finally, they had married soon after she had finished her schooling. Her parents, also from up north, had seen him as the ideal catch for their little girl. Consequently she had never needed to hold down a job. He had provided for her as soon as they had returned from their honeymoon in Europe, which turned out to be a six-week escapade of glorious bliss interspersed with a little sightseeing. Physically at least it had started out to be the perfect marriage, much to the delight of both sets of parents.

When he had left school his instincts had led him to a position with a stock brokerage firm as a trainee under an aging gentleman who had later become his mentor. Thanks in part to his parent's social and business contacts, he had quickly built up an extensive and very exclusive clientele, whom he served consistently and competently. His expanding business had allowed him, before his wedding day, to buy an expensive house in Coral Springs, one of the more affluent and exclusive suburbs west of Fort Lauderdale and almost in the Everglades, that river of grass which runs from Lake Okeechobee to Florida Bay.

Unfortunately for his chances of a normal and unexciting life, his expanding business had dictated that he spend more and more time with his clients to the detriment of his marriage. The arguments between them had been mild at first, accusations of his being married to his job was the most common complaint, and the making up afterward had almost made the conflict worthwhile, but soon the feelings had started to affect all their activities, both together or apart, and things that they had enjoyed doing together were soon left by the wayside.

He couldn't even guess at which point in time his wife had started seeing other men clandestinely, but sometime about five years ago, he had started to notice little things changing. By that time, their beautiful house by the lake seemed less welcoming after that long day at work, and was slightly less clean and tidy than usual and that she was never there on the few occasions when he called home but she always seemed to be able to come up with a reasonable explanation to his questions. His suspicions were further raised when a neighbor innocently inquired about the Ferrari in which his wife had been picked up the day before, and he knew no Ferrari owner who would have any business picking up his wife, at home, in the middle of the day.

Ultimately, it all came to a head when a business deal had fallen through and, instead of returning to his office, as he normally would have done, he went home in the middle of the afternoon and found his wife in bed with a total stranger.

Even through the pain, he still felt a certain amount of pride because of the way he had handled that situation; displaying no anger, producing no histrionics, and throwing no accusations at either of them, he had simply stood there and watched while the stranger had gotten dressed and drove away in his Ferrari. He had then sat on the edge of the bed and explained to his wife in very simple terms why she ought not contest the divorce and why not to expect anything in the settlement except the clothes she had accumulated in her wardrobe, since she had been wearing none at that time. He still thanked heavens that there had been no children involved. Perhaps if there had been, things would have worked out very differently.

After the divorce, she had taken up with the Ferrari guy, leaving Jack to wonder if there had ever been any love between them or if it had just been familiarity with each other that had made his marriage plunge off the deep end. Either way it had left him gun-shy, unable to trust his broken heart to anyone. He had become more of a loner, pleased with and pleasant in the company of others but much preferring his own solitude.

He had sold the Coral Springs home, at a tidy profit, and had rented a two story, two bedroom townhouse overlooking the Intracoastal Waterway. His business suffered a small setback as affairs of the heart and recovery thereof had taken precedence, but eventually he had migrated back into the world of the living one small step at a time.

His love of boats dictated his attendance at each year's Fort Lauderdale International Boat Show. The sight of all those beautiful boats instilled in him the idea that living on a comfortable motor yacht would be preferable to renting a townhouse, and when he saw the Neptunus 70, he knew it was just a matter of time before he bought her.

She was a thing of bewitching beauty to his eye, 70 feet of solid, practically bulletproof fiberglass, with a beam of 21 feet and a semi displacement hull which drew only 5 feet of water, an important requirement for someone like him, who planned to cruise in the shallow waters of the Bahamas.

She was definitely not a go-fast boat, as so many South Florida boats are. However, if pushed hard, she could reach 33 knots. He reasoned that if he wanted an adrenaline rush all he had to do was to take his car onto Interstate 95 during rush hour to experience that kind of feeling, especially when the snow birds from up North were down.

Her twin Caterpillar C32 - 1450 horsepower engines pushed her along at a top speed of 33 knots but most of the time she would cruise along quite nicely at 10-12 knots and at 9 knots her 1850 gallons of diesel fuel gave her a range of over 2000 nautical miles, which was sufficient to cross the Atlantic, if necessary.

Shortly after purchasing the boat, he had taken on a trainee in the business, and, acting as mentor for the new kid just as the old man of the firm, now dead, had once done for him, had been able over several years to transfer most of his workload over to his prodigy. He had still kept a few of his more select and lucrative clients and had, amazingly, found himself with lots of spare time on his hands, which he had used constructively to work on his boat, something he had found himself surprisingly good at, and also had taken the boat exploring in the South Florida, the Keys and the Bahamas areas.

He was suddenly aware that he was at Las Olas Boulevard already and, turning left, ran across the sand and onto the pedestrian walkway beside State Road A1A. Being so early in the morning, he walked past closed stores westward for one block to the southbound lanes of A1A, then started running south past the Swimming Hall of Fame and Bahia Mar, around the triple bend in A1A until he was once again at Pier 66.

After he had taken the Wall Street Journal out of his mailbox, he walked down B dock towards his boat 'Final Option', a name he had chosen in preparation for his departure from the stock brokering business. At 6:30 a.m., the world was finally beginning to stir around him, and he greeted several friends and acquaintances on his way past their boats. However, knowing his routine, they didn't stop him to chat.

When he reached his boat, he climbed the aft stairs onto the aft deck, unlocked the saloon door, stepped inside, relocked the door again and went below to shower and change. He always made it a point to lock up behind himself, because one could not be too careful these days. Although Pier 66 had good security and only minimal trouble with break-ins or vandalism, removing temptation was easier than dealing with the consequences.

After his shower, he glanced in the mirror, rubbing his chin and finding a little stubble but not enough to bother shaving. He dressed in his normal uniform, blue jeans, white golf shirt, boat shoes, baseball cap and sunglasses, and left the boat locked as he walked to his Isuzu Rodeo SUV. Again, he could not see the necessity to spend 50 or 60 thousand dollars on a vehicle, when one that served his purposes could be acquired for eighteen thousand.

Exiting Pier 66 he drove west on the 17th Street Causeway, turned right on U.S.1 and stopped at his usual breakfast place. He sometimes ate breakfast on board, but usually he preferred company, even that of strangers, if only for the noise. As he ate he perused the highlights of his Wall Street Journal, and made some notes on items he would have to check later. But first, he had a propeller to replace on his Novurania Rib semi-inflatable tender, the result of an early morning encounter with a rock in Whiskey Creek, and after breakfast he drove to the Yacht Chandlers to get it.

"Morning, Jack," the man behind the counter recognized him as soon as he walked in, because he was a regular customer. "What can I get for you?"

"Morning, Ben. Has the new prop for the Novurania come in yet?"

"I think so. Let me look in back."

While he waited, Jack looked around the ship's store, trying to find another useful gadget which he could mount on the boat. It seemed he was always trying to find another excuse to putter around on his boat. He picked up the latest copy of Southern Boating, which turned out to be the annual Bahamas Swimsuit edition.

"Here it is," said the clerk, returning with a brightly colored box. "Shall I put this on your account?" Each month Jack received a bill from the Chandlers for somewhere between $100 and $1000.

"Yes, please, and this magazine, too."

The clerk wrote out a sales slip for Jack to sign and then went on to the next customer. He left and walked to his SUV, where he placed his purchases behind the driver's seat, got in and drove back to the boat.

Jack spent the rest of the morning replacing the damaged prop on his inflatable, vowing never to run aground again, and chatting with his neighbors working on their boat until shortly after 1 p.m., when he finished up and walked the couple of miles to Grandpa's on Fort Lauderdale Beach.

He liked Grandpa's. It was his kind of place, where a person could watch a ball game on one of the many TVs, play a game of pool or just sip a beer while watching the numerous nubile young female bodies prancing along on the beach and A1A's sidewalks.

Today, seeing that the sun was way beyond the yardarm, he ordered a Dark and Stormy, a combination of Goslings Black Seal Bermuda Rum and Goslings Ginger Beer just for a change and, choosing an outside table, sat down in the shade of a palm tree. He reached into his pocket and came up with a small, rum flavored cigar and a lighter. For $100 a month, an ex-Cuban cigar maker he had met in Key West many years before, sent him a sealed box of 50 of the specially selected, hand rolled, rum flavored cigars which was his one foray into the drug world, unless you are counting alcohol and caffeine.

As he sat, savoring his cigar, sipping his drink, and appreciating all the young ladies in their skimpy bikinis walking by or sunbathing on the beach, a rather spectacular, long-limbed honey blond bombshell in a black one-piece and a brightly colored sarong walked past him on the sidewalk, eying him appreciatively. She slowed her pace to a crawl by pretending to window shop for a new bathing suit, all the time throwing inquiring glances in his direction, but apart from smiling pleasantly, he ignored her. He was not ready for any one night stands yet. The desire would probably come back in time, but until it did, he was not about to force something which wasn't there.

He did love this time of the year, when the days were not too hot and humid, and the nights were refreshingly cool. In a few months, it would be oppressively sweltering day and night, and all of God's creatures, man and woman included, would be searching for a rock under which to hide from the searing sun. While the winters in Florida were pleasantly mild, the summers could be brutal.

Reflecting on the schooner he had seen that morning, an idea suddenly struck him. To escape the searing heat of the coming summer, why not take his boat to New England for the season? With his cell phone, which he carried everywhere with him, the computer on the boat with its Internet connection, e-mail, and overnight letter and package service from various companies, he could conduct his business successfully, what little he had left, from on board his boat, anchored anywhere in America; or anywhere in the world, for that matter.

Suddenly excited, he took out his notebook and Parker pen, a gift from a client, and started to put his thoughts down on paper. He thought about times, distances, equipment, crew, paperwork, insurance, arrangements, maps and guides, weather and communications, and after an hour, came up with a rough working plan while consuming two more Dark and Stormies.

Just then his ever present cell phone rang for the first time that day. One of the few clients he had left wanted to place a buy order on the stock exchange. Jack made the necessary notations in his notebook and, after a few minutes exchanging pleasantries, hung up and called his prodigy at the office and gave him specific instructions on how and when to place that order.

Business seemingly concluded for the day, he paid his tab and started walking down the pedestrian walkway between A1A and the beach. He appraised with great appreciation the many young women on the white sand, who were mostly snowbirds on this Tuesday afternoon, people from the northern States and Canada who were here in Florida for anything from a few days to a few months duration, and who were instantly recognizable by either their pasty white or their lobster red skin depending on the amount of time they had been exposed to the sun on the beach. But he also looked with appreciation at the ocean, flat calm today, and the boats which sailed and powered upon its surface. Whenever he saw another boat going somewhere, he felt like taking off in his own, regardless of the consequences, and leaving this rat race behind him.

Although his investments earned him a better than average living, he was still uncertain if it could sustain an extended period of traveling, and going into debt was the one thing he desperately wanted to avoid. Even more than marriage, consumer debt killed a person's spirit of adventure and freedom. Debt condemned you to a specific place, more than likely enslaving you to a routine and boring occupation at a place you didn't like but couldn't afford to quit, putting in your required number of hours each week working for and with people you detested. Still, for him, the call of the open ocean was strong and persistent, and getting louder all the time.

He crossed A1A and climbed the steps to Beach Plaza, the new multi-story hotel-shopping complex built on the site of a former Spring Break favorite bar/lounge/nightclub of ill repute, which was torn down when the good city fathers of Fort Lauderdale, looking out for their flock, had decided in their ultimate wisdom, that Spring Break was too much fun, and brought in too much money, and that the tourist business in Broward County would be just fine without those millions upon millions of dollars which they eventually gave away to Orlando, Daytona Beach and South Padre Island. The county almost died before the 'family-oriented' people started to come, but even today it was but a shadow of its former self.

After looking in the windows of some of the fashionable stores on the ground floor, and checking out the latest movies playing at the ten screen theater, he went upstairs to Hooters, where immediately upon entering, he spotted an old friend behind the bar.

Twenty-four year old Janine Beaumont was a tall ebony black Bahamian girl whose beauty and ample proportions had made her one of the poster girls for the establishment for which she worked. She was also an extremely warm and caring person and one of Jack's few confidants, a shoulder to cry on in times of trouble and almost a little sister to him. He trusted her judgment completely, and was totally at ease in her company.

She was delighted to see him, and quickly made arrangements for Lisa to take over the bar so she could take her break and they could sit and talk without interruptions. When Lisa was safely positioned behind the bar, Janine brought a beer for Jack and a Coke for herself to the table which he had chosen on the terrace. This caused a general ripple in the entire establishment as dozens of mostly male heads turned to follow her stately, graceful progress across the room to the table, followed immediately by an almost audible groan as she put down the drinks, leaned over and kissed Jack, and sat down in the chair next to him. He glanced around the room in smug satisfaction and the looks that greeted him ranged from utter contempt to 'oh, well, what the hell'. He turned back to Janine, trying to catch what she was saying.

"Jack, it's so good to see you." She said. "Where have you been? I haven't seen you for ages."

"Oh, I've been around. Here and there and everywhere," he said sheepishly, feeling guilty and very aware of the considerable amount of time that had passed unnoticed since the two of them had last sat and talked.

"Hey, c'mon," she said, sensing the uneasiness he felt, "I don't have any claims on your time. And I wouldn't want you to feel obligated to come and see me. I just missed you, O.K?"

Jack relaxed, knowing once again why she was such a good friend.

"Listen," he said suddenly. "I have this crazy idea and I want to run it by you so you can pick holes in it. I know it sounds weird but I want to take the boat to New England this summer ...." He proceeded to get out his notebook and started to outline the entire trip for her as she sat listening intently and absorbing the details of the plan. She didn't interrupt him until she sensed that he had finally run out of steam when he said, "....So what do you think?"

She sat deep in thought for a few seconds, and then said, "O.K. Couple of things right off the bat. You are talking like you expect me to come with you..."

"Yes," he interrupted.

".... and that ain't gonna happen. I can't take a whole summer off from my job, because I wouldn't have a job to come back to. And I can't afford to miss all that work or all that money; I have bills to pay. I've just signed a new lease on my apartment and I wouldn't want to pay on that place if I wasn't here...." Janine was like most women, once you let them get started, you could only stop them with great difficulty and perseverance. "...And don't tell me that you'll pay me to work on your boat because I would only feel obligated to you and then we would probably end up sleeping together and that would spoil our unique relationship and I wouldn't want that because it would be the end of what we have now." She paused for breath and Jack jumped right in.

"Whoa, hold on there! I'm not forcing you to come. I just wanted you to be the first to know so that we could keep our relationship like it is. You know, with me, you have the right of first refusal."

"Thank God! For a moment there I thought you were asking me to run away with you, and I honestly don't know what my answer would be."

They simultaneously reached for their drinks as a moment of embarrassment allowed itself to dissipate, and slowly the atmosphere returned to normal as Jack reached hesitatingly for her hand and she didn't pull away so he held her sensitive fingers in his and stroked softly until she smiled and relaxed in his company.

"You know who you ought to go and see?" she said after a while.

"Who?"

"Sean!"

"Why?"

"Because he is your best friend, he's a boat nut like you, and he has the contacts to help you get a crew for your adventure, or at least for the beginning of it."

He thought for a moment and then said, "You know, you are probably right."

That evening, Jack went to dinner at the Four Leaf Clover, an Irish American pub owned by his good friend, Sean Brady. Originally from Dublin, Ireland, Sean had turned up in Fort Lauderdale some ten years earlier, and immediately bought a ramshackle building in the downtown area and quickly transformed it into the most popular and authentic Irish pub in South Florida. No one knew where Sean's money had come from, and he wasn't saying. They only knew that he had plenty of it; more, seemingly, than even his hugely successful restaurant could generate. His well known and easily recognized boat 'Leprechaun', a fifty foot bright green Cary, was the exact opposite of 'Final Option', Jack's slow, comfortable yacht. The Cary was loud, opulent, brash, sleek and fast. It barely made it from port to port before having to refuel, but its twin 2850 h.p. racing engines and Arneson drives moved it from Point A to Point B in one hell of a hurry.

Sean and Jack had met at the annual Columbus Day Regatta off Elliot Key in Biscayne Bay south of Miami several years earlier, when Jack and his wife had owned a 27 foot Chris Craft weekender, and had sometimes had a good time together on the water. The two men had struck up a friendship when they had, by sheer chance, been rafted together for the long weekend. They discovered that they both had a love for Killian Red beer, good Irish whiskey, and beautiful women, all of which were present in abundance on those long weekends on Biscayne Bay.

Later, when Jack and his wife had come to Sean's establishment at his invitation, they had also discovered that they were at about the same level in darts and pool, resulting in many friendly, close and hard fought games between them. They also liked the same kind of music, from U2 to Enya, the Corrs and Sting to modern Jazz and, surprisingly, Latin jazz and Caribbean rhythms including Reggae, and this led to many outings together to attend outdoor concerts and art shows which occurred almost every weekend somewhere in South Florida. They had never missed the free Jazz Brunch by the New River on the first Sunday of each month and had, by mutual consent, started to spend many weekends together, Jack with his wife and Sean with, seemingly, a new and different woman each time.

It was on one of these outings that Sean had turned up with Janine and from the start Jack had felt a kinship with this young lady who was seemingly intelligent beyond her years. It was Janine who had convinced Jack, after his divorce, that Sean was not one of those men who had spent time with his wife behind his back and therefore the friendship between them continued to this day, even though, like Jack's parents, Sean saw more of Jack's ex-wife than he did of Jack.

He was greeted enthusiastically at the door of the pub by Katie, one of the authentic Irish lasses employed by Sean and immediately shown to a table by the dartboards, of which there were many. He ordered a Smoked Salmon and Capers appetizer and a Killian Red and settled down to wait, while watching a group of not-so-expert dart throwers obviously enjoying their game despite their lack of skill. He knew Sean would be out to see him from the back room as soon as word was passed to him that Jack was out front.

He was halfway through his meal, being fussed over by Katie and several other young waitresses, when Sean finally appeared.

"So, you old pirate, what have you been up to lately? Robbing old ladies out of their life savings, I suppose?"

Sean's easy manner made Jack smile and he countered with, "No, I usually leave that to crooked inn-keepers like yourself."

Anyone who didn't know the two men would have assumed that they were enemies, but this good natured ribbing of each other's professions was only an outward sign of the strong friendship which had built up over the years.

Sean sat down and, as if by magic, two bottles of Killian Red appeared before them. They clinked bottles and drank deeply, each saluting the other.

"So." Sean said, wiping his lips with the back of his hand, "What brings you here? Besides the great food and good company, I mean."

"Well, I've had this idea which could be crazy but I wanted to run it by you to get your thoughts on it. I am thinking of taking my boat to New England this summer and I know I can rely on you to give me all the pros and cons of the plan......."

Jack was halfway through the plan when Sean suddenly said, "Wait a minute! You are talking about taking your boat to all these places up north where it would be just as easy, quicker, more convenient and cheaper just to take your SUV. Why not go the whole hog and take the boat to Europe? You've got the range and you know you keep telling me how much you enjoyed your honeymoon over there. Your boat could make it across the big pond, mine couldn't, not enough range, but you'd have to take a crew with you because it would be a long, slow trip."

Jack thought the suggestion over for a while and then, nodding his head, said, "You know, that's a hell of an idea, and you're right, I could make it across and I would need a crew, so how about it?"

"Hell, no, not me. I've got a business to run. I can't afford to take time off. Besides, you know me. There's nothing I like better than blasting down Biscayne Bay with a load of bikinied women on board, you know that! A long, slow trip to Europe doesn't interest me in the slightest. I'd probably hop a flight to where ever you ended up and meet you over there, though. Might even spend a couple of weeks if you're somewhere interesting."

At that moment, Katie came over to inform Sean of a phone call in his office, and he left to take it while Jack indulged himself in another Killian Red.

A few minutes later, a commotion by the front door caught his attention. A red faced overweight man was arguing with Katie about something on the bill, becoming increasingly agitated and verbally abusive. Kevin, the club bouncer, was quickly moving into the area to intervene in the argument, but what caught Jack's attention was not the altercation, but an apparition of beauty behind the hot-headed customer. Standing behind the shouting man and obviously trying to get into the establishment, was perhaps the most beautiful woman Jack had ever seen.

She stood about five and a half feet tall, with her straight, auburn brunette hair caught by an elaborate antique silver barrette, which formed a ponytail that reached down to her lower back. She could have won any beauty contest she cared to enter hands down. Her slim figure was augmented by adequate, but not excessive, curves in all the right places, and the black designer T-shirt she had chosen to wear clung to her upper body. Her long thin legs, clad in slightly tight, unfaded black jeans gave her the look of a gazelle. Her naturally pale skin had been comfortably tanned and she wore a minimum of makeup, simply because she didn't need it and she was smart enough to realize it. However, her most striking feature, and what caught the attention of most people, was her startlingly clear, deep blue eyes. Even across the darkened and smoke-filled room, their brilliant color and intensity were quite apparent.

Jack realized he was staring openly at her, like a small boy standing outside the window of a toy store, and she suddenly became aware of his scrutiny. Those intense blue eyes flicked quickly across the room and when they settled on his face recognition registered in her manner and she gave him a ghost of a smile and suddenly her eyes took on an electric sparkle directed at him. Jack felt his pulse quicken and, being unable to understand the open invitation in those beautiful eyes, averted his own eyes, telling himself to quit acting like a schoolboy.

When he finally gathered up the courage to look up again, she was no longer there, and the disturbance at the front door having been quelled by the bouncer, the room looked normal, as if the incident had never happened. Jack started to scan the room, but was distracted by Sean's return, wearing a slight frown on his boyish face.

"What's up, old son?" said Jack as Sean sat down.

"Oh, nothing really. Just an accounting problem with one of my distributors." Sean seemed distracted for a moment as if he wasn't there, when suddenly he gave a little shake of his head, pulling himself back into the present and then asked, "What was all the ruckus about?"

"Just another dissatisfied customer objecting to the outrageous prices you charge for your watered down rotgut whiskey. Kevin took care of him; you'll probably get the hospital bill in the morning."

Sean finally grinned, "Good thing you ain't a lawyer, you'd probably be representing him."

They both laughed and Sean, glancing over Jack's shoulder, said, "Come and join us, Shannon, maybe together we can browbeat this guy into submission."

Behind him, Jack heard a soft but husky, slightly accented voice answer, "Sure, why not?" and as he turned he saw the object of his earlier scrutiny directly behind him. Before he could rise to do the gentlemanly thing, he watched as she pulled up a chair and sat down beside him. She was watching his face and still wore that ghost of a smile, which broadened slightly as she read the confusion on his face. Jack, inexplicably, felt himself break into a sweat.

Trying to be flippant, he said, "How about an introduction, Sean?"

"Sure, I guess," he said, frowning. "Shannon O'Loughlin, meet Jack Elliott. Jack, this is Shannon."

Jack turned and, extending his hand, said, "A real pleasure to meet you, Shannon."

A genuine smile broke out upon her face as she took the offered hand, and she answered cryptically, "Oh, but we've met before, Jack."

"We have? I'm afraid I don't remember."

"I don't suppose there is any reason why you should, but it was right here several years ago, in the company of many people at one of Sean's famous get togethers, but you were very married at the time and your wife was with you, so you probably didn't notice me."

"Hey, I can tell you that I don't know why I don't remember you, but it can't be that I didn't notice you. I was married that's true, but I wasn't dead. Only those who are blind and deaf, the totally insane, and the dead and buried would not notice you."

She actually blushed and averted her eyes and Jack felt embarrassed by her show of modesty. In an attempt to show apology, he touched her shoulder, and felt an electric tingle probably caused by static electricity. Her head lifted and her eyes widened to show him that she had also felt it.

Sean suddenly stood up. "Now that you two have been properly introduced, I guess I'll leave you alone." And then he turned and did just that.

Small talk was not Jack's strong suit, and having had limited experience in the genteel art of enticing young females for personal gain, he was temporarily tongue-tied, but he made the attempt at what he thought was an original opening line.

"So, Shannon, what do you do for a living?"

After a slight pause and a look usually reserved for the temporarily deranged, she replied, "I'm a travel agent; or more correctly, I work for a travel agency."

"There's a difference?" It was a question, not a statement.

"Sure there is. I work at a fixed salary, plus overtime after forty hours, for a group of travel agents who work on a strictly commission basis, translating their documents, answering mail and taking phone calls from people who don't speak or write English. I handle the Spanish and French speaking customers and then pass them on to the agents."

"You must run up quite a large long distance phone bill."

"Yes, we do, but you'd be surprised at how much of my work is local, from people who make their homes and their living right here in South Florida at the good will of the people of America, but who still refuse to learn to speak English because they think that the general public will cater to them, and unfortunately, that's exactly what's happening."

"It sounds like quite a challenge, but who makes the most from the deal, you or the agents?"

"Usually the agents, but sometimes me, because I get my salary from the agency regardless of the number of customers. During the lean times, the commissioned agents sometimes have to take second jobs to supplement income from commissions which aren't there."

"Is it interesting work?"

"Like anything repetitive, it becomes boring after a while, but it's a living. I have to admit, though, that sometimes I have to fantasize that it's me taking all those exotic adventures."

"Do you like to travel?"

"I don't know. I've never been anywhere. I mean, I was born in Ireland and I moved to the States, but I wouldn't call it traveling since it was basically a trip from one place to another. But, you know, I think I would like to travel. I've always enjoyed meeting new people and the idea of seeing new places certainly does excite me."

Jack did not even see the minefield into which he had blundered so he blindly, happily jumped right in with both feet.

"Well, one of the reasons I came here tonight was to talk to Sean about traveling abroad in my boat this summer. I was ready to go to New England, but Sean has just about convinced me to take it to Europe instead. If I went, I would need a crew because it would probably take ten to twelve days to cross the Atlantic and I wouldn't do that by myself."

"Wait a minute, am I getting this right? Are you asking me to come with you on this journey of yours?" she asked, somewhat incredulously.

He hesitated for a while, finally seeing the corner into which he'd painted himself, until at last, making up his mind, he swallowed the remainder of his beer without tasting it, and replied, "Yes."

Now it was her turn to hesitate. Katie, without having been asked, brought two more bottles of Killian Red, and sensing the tension and indecision in the air, left without a word.

They both reached automatically for their bottles, and as their eyes locked on each other's face, a silent communication flowing between them, full of questions but producing no answers.

"You know," he said, breaking the awkward silence, "you don't have to make up your mind right now. It's not like I'm taking off tomorrow. This trip will take a lot of planning and there will be arrangements to be made, provisions to be bought and stowed and documents to be procured from the various countries we might visit. And to top it off, you might not even like my boat."

When she still didn't say anything, he continued desperately, "Tell you what, why don't we take a short trip, say, down to Islamorada, this weekend if you're free and we'll get Sean and whoever he's seeing at the moment to come with us?"

Finally she relented and said, "That sounds like a good idea; at the very least, I could see if it was something I really wanted to do."

He raised his bottle and said, "Here's to a plan."

She raised her bottle and they clinked them together and drank deeply. Something inexplicable passed between them and the atmosphere turned comfortable.

Jack excused himself to go make arrangements with Sean, leaving her alone with her head swimming with the possibilities of this chance encounter.

As Jack approached Sean, a broad grin broke out on the younger man's face, and he asked, "Well, old man, are you making time with one of my favorite ladies?"

Jack was shocked to hear himself say, "It could be, it just could be."

The two men stood looking at one another for a minute, both of them grinning from ear to ear like a pair of lunatics.

"Sean, I've asked Shannon to come to Islamorada with me on my boat this weekend and I want you and your current lady to come with us. Can you make it?"

Even as he asked the question, Jack was of two minds. Half of him wanted Sean to say no, so he could be alone with Shannon; the other half was afraid that she wouldn't come unless there was someone else on board to chaperon.

Sean settled the question by saying, "Sure, I'll come and I'll even bring the beer. You just make sure that you bring the steaks for Saturday night."

"Great. I'll see you then. Saturday morning, 6 a.m. O.K?"

"O.K."

As Jack retraced his steps back to Shannon, he felt a certain lightness in both his step and his heart. A plan had been formed, something out of the ordinary, and he was already looking forward to the weekend.

As he sat down next to Shannon, he said, "Sean says he'll be able to make it, so are we on?"

"Sure," she said, smiling brightly and illuminating the whole area around them. "Where and when?"

He replied automatically, "Saturday morning, 6 a.m., Pier 66, B Dock, the name of the boat is 'Final Option'. Will you be able to make it?"

"I don't see why not." She finished her beer and abruptly stood up. "It's been a real pleasure, but I've got to go. I'll see you Saturday morning."

"So soon?"

"I don't know about you, but since it's after midnight, I have to get home and get my beauty sleep. Besides, my employer has this stupid rule that all employees must remain fully awake during their entire workday. It's a bitch but I usually try to comply."

"Point taken. But you don't really need the beauty sleep, seems to me you've already built up a hell of a surplus. Can I give you a lift?"

"No, but thanks, I have my own car. I'll get Kevin to bring it around."

"O.K. See you Saturday."

As he finished his own beer, he watched her walk over to Sean, speak a few words to him, peck him on the cheek, and then turn and wave at Jack as she exited the front door.

"A date," he thought to himself, "It has been such a long time since I've made a date for myself." And then, with sudden insight, he realized that this was the first date he had ever made for himself, his parents having set up his first date with his ex-wife, and since then he had not gone out with another woman except in groups arranged by someone else, usually Sean. It was quite a revelation, and somewhat of a shock.

Shortly thereafter, Jack also left, waving at Sean as he said goodnight to Katie and Kevin, and then drove his Rodeo back to the boat and to his empty, lonely bed.

Chapter 2

The sun, casting off its cloak of darkness, burst forth upon the day with fire to light the bright blue of the sky. Nary a cloud obscured this brilliant display of color and the weather forecasters promised that it would last the whole weekend. Jack was already up and had finished the preparations on the boat when this glorious event occurred and he stopped to witness the sun climb quickly out of the ocean into the sky.

He reflected ruefully on yesterday's phone conversation with his mother, the only jarring note of the last few days, which had been filled with happy anticipation of the coming weekend. When his cell phone had started it's ringing at 6 p.m. the previous evening, he had expected one of his clients or Sean was calling, but his mother's voice had startled him. She rarely called him at all and never on his cell phone, preferring to leave a somewhat cryptic message on his answering machine to ensure that he would call back.

After the usual pleasantries and some idle chitchat about mutual friends, she got to the point of the call.

"Rain and Stephan are coming over this weekend. It would be nice if you could join us."

"Sorry, Mom, I can't. Sean and I are taking the boat to Islamorada tomorrow morning."

"Oh, Jack, how long has it been since you came to see us? Couldn't you postpone your trip? I'm sure Rain would love to see you. Couldn't you come? For me? I'd love to see you."

"Mom, I just can't. I've promised some people that we'd go to the Keys and it's going to be a beautiful weekend. Besides, I don't particularly wish to spend any time with Rain and especially Stephan. Don't forget he's the reason I'm divorced, remember?"

Rain, short for Lorraine, was his ex-wife and Stephan, her Ferrari-driving boyfriend, a personal injury attorney who gave even other P.I. lawyers a bad name, were two people he definitely did not want to see under any circumstances, which was why he seldom went to his parent's house anymore. His mother still had the crazy idea that if she kept bringing them together; they would someday get back together again. The truth was, like most people, she could barely tolerate Stephan, but put up with him because of Rain.

She had been very upset and had hung up on him, and although he had tried to call back, he had only gotten the answering machine. He had waited for her to call back, but as yet he hadn't heard from her.

His mood improved remarkably when he glanced down the dock and spotted Sean struggling under the load of two cases of Killian Red, followed closely by Katie bearing several bottles of Jameson's Irish Whiskey. Jack jumped onto the dock and ran to help Sean and when he reached him, relieved him of one of the cases.

"It's about time you showed up. I was about to have a hernia."

"Let me give you Stephan's number; you could sue the beer company."

"Or you, seeing you made me bring all this terrible stuff."

"Yeah, right!"

Sean and Katie had both brought changes of clothes with them and they were in Sean's car, a vintage 1971 426 Hemi 'Cuda which he had rebuilt from scratch by himself and was his pride and joy, and, after stowing the booze, they all went back to get them. As they were walking back to the boat, Jack had the chance to really notice Katie for the first time outside of Sean's club, and he definitely liked what he saw.

Trim and petite, she stood only about five foot one and probably didn't weigh a hundred pounds soaking wet. This morning she had chosen to wear a bright multi-colored Hawaiian shirt knotted at the waist over a pair of white, very short, shorts. She was wearing boat shoes, which pleased him a lot because the teak decks on his boat were too easily damaged by street shoes and sandals.

When they got to the boat, they took their duffel bags down below and claimed the forward cabin, which, like Jack's midship cabin, had a double berth in it. The third cabin had two single bunks and was usually used for storage, and it had taken Jack several hours to clean it sufficiently for occupancy, for he had assumed that Shannon would occupy this cabin for the weekend. When they reappeared, he offered them coffee which they took to the flybridge, while waiting for Shannon to arrive.

They didn't have long to wait, sitting there amongst the bustle of other people preparing their boats for this first warm weekend after a late winter cold snap.

Presently, she came strolling down 'B' Dock, only a fashionable ten minutes late. She was not hurrying, but had a large, apologetic smile upon her face, and walked with a jaunty spring in her step. She was wearing a close-fitting, electric blue crop top and a pair of reasonably tight, white Levis, boat shoes and a black baseball cap with a Porsche logo on it, and carrying her own duffel bag. She looked like a million dollars and, as she approached the boat, all preparations on the other boats came to a standstill as heads swiveled and necks craned in order to get a better view. She took all this attention in stride and when she arrived at the boat, stepped up to the aft cockpit as if she had been doing it all her life.

Leaving her dufflebag in the main saloon, she climbed the aft ladder onto the boat deck, where the Novurania and a Yamaha Waverunner were stored, and joined the others on the flybridge where she accepted a cup of coffee from Sean. Confidently, she didn't offer any explanation for her lateness, but simply joined in the conversation as if she had been there all along.

After a short while, Jack went down to the pilothouse to start and warm up the engines, while the others shortened up the lines, brought in the extra fenders and stowed all the loose gear belowdecks.

After conducting a quick but thorough inspection of the boat from stem to stern, Jack went up to the control station on the flybridge where he had a commanding view all around the boat. Both women had obviously spent at least a little time aboard a boat, because they both went to all the right spots, let go the correct lines as instructed by Sean, and stood by with fenders at the bow and stern in case of trouble. Because they were definitely not your typical, 'sit on a seat with a drink in hand and let the men do the work' women, these two were already impressing the hell out of him.

Jack deftly backed the boat out of the slip and, playing a tune on the throttles of the twin engines, swung it into the channel between the docks. When he was pointed north, he went from reverse to forward and gently exited the marina. As he reached the restaurant on the end of 'A' Dock, he made a wide, sweeping, 180 degree turn to port, and then slipped smoothly into the flow of traffic on the Intracoastal Waterway, passed under the 17th Street Bridge and into Port Everglades.

Sean and the two women, having stowed the lines and fenders, joined him on the flybridge in time to enjoy the spectacle of the early morning exodus of boats through the Port entrance and into the open sea. With just a slight on-shore breeze coming out of the east to replace the rapidly warming, rising air over the land, the ocean was flat and calm, unruffled except by the wakes of the many boats heading offshore for the day.

Setting 150 degrees on the autopilot and 3,000 revolutions on the engines, which headed the boat slightly south of south-east at about eighteen knots, Jack and his companions settled down and relaxed for the one hundred mile journey, while the four blade stabilizers effortlessly smoothed out the almost unnoticeable swell. Sean popped an Enya CD into the player and soon music, as well sunshine and a fresh, salty breeze, filled the air around them. Katie went below into the galley and soon returned to pull four Bloody Marys and toasted and buttered English Muffins from the dumb waiter, which joined the galley with the flybridge.

Jack reluctantly took his drink, but only sipped at it. He was, after all, the captain and was, as such, responsible for the safety and navigation of the boat and its occupants. He did, however, wolf down his muffin.

The sun, as it rose higher in the sky, turned hotter and soon the clothes started coming off quickly. Katie's Hawaiian shirt and short shorts gave way to a tiny slip of a string bikini, strikingly pink and black, with the top tied only loosely. Sean shed his T-shirt and Sportif boat shorts and was wearing Speedo briefs, and Shannon was minus the white Levis and was wearing a bikini; electric blue to match her crop top, which had joined the rest of the excessive clothing in the locker under the seat of the dinette on the starboard side aft of the flybridge. Her bikini was not quite as small as Katie's, but left very little to the imagination, nonetheless. Jack, not having had to travel to the boat, was still wearing his favorite green and black America's Cup swim trunks, but had shed his T-shirt.

Revealed in the bright sunlight, Jack noticed that, apart from height and hair and eye color, there was little difference between the two women. They both had that long, lean, healthy outdoors look and although Shannon was more curvaceous than Katie, who had a slightly tomboyish figure, they were both shining examples of true femininity.

They sat around all morning, talking and laughing, as the boat bore them steadily toward their destination. Their course took them offshore to where the gray-green coastal water changed abruptly to the brilliant, shimmering blue of the Gulf Stream, a warm water current which affected the weather positively in Bermuda, Greenland, Iceland and the British Isles and kept ports as far away as Murmansk in northern Russia ice free all the year around. The weed line which marked the boundary between the two distinct bodies of water was the best place to find Jack' favorite seafood, bull dolphin, the fish not the mammal, which was also called mahi-mahi in restaurants after a distant Hawaiian cousin.

At one point, just south of Miami's Government Cut, Sean turned to Jack and said, "You know, if we'd taken my boat, we'd be there by now."

"Yes," he conceded, "but then we wouldn't have had the time for all this stimulating conversation, and we'd have had to stop for gas twice at the very least."

Sean laughed and said, "True, how true."

At that moment, Shannon abruptly stood up and, pointing toward the bow, asked, "What's that?"

Right there, riding the bow wave, a sleek gray form undulated hypnotically under the water, moving forward of the boat, only to reappear a few seconds later on the other side of it, and effortlessly keeping pace and even outrunning the boat.

Sean said, "Dolphin, the mammal not the fish. You know, Flipper." And Shannon immediately disappeared down the companionway steps and out along the port side deck to reappear on the fore deck, where she lay down on the bow anchor platform to watch the dolphin playing in the bow wave. She looked so enticing lying there that Jack felt stirrings he hadn't had for a long time. The combination of her natural beauty and the sunlight sparkling off the water, combined with the salt spray on his sunglasses gave her an ethereal quality, like suddenly coming upon a woodland nymph by a stream after tramping through miles of unending forest. He stared for a long time until, as before in the club, she sensed that she was being watched and slowly turned around, the dolphin forgotten, to confront him watching her.

This time he didn't avert his eyes, but let a grin slowly develop on his face, which very quickly became a full leer when she assumed an extremely sensual, if not erotic, position and gave some unmistakably provocative signs at him. Torn between his duty to maintain control of the boat, and running to her, he shook his head, trying to clear the cobwebs from those parts of his imagination that had lain dormant for so long.

Sean and Katie, standing beside him, exchanged glances, then grins, and finally high fives.

Jack was startled out of his reverie at the sound of palms slapping together and at an indication from Sean, he looked down at himself to where what he was thinking about was quite apparent. He turned and once again looked forward, and he saw her walking seductively back toward him. She disappeared under the overhang of the upper deck and he waited with anticipation for her to reappear up the companionway steps. He saw her head first as she peeked over the edge of the hatch, but his attention was ripped from her face as, out of the corner of his eye, he saw Katie nonchalantly remove her bikini top and throw it at him. He was torn between a sense of modesty, indignation, and admiration as he watched her pirouette in front of him as Sean, sitting back in dinette seat, took another long pull on his beer.

Finally finding his tongue, he managed to say, "You realize, of course, that I'll never be able to look at you at the Club after this without seeing you half naked like this."

She gave him a sexy, wicked grin and said, "Of course you won't, and that's the whole point of this trip. You know, you *have* been ignoring me lately."

Unnoticed by all, Shannon had come all the way onto the flybridge, and as he felt her hands on his shoulders, he turned and looked into her eyes. At least she was wearing both parts of her bikini, but she was looking at him in a very strange way. The intensity of those sparkling, deep blue eyes seemed to be searching his soul for an answer to an unasked question.

He wilted under her scrutiny and, placing his hands on her tiny waist, allowed his eyes to travel downward covering the full length of her perfect body and pausing at all the pertinent points along the journey, and finally coming to rest on her feet as he stood before her like a whipped puppy.

He saw her pouting at him as her hand raised his chin until their eyes met and then, impulsively, she kissed him, gently at first like a mother might kiss her child's skinned elbow, but becoming stronger and longer until her tongue searched for his, and finding it, they came closer together and their bodies intertwined.

As they finally came up for air, Jack looked over Shannon's shoulder to see Katie and Sean removing the cover on the Jacuzzi, which had replaced the bench seat on the port side aft of the flybridge. Nervously he quickly scanned the horizon, but he saw no other boats, in fact a small gray smudge on the western horizon was all that showed of the coast of Florida.

Resigning himself to allowing his boat to be turned into a floating bordello like Sean's, he relaxed and luxuriated in the feel of Shannon's soft, warm body next to his, while still keeping a weather eye out for other traffic. His heart soared when she whispered; "You have no idea how many years I've waited for this to happen."

Around two in the afternoon, having skirted the reefs around Pennekamp State Park, they arrived in the waters off Islamorada. They entered the channel that led to

Holiday Isle, which had recently undergone renovations and modernization and had grown immensely from the island dive it used to be. By prior arrangement they docked at the last slip at the southeast end, right by the little park at the end of the peninsula of land that formed the boat basin. Before arriving they had all gone below singly to get showers and a change of clothes, so they could arrive fresh and salt-free at the popular watering hole.

Katie had put on a slightly more modest version of her pink and black bikini, this one in a Dusky Rose color and she had combined it with a bright yellow sarong worn very low on her hips. Lightweight yellow sandals completed her outfit. These colors combined with her skin and hair coloring to make her look absolutely stunning, far outshining Sean, who had donned a loose, white guayabera shirt, which he had picked up in Puerto Rico some years earlier, over a pair of black swim trunks and boat shoes.

Shannon chose a slinky, radically cut black one-piece which showed off her figure to perfection and combined it with a pair of loose fitting white sea cotton pants and black sandals. Neither woman wore makeup or jewelry. Neither one needed to.

Jack was his usual self in a white T-shirt with Final Option written on it, navy blue swim trunks and boat shoes.

As soon as the boat was secured and washed down, the two women immediately disappeared over to the pool, where they claimed a couple of lounge chairs while Sean and Jack were left to sample Holiday Isle's most popular drink, the Rum Runner, for which they are justifiably world famous. They did this sampling while watching the scores of delectable young women cavorting about in the pools, on the beach and in the many boats and water toys visiting on this weekend.

When the women joined them, they all spent the afternoon drinking and snacking, playing beach volleyball, swimming and simply sitting in the lounges, soaking up the sunshine. They watched a bikini fashion show and listened to some passable reggae played by a local steel band. The women managed to squeeze in a little shopping and the boat started to fill with new clothing, jewelry, and knick-knacks. As the day drew to a close, Sean suggested steaks and they all gravitated back to the boat, where Jack set up the grill on the aft deck, which overlooked the boat basin. Jack preferred to cook over charcoal, rather than propane, because of the flavor they added to the steaks. The process of burning down also added to the time it took to prepare the steaks, and the anticipation of the mouth-watering meal. Sean, amongst others, swore that Jack's steaks outshone any others that he had ever had before, even at high-end steak houses.

As the steaks went on, the fire having burned down sufficiently, the boats in the basin, now in darkness except for the full moon and a few shoreside lights, were rocked violently by the wake of an arriving speedboat.

"What a jerk, there is always one in every crowd," said Jack, with Sean enthusiastically nodding agreement. The 98,000 pound displacement of the Neptunus had ensured that they had not been terribly inconvenienced but some of the lighter boats were pitching and yawing to the point that their pristine decks were covered with the remnants of their owner's dinners, having spilled from the backlash of the wake the speedboat had left. Angry shouts and curses rang out from all sides of the basin at the offending vessel and, as the two men on board were illuminated by a spotlight from one of the gyrating boats, they gave the customary international one finger salute to the general population.

Amid the chaos of their actions, they quickly tied up and disappeared ashore in the direction of the bar. Silence descended slowly on the basin as the waves declined, the messes were cleaned up and the atmosphere calmed into another balmy Florida Keys night, laid back, relaxed, a drink in one hand and a girl in the other type of night. Jack had returned to his role as chef du jour and was busy preparing the steaks on the grill to everyone's liking, and therefore missed the start of the actual incident that was to change the lives of all on board. Later, he would recollect, that the first thing he was aware of was loud angry voices that intruded on the U2 CD they were playing softly and a body that came hurtling out of the darkness of the park, narrowly missing the stern platform on the boat, and landing in the water only feet behind the boat.

A huge fountain of water erupted, some of it splashing into the cockpit, catching everyone off guard and causing a minor crisis as they tried to avoid getting drenched. Moments later, a weak voice reached out of the darkness pleading for help. Sean was the first to react, pulling off his shirt and diving into the water in the direction of the voice. Fortunately, he surfaced a few feet from the struggling figure, who, unfortunately, immediately tried to clamp on to him the way a drowning person will when in trouble, endangering them both.

With an expert move, learned in diving classes, Sean had the man on his back, one arm wrapped around the upper body supporting the man with his head above the water's surface despite his attempts to drag them both under.

Steaks forgotten, Jack caught a glimpse of the two men from the speedboat on the dock, watching all the action, before he went down the steps onto the swim platform to help Sean manhandle the now limp form aboard the boat.

The man looked to be in his late 60's, with a shock of white hair and a 3 day stubble on his chin, and the unmistakable veined nose of a heavy drinker. His clothes, apart from being soaked through, were baggy and wrinkled, and his workman's boots had definitely seen better days. Quickly turning around, Jack looked for the two men on the dock, but they had gone.

Laying on the swim platform, the old man started coughing and spluttering, and unaided he rolled over and let the water he had swallowed drain from him. When Jack reached down and touched his shoulder to reassure him, the man drew himself into a defensive posture and started cursing him in German. With reassuring words, Jack calmed him down and then asked, "Are you all right? What happened? And who are you?"

For a second a look of total incomprehension dominated his face. Finally, realizing that he was not about to be attacked, he collected himself sufficiently to reply slowly, "Name's Captain Pete Olsen-Smith and those two Nazi bastards over there beat the hell out of me and threw me into the harbor to drown."

Closer examination of the man's face revealed bumps and abrasions which didn't seem likely to have happened from a simple fall into the water in which nothing was struck on the way down.

"Is that steak I smell cooking?" he suddenly asked, catching them all off guard.

Even in all the excitement, Katie, bless her heart, had remembered the steaks on the grill and had moved them to the side so they had not been reduced to charcoal.

"You know, I haven't had a steak for months. I don't suppose you could spare one for a hungry man?" he asked, looking at the grill and the set table in the cockpit.

Before Jack could speak, Shannon said, "I'll split mine with you. I am not very hungry after all the stuff I've eaten this afternoon. A girl has to watch her figure, you know."

"Very well," said Jack, "set another place and let's eat." He turned and looked curiously at the old man and asked, "You don't happen to have any dry clothes on you, do you?"

This time Sean spoke up, "He's about my size, I think. Come on, old timer, let's get you into some dry clothes."

With difficulty, the old man stood up and, helped by Sean, went below to change.

Katie and Shannon made the final preparations for dinner, setting a place for another person, tossing the salad, and getting the baked potatoes out of the oven.

Everyone turned to look as Sean and Capt'n Pete emerged from below. They had both cleaned the harbor water off themselves and the old man was wearing an old pair of faded blue jeans and a white T-shirt that Sean kept aboard for those times when Jack browbeat him into helping with the maintenance on the boat, and while they were admittedly not stylish, at least they were dry. Sean had also found something dry, although for him this was probably stretching things, at least as far as clean clothes were concerned. All the food being on the table, they all sat down and started digging in, except the old man, who stood by grinning sheepishly and looking at Jack.

"Are you sure it's O.K?"

"Sure. It's O.K. Sit down and eat." Jack said.

"Have a beer," said Sean, as Capt'n Pete took the last empty seat.

"Never touch the stuff," the old man said, surprising them all, "...but I'll be havin' a wee drop of that good Irish whiskey though, if you be offering."

Instantly they erupted into laughter, for this stranger had mimicked Sean's strong Irish accent very closely indeed. Sean grabbed the bottle of Jameson's and poured a good measure into the glass in front of Capt'n Pete, as they would soon be calling him. Sean asked him with the innocence of youth, "Ice, water?"

The man, caught in the process of lifting the glass to his lips, paused and looked straight into Sean's eyes, "Wouldn't want to contaminate it now, would we?" he said with a crooked smile on his face.

They all started on their steaks, and Jack inquired, "So, tell us what happened?"

"I really don't know for certain. I was sitting at the bar and having a drink and starting on my plate of food, you know, they have that happy hour spread of nachos and wings and stuff. Sally, the barmaid, she always gets a plate ready for me so as I don't have to get in line with all the others."

"Anyway, I was just starting on my food when those two jokers came in and said they wanted to talk to me, and the next thing I knew they grabbed me by my arms and hustled me right out of there and dragged me over here to the park."

"Didn't anyone try to stop them?" asked Shannon.

"Hell, no. Around here everybody minds their own business."

"Do you know who they are?" asked Sean.

He hesitated slightly, "I can't say that I ever met them before but they were the two idiots on that speedboat that caused all that commotion here a while back and I know that the speedboat is a tender to the big yacht that's anchored over there." He pointed vaguely in the direction of the sea, indicating with a sweep of his arm the overall encompassing of an area which included a number of boats anchored in a small, protected cove on one of the offshore islands far in the distance.

As if to emphasize the point, the speedboat in question shattered the evening's calm by starting the engines and casting off. In vivid contrast to its arrival, this time it proceeded at a leisurely pace, its turbo charged engines throbbing with unleashed power, and as it passed the stern of the Neptunus with the five people dining in the aft cockpit, on its way out of the boat basin, both men in it looked intently at them. If looks could have killed, all five of them on the motoryacht would have been instantly incinerated.

As the rumbling boat passed the outer markers of the basin, both throttles were firewalled and the boat disappeared at a rapid rate of speed into the darkness in the direction of the anchorage on the offshore island, and shortly the noise of its passage disappeared, too, to the relief of all the people in the basin.

No one spoke for a while, all preferring to concentrate on his or her rapidly cooling meal, but inevitably the conversation came back to the same subject.

"Did they say what they wanted from you?" Sean asked, filling the old timer's glass for the third time.

"No, not really. All the time they were beating me, and taking pleasure in it let me tell you, they were shouting something about getting even, and Nazis, and wanting information out of me, but I have no idea what the hell they were talking about. I just want to be left alone to live a nice quiet life."

"Where *do* you live?" asked Jack, suddenly worried about the old man's safety.

"I have an old trailer in the recreation area on the next Key down and my truck is in the parking lot out front."

"Maybe he'd better stay here for the night, just in case those guys come back." Sean suggested, catching Jack' drift.

"That might be a good idea," agreed Jack, "if you are willing," he said to the old man.

The old sailor nodded his agreement to the suggestion. "Don't want to be no trouble to nobody, though."

"I'm afraid you'd have to sleep in the main saloon, though."

"Don't be ridiculous," Shannon interrupted, " he can sleep in the starboard cabin. It's empty."

Jack swung around and raised his eyebrows questioningly at her, but she just gave him a sweet little smile and a tiny shrug of her shoulders. He saw the grins forming on the faces of Sean and Katie and suddenly realized that the thing he had not dared to think about all day was about to happen, and silently he thanked this stranger who had come into their midst at such an opportune moment.

The matter apparently having been settled, and as it was still too early to retire for the night, they all went to the flybridge and paired off, Sean and Katie taking a seat on the cover of the Jacuzzi, Jack and Shannon relaxing in the dinette and Capt'n Pete keeping company with the bottle of Jameson's on the helm seat. With Sean's encouragement, Capt'n Pete told his tale and an interesting and intriguing story it was.

He told them that he had been born in England of a Swedish mother and an English father, and had immigrated to the States in 1949, had grown up right here in the Keys. He had worked on many boats during his lifetime on the water; first in the Navy as an ordinary seaman, then as a commercial fisherman, and finally on numerous private yachts, where he had worked his way up from deckhand to Captain, on the last boat upon which he worked.

He had a 3,000 ton Captain's License but had been unable to get work on any boat lately because of the drinking habits he had acquired over the years. Now he was reduced to working at the odd jobs sympathetic marina owners would give him, and the occasional boat delivery for people who put more faith in the piece of paper he carried than in what their own eyes told them of his ability to finish the job, simply because he worked cheap. So far, he'd been lucky; he hadn't sunk one yet, but he had deteriorated to the sorry state that now sat before them.

After his tale was told, the old man innocently inquired about the situation which prevailed on this boat, more to break the silence than for any desire for information and Jack, surprising himself, told him of their plans for the trip to Europe.

Capt'n Pete listened politely at first, but as the anticipated adventure was unfolded before him, his eyes grew brighter and his attention was caught and held. He began making suggestions; some trivial, but some important.

"So what you're telling me is that you and this slip of a girl are going to take this fine vessel and attempt to cross the Atlantic Ocean on her own bottom. Am I correct?" he asked, questioning Jack and indicating Shannon with a wave of his hand.

"I question your use of the word 'attempt', but essentially that's correct, assuming that you mean the boat's bottom and not the girl's." answered Jack.

Shannon threw a playful punch at him.

Turning on Sean, he asked, "And you two?"

Sean answered, "Hell, don't look at us, we're just along for the ride for this weekend only."

"Fine, then, let me ask you this," he turned and looked Jack squarely in the eyes, "Have you ever been offshore in any official capacity aboard a small boat?"

Jack answered, defensively, "We've taken this very boat to the Bahamas several times."

"The Bahamas. Hah! That's a cakewalk. A ten year old could do that!"

Jack' eyes narrowed, and then he grinned, "So, just what is it that you're proposing. Or are you just jerking my chain for the fun of it?"

"Well, if you are willing and can come up with a decent salary, I'll help you take this boat across the big pond. I've done the trip over and back seventeen times, in various boats, and if anyone can get you safely across, I can, despite current appearances."

Jack looked skeptical, then doubtful, and then thoughtful, and finally said, "Tell you what I'm going to do. Let me sleep on it, and I'll let you know in the morning."

Shannon suddenly said, "Speaking of sleep, it's way past my bedtime. I'll see you all in the morning."

A chorus of goodnights was followed by Katie's decision that she, too, was exhausted and was going to bed, leaving the three men sitting in silence making a dead soldier out of the bottle of Jameson's.

The boat basin itself was quiet at one in the morning, but occasionally the sounds of a jukebox, partying and laughter drifted on the light breeze across the water from the bar at the hotel. Lights danced gently on the almost calm water and a billion stars blazed in the heavens. The full moon looked down upon them as they sat, relaxing, not saying much, but just winding down from the unusual day.

Eventually, the full day in the sun, the afternoon's partying and the evening's excitement took their toll and by mutual consent, they all decided that enough was enough. After locking up the boat for the night, and settling Capt'n Pete into the starboard cabin, Sean and Jack said goodnight and retired to their respective cabins.

As Jack entered the darkened midship cabin, unsure of what to expect, his hand reached out automatically and flipped on the light switch. He liked to keep the light in stateroom slightly subdued, so the scene that greeted his eyes was not harshly illuminated. In fact, it had a hazy, dreamlike quality to it, although that could have been partly due to the Jameson's.

She was laying on her back in his bed, her long dark hair splayed out on his pillows and her body covered only by a thin, white sheet. The moment the light came on, her eyes opened slowly and that mischievous smile of hers formed on her face. She sat up slowly, allowing the sheet to fall from her breasts and causing Jack to gasp deeply for breath. With a deliberately slow movement of her hand, she removed the sheet to reveal her superbly formed, totally naked body that had been almost hidden beneath it. Then she deftly tossed the sheet aside as she languished back onto the pillows, both hands behind her head.

As she lay there, moving slightly and seductively, she asked him, "Well, old man, are you going to stand there and just gawk all night? Or are you going to do something about it?"

Jack was tongue-tied, and he had to hold onto the wall to keep from falling over at the sight of such beauty before him, and when, after a long pause he still hadn't answered her, she commanded him, "Will you get your clothes off and come join me."

And he did.

The next morning dawned bright and clear, with the promise of another long, hot day. Unfortunately, none of the people on the boat were awake to see it, for they had all, somehow, forgotten to set their alarm clocks before retiring. It being Sunday, even the young people preferred to sleep late.

Somewhere around nine a.m., Jack suddenly jerked awake, momentarily disoriented by the presence of a naked lady in bed with him. It was such an unusual occurrence that it took him a few moments to recall the events of the previous day, but when it all came back to him, he felt a warm glow inside. As he looked over at the radiant face beside him, she slowly came awake, and seeing him watching her, gave him a dazzling smile that lit up her face and made her more beautiful than he'd ever seen her before.

"Morning, sleepyhead," he said as he reached for her, remembering fondly the pleasures of the night before, but she drew away from him. Relenting slightly, she gave him a quick peck on the lips, said, "Got to go," and disappeared into the head. As he watched her walking away as naked as a jaybird, he couldn't help wondering what wonderful circumstances had come together to create such an exquisite creature. He lay back, suddenly frowning as his nose detected unfamiliar odors in the boat. He stood up and slipped into a robe and went topside to the galley where he found Capt'n Pete frying bacon and scrambling eggs.

"Hope you don't mind?" he said, "I got hungry and no-one was up, so I helped myself. Have some coffee."

As he helped himself to a cup, Jack said, "Don't tell me you're a gourmet cook, too?"

"Been on my own all my life, I had to learn to cook in self defense."

Awakened by the smells of breakfast, everyone appeared at once, Sean and Katie first and then Shannon, looking sheepish and glancing surreptitiously at them to see what kind of reception last night's sudden impulsive decision would bring.

But there were no sly grins, no winks, and no change in the way she was treated. Life simply went on and they were all relaxed with one another. Surprisingly, even Capt'n Pete was in an expansive mood, regaling them with more stories of his youth as they ate breakfast in the main saloon. Jack and Shannon had taken the seats in the dinette, while Sean and Katie shared the main table with Capt'n Pete.

He had hedged around the subject for a while, until he finally asked, "So, have you come to a decision yet?"

Without thinking, Jack replied, "To tell you the truth, I hadn't had a chance to think about it yet." To cover himself, he added quickly, "But we can talk about it now, if you like."

"O.K."

"You have to understand first of all that I am not one of your typical filthy rich boat owners, so I wouldn't be able to pay you a lot," he went on, "Perhaps a thousand a month plus room and board, health and accident insurance, and a bonus at the end of the trip would be the maximum I could afford."

"O.K."

"In addition I would guarantee you a return air ticket from wherever we were at the time to home, in case you decided to leave or we decided that we didn't need you anymore."

"O.K."

"And you would need to recognize that I was the Captain, not just the owner of the boat and my decisions would be final."

"O.K."

"And you'd need approval from the other member of the team, whoever that turns out to be."

"O.K. But wait a minute," he said, looking at Shannon, "I thought you were the one who was coming."

Shannon hesitated, weighing the consequences of her decision and then, with conviction, she answered, "Of course I am."

He looked quizzically at Jack, who shrugged his shoulders and said, "Don't look at me. That decision has just been made and this is the first I knew of it, too." Turning to Shannon, he asked, "So, do you want to go to Europe with me on this boat?"

"Yes, of course I do."

"And would you approve of Capt'n Pete coming with us?"

"Yes. I think someone with his experience would be an asset to us on this voyage, don't you."

"Yes, I do. Now it's up to you, Capt'n Pete."

"Well, the money, terms and conditions are all right with me, and I appreciate the vote of confidence from you, young lady, but if ever it turned out that we were in any danger I would expect you to listen to me and follow my advice. I do have a lot more sea time and experience than you do"

"Fair enough. When could you start?"

"I can't see any reason not to start right now. There certainly isn't anything of importance keeping me here at the moment. But if we are going back to Fort Lauderdale today, I'd need a lift back down to pick up my truck and trailer after I'd found a place to store them."

"I don't foresee any problems with that arrangement. Welcome aboard, Captain."

They shook hands on the deal, and then Capt'n Pete said, "We'd better get going if we're going to get back to Fort Lauderdale before dark."

Breakfast having been devoured despite all the conversation, the two women cleared the interior of the boat in preparation for the trip back, while Capt'n Pete did a thorough safety and familiarization inspection of the boat, accompanied by Sean, who knew the boat intimately from his many previous visits.

Jack went down to the Marina Office to pay for their dockage, and while there the dockmaster asked him, "That's not Capt'n Pete on your boat, is it?"

"Yes it is," Jack replied, his curiosity raised. "Why?"

"I'd be careful around that man if I were you. I've heard some stories about him and his behavior that would curl your hair. Besides, everyone knows that he's a drunk."

"Really? What kind of stories have you heard about him?"

"Well mainly that he's unreliable and has his own way of doing things and when he doesn't get his own way, he has a nasty temper. Damn near killed the owner of one of the boats he worked on a while back."

"And who has been telling you these stories?"

"People who he worked for in the past. Reliable people who have been coming here for years."

"Well, so far he's only coming with us as far as Fort Lauderdale." As soon as the words were out of his mouth, he regretted his announcement, suddenly remembering that the two men last night had acted with impunity, and how no one had tried to stop or reprimand them, especially when they were hauling an old man out of the bar against his will. As he paid his bill, he glanced around and became aware of the flitting eyes of the other customers who were staring at him although trying not to be obvious and who had been surreptitiously taking in the conversation. He didn't at all like some of the looks he was getting, so he left in a hurry.

Maybe it was paranoia, but as he walked back to the boat, he sensed that he was being watched. He turned around abruptly several times but could not catch anyone paying him any special attention. But still the feeling lingered.

As he arrived back at the boat, he noticed that preparations were well under way to put to sea. Seemed like Capt'n Pete had things well in hand, because it had not taken him very long to familiarize himself with the layout of this particular boat. As he embarked he noted with pleasant surprise that a lot of the things that he was meticulous about in the preparation of the boat for sea had already been accomplished in his absence.

Jack joined Capt'n Pete on the flybridge as Sean and the girls stood by the lines and fenders, and Capt'n Pete asked, "Do you want to take her out, Jack?"

Not even Sean had taken this boat out of its slip before, and in fact, Jack did most of the driving by himself even when there were competent and qualified people aboard to relieve him, but he hesitated for only a second before saying, "If you are going to run this boat clear across the Atlantic, no time like the present to get started."

Capt'n Pete nodded once, and in a quiet but commanding voice began giving only the absolutely necessary instructions to Sean and the girls, acknowledging their expertise with this boating procedure. With a minimum of fuss and without any unnecessary movements, Capt'n Pete quietly extracted the boat from its slip and then turned, saluted the bystander on the dock who had helped with the lines and waved at a boat captain who was watching the action. The man didn't wave back, but just stood there and glared.

"Who is that?" Jack asked.

"Just someone who told me once a short time ago that I would never get to work in any capacity on another boat if he had his way."

Once clear of the boat basin, and into the channel which led through the reef towards the open sea, everyone, having cleared the deck of lines and fenders, gathered on the flybridge. The boat ambled along at the blazing speed of fifteen knots, but thanks to intelligent design and a lot of engine room soundproofing, only the waters parting for the hull's passage and the apparent wind caused by the boat's forward motion could be heard. Everyone was conversing in normal voices, and the breeze was more than welcome, for the day was already shaping up to be a scorcher.

Capt'n Pete sat in the helm seat, constantly making minute corrections to the boat's course in order to keep them in the middle of the channel. The boat only drew five feet of water, but some of the sandbars and reefs on either side of them were covered by only inches of water, and at times the channel was extremely narrow. It was a place for a great deal of precise and careful navigation.

Capt'n Pete looked as if he had been running this boat for years, knowing instinctively where to look to gather information from the various instruments on the panel of the helm station, and alternating this with the old time sailor's long, slow scans of the horizon, consulting the map in his head, which had been built up over many years in these waters.

"Oh, oh. Looks like we have company, and I don't think that it's good company," Capt'n Pete said, indicating a roostertail of spray out in the ocean in the direction of the offshore islands. The boat causing this plume was just a speck but it was growing larger by the minute, and was soon recognizable as the speedboat that had caused the ruckus the night before. They watched helplessly as it bore down on them, on a collision course. They had almost made it to the end of the channel, where they would have had room to maneuver, but the other boat, with its superior speed, got there first, slewing to a stop and settling in the water in front of them, effectively blocking the end of the channel.

Capt'n Pete automatically reached over and pulled back on the throttles and brought their boat to a stop only a few dozen yards away from the side of the speedboat. The same two men from the night before stood watching their progress come to a halt. Both men wore the usual uniform of hired crew, boat shoes, white shorts with a nautically themed canvas belt, and a short sleeved white shirt with gold ringed epaulettes and a boat name on one side of the chest. The distance was too great for Jack to make out the name of the vessel but it was in bright green embroidery. Both men looked amused but neither was smiling.

The tall blond man reached down, flipped on a switch and spoke into a handset he held. An electronic voice clear enough to recognize the German accent issued from the loudhailer.

"Good morning, Mr. Elliott. I am terribly sorry to inconvenience you like this, but it seems that I have some unfinished business with your Capt'n Pete that cannot wait. We will come alongside to allow him to come with us, if you would be so kind, then you can be on your way."

Jack looked over at Capt'n Pete and raised his eyebrows, and got a shrug of the shoulders in return. He picked up the microphone, thumbed the switch and said into the instrument, "I have spoken to my Captain and he assures me that he has no business, unfinished or otherwise, to discuss with you. So if you would be so kind, back off and allow us to pass."

The effect on the two men was startling. The shorter, less blond man slid his hand behind him and pulled an automatic handgun from the small of his back and assumed a shooter's stance with the gun held in both hands but aimed skyward. The tall blond man seemed to lose all semblance of civility and literally screamed into the microphone, "I am sick and tired of your damned interference. This could have been settled last night, but you had to stick your nose in where it wasn't wanted. You have ten seconds to hand that sorry son of a bitch over OR ELSE!!!"

Jack looked around desperately for help but saw no other boats anywhere near them. He did notice, however, Sean, who had disappeared down below when the fracas had started, standing in the companionway holding the two 12 gauge pump action riot guns Jack kept aboard for insurance. He knew that they would be fully loaded and ready to go, which boosted his confidence, and so he yelled right back, "And you've got about two seconds to move your butt before I run right over that piddle ass little boat of yours, and start yelling 'PIRACY' to the Coast Guard over the radio!"

He dropped the mike, grabbed one of the riot guns from Sean, who had come up beside him and yelled, "Everybody! Get down! Capt'n Pete! Full speed ahead!"

Capt'n Pete reacted immediately, firewalling both throttles in forward, as the girls dove to the deck behind the spa for the protection the water in it would give them. The heavy boat squatted at the stern as the twin 1450 horsepower Caterpillar diesels turned the four bladed props, which pushed copious amounts of water from under the hull and started her moving forward. Jack prayed silently that his stoutly constructed hull would stand the impact of a ramming, but the other skipper wasn't willing to find out, for he was just as quick off the mark, and gunned his boat clear of the onrushing Neptunus. Sean and Jack walked around the flybridge and onto the boatdeck, their riot guns aimed and following the progress of the speedboat as the 98,000 pound hull of the motoryacht just barely missed hitting her stern, her wake pushing the Neptunus's bow a little to starboard. Fortunately the sudden acceleration of the speedboat had knocked the man with the gun to the deck, and by the time he recovered his dropped weapon they were out of effective range, so no shots were exchanged.

As 'Final Option' proceeded towards the maneuvering room of the open ocean, Sean and Jack watched fascinated as the speedboat got herself in trouble. Her sudden acceleration had taken her past the edge of the channel and into shallow water where her props, still racing at full speed, were churning up the sand on the bottom. While they watched, one of the props must have hit something solid because the hub disintegrated, literally sending propeller blades flying through the air, and bringing the boat to a shuddering halt as she ran aground hard, knocking both men off their feet. She seemed well and truly stuck as the blond man rocked the boat with alternate bursts of forward and reverse throttle on his remaining engine, but it was doing little good. Finally realizing his dilemma, he shook his fist at them and yelled a lot of choice words at them, but by then, they were too far away to hear them. Prominent on the stern of the speedboat, Jack noticed some green writing. Grabbing his Nikon 12 X 50 binoculars, he read, "Tender to M/V SHILLELAGH."

Everyone visibly relaxed as the distance between the two boats increased and the danger lessened, and Sean put away the riot guns, but not too far away. Jack continued to watch through the binoculars at the stuck speedboat that dwindled in the distance as the Neptunus went on its leisurely way. Before they passed from view entirely, Jack saw a second, identical speedboat appear and attempt to pull the first off the sandbank.

"Let's stay offshore as far as Key Largo, but keep close to the reef in case they come after us. I want to be able to duck inshore to a populated area if I see them coming," said Jack.

Capt'n Pete nodded agreement and adjusted their course to take them barely south of the fringing coral reef upon which so many ships over the centuries had come to grief. It seemed that most of the reefs in the Keys were named for the ships that had hit them. Nowadays, of course, boaters had the advantages of accurate charts, reliable communications, and the GPS satellite navigation system, which was extremely accurate and showed their actual position on an electronic chart in real time. Somehow, though, even with all these aids to navigation, there are still a few ships, through their own carelessness or stupidity, which manage to hit the fragile reefs each year.

By the time they reached the channel into Key Largo there was still no sign of pursuit, so by mutual agreement, they stayed in the open ocean where they could use the autopilot rather than struggle with the vagaries of the marked channels inshore, which required a boat to change course every half mile or fifteen minutes, whichever came first. They moved a little further offshore to take advantage of the favorable push of the Gulf Stream. They all agreed that trying to go north on the Intracoastal

Waterway on such a beautiful day would be like traveling on I-95 during rush hour in the snowbird season.

As they proceeded towards their goal, every hour or so Capt'n Pete would turn over the controls of the boat to Jack and proceed to the engine room through the crew quarters to check visually that everything was in order. Despite all the systems and sensors on the boat, he preferred an eyes on approach.

At lunchtime, which came soon after passing Key Largo due to their late departure, the question of Capt'n Pete's sobriety seemed to be settled when the others enjoyed their first beer of the day with the smoked kingfish dip, havarti cheese and crackers lunch that Katie had prepared. Even when encouraged with a new bottle of Jameson's, Capt'n Pete politely declined the alcoholic drinks and had root beer, saying, "I'll do my drinking when this boat is safely in its slip."

And so the afternoon passed pleasantly, the excitement and danger of the morning all but forgotten. Apart from a few sportfishermen and a helicopter which passed over them heading north, the sea was calm and empty and so they simply relaxed in the sunshine. Everyone changed into swimsuits except for Capt'n Pete, who was still wearing Sean's jeans and T-shirt, although his own clothes had, by now, been cleaned by Katie in the boat's own washer and dryer, drawing a comment from Capt'n Pete that she would make someone an ideal wife; smart, beautiful and handy, too. The comment raised Katie's eyebrows toward Sean, silently asking him if he was listening. He, of course, totally ignored the look and the implication and continued staring at the distant horizon.

Around five in the afternoon, having made excellent time due to the helping hand of the Gulf Stream, they spotted the tower of the Point of Americas condominium at the entrance of Port Everglades and set their course towards it. As they successfully transited the entrance, which was extremely congested, and came into Port Everglades proper, Capt'n Pete asked Jack, "Do you want to take it from here?"

"You've brought us this far. I don't see why you shouldn't finish the voyage," Jack said without hesitation. In heavy traffic, they proceeded north up the Intracoastal Waterway, Capt'n Pete paying particular attention to Jack' directions. In short order, and again with a minimum of fuss, they were securely tied up at her home slip at Pier 66.

That night, they all enjoyed Sean's hospitality at his club, where Capt'n Pete, true to his word, did do his drinking after the boat was safely in its slip.

Chapter 3

The past week had been an extremely busy one for everyone. The preparations for the trip had been started and, at least for Jack, events seemed to be happening faster than he had expected.

On Monday, Capt'n Pete had gotten a lift back to the Keys with a friend of Sean's who happened to be going down for a little fishing. Sean's friend, Riley, had turned out to be a bear of a man, but was described by Sean as a gentle giant who wouldn't hurt a fly. He had taken Capt'n Pete into the cab of his loaded pickup truck with a simple nod of his head and they had left immediately.

After a long talk with Jack on Monday morning, Shannon, who had stayed on the boat Sunday night while Capt'n Pete had gotten a hotel room for the night, had gone to the travel agency to hand in her resignation in order to work on the boat full time, organizing and provisioning it for the upcoming trip. She had also negotiated a salary equal to Capt'n Pete's, much to Jack's chagrin, and had terminated the lease on her apartment in order to move onto the boat full time. Those things she wanted to keep but couldn't take with them on the trip had been placed into storage, and the rest sold off, given away or trashed.

She had moved onto the boat officially on Tuesday and had spent the day moving her things into every nook and cranny she could find, until finally Jack had to point out that soon there would be no room left for people, and not enough reserve buoyancy for fuel. She had pouted a little but agreed that there were some things that she didn't absolutely have to take.

Capt'n Pete arrived back from the Keys on Wednesday morning driving his battered but still serviceable pickup truck and towing a totally dilapidated travel trailer behind him. The Pier 66 management was not completely overjoyed to see these still moving corpses of former vehicles in their parking lot and tactfully suggested that they be removed before they were towed away.

Jack had arranged for a Lanai room at the Hyatt Pier 66 hotel at a reduced rate and soon Capt'n Pete's few belongings had been transferred to either the room or the crew quarters on the boat. The trailer was consigned to a storage facility in Davie, where it would feel at home with more of its kind, and the truck had been parked across the road at the Harborview Shopping Center, where it fitted right in.

Capt'n Pete and Shannon were given their own sets of keys for the boat and Jack's SUV, and Shannon had also placed her car, a white Corvette convertible, into the carpool for the use of all.

A full day planning and strategy session was held Thursday starting beside the pool in the center of the Pier 66 resort, where the sounds of children playing and waterfalls splashing mixed with the tropical landscaping to almost give one a sense of escape from the city, except for the seventeen story hotel building which towered over them. They eventually ended up at the top of this tower at, naturally, the Piertop Lounge, a revolving lounge which completed one revolution every 66 minutes, and gave the viewer a unique perspective on Fort Lauderdale, its port and the surrounding area. Plans, itineraries and schedules were hammered out and specific tasks, projects, and duties were assigned to each of them.

Friday would be another day of organizing and ordering, mainly paperwork, passports, visas, health certificates, cruising permits for each country they would visit, insurance for the boat and its occupants, notarized ownership and registration papers, etc., etc.

Jack and Shannon got up early, and went to roust Capt'n Pete out of his slumber only to find him drinking coffee on the balcony of his lanai room overlooking the canal beside the hotel. They joined him and had been discussing the assignments that had been completed for a couple of hours and had come to the tasks for the day when Capt'n Pete suddenly stood up and let out a string of salty swear words, for which he immediately apologized to Shannon, but kept looking towards the Intracoastal. There, just swinging into view from behind 'A' dock, was the apparent object of his wrath. As he looked at it, Jack could not understand Capt'n Pete's outburst. The boat, a ship really, was a 165 foot long Feadship, all gleaming white and pristine, with a Bell Jet Ranger II helicopter on the aft deck between the two ships boats.

A vessel to be admired, not scorned, Jack thought, until he searched for its name and found, in bright green script, the word 'SHILLELAGH'. Now he understood Capt'n Pete's annoyance, and he felt his own anger rising. It lasted only a moment, though, and he had to suppress a smile when he noticed, on the speedboat facing them, the bent and useless outdrive with the missing propeller.

"Off the balcony, now!" instructed Jack, as he walked over and picked up the phone. He called the front desk and spoke with George, the concierge.

"This is Jack. If anyone asks for Captain Peter Olsen-Smith, you've never heard of him."

"I don't believe we have anyone by that name registered here, sir," said George.

"Good man," said Jack, hanging up.

"Capt'n Pete, stay in this room until we come and get you, and don't let anyone see you. Come on, Shannon, let's go for a walk."

After Jack and Shannon left, Capt'n Pete got busy phoning the various embassies in Miami for visas and cruising permits, which was, after all, his assignment for the day.

As they were walking back to 'Final Option', Jack wondered how the people on the yacht had found them so easily. Perhaps it was just that Pier 66, being the closest full service marina to the Port Everglades entrance, was a natural place for a boat the size of the 'Shillelagh' to stop for refueling. As they emerged from the central courtyard of the hotel, Jack stopped so suddenly that Shannon nearly walked into him. There on the aft deck of the Feadship was his answer. He recalled the helicopter that had passed over them on their way back last Sunday, and he had seen or heard several choppers over the marina during the week.

They made a quick stop at the boat, where Jack picked up one of his cameras. He chose a Nikon Coolpix P100 digital camera with its 26 times optical zoom lens, rather than his Nikon Coolpix 4300 digital camera, because of the long zoom on the larger camera. Checking that the 16 Gigabyte card was loaded into the camera and the battery was fully charged, he took Shannon by the hand, and said, "Let's go."

"Where are we going?" Shannon asked nervously.

"Over to the Pelican Bar for a drink."

"I guess we *could* have an early lunch."

"No food, just beer or drinks. I just want to sit on the observation deck and watch what is going on. I just hope that no-one recognizes us from last weekend."

The Pelican Bar was the second story of the marine store at the outward end of 'A' dock and half of it was a deck strewn with tables, chairs and umbrellas overlooking the Intracoastal and, incidentally, all of 'A' dock. The only trick was to get past the yacht, which was even now tying up to that dock.

Fortunately, even the most jaded boat watchers were turning out to watch this operation and quite a crowd had gathered. Jack and Shannon eased their way through the people and just when it looked as though they would make it, the crewman on the bow line turned and almost ran into them. A spark of recognition showed on his face as they passed but he made no move to stop them. Jack remembered him as the shorter of the two men in the speedboat, the one who had drawn the handgun.

They made the end of the dock and climbed the outside stairs to the Pelican Bar. Selecting one of the few tables left, they ordered from Jenny, the waitress, two Heinekens at Shannon's insistence. Even though the sun was nowhere near the yardarm yet, she was certain it was 5 o'clock somewhere.

As they sat and sipped their beer, they surreptitiously watched, and photographed, the post voyage activities on the yacht, the crew setting and adjusting the fenders and lines so as to keep the big boat off the pilings. Already one crewman was preparing a hose, buckets and soap to wash away the salt spray. It looked as if they were prepared to stay a while.

Shannon saw the big blond man first and tapped Jack on the arm, indicating him with a nod of the head. He was coming out of the side door of the bridge accompanied by an elderly gentleman, obviously the owner of the boat, for he was impeccably dressed. They were deep in conversation, talking as equals, even though there was no doubt who was the crewmember.

Jack was staring at them when the big man turned and saw him. Their eyes locked and the conversation stopped abruptly. The old man turned to see what the blond man was looking at and, as soon as he caught sight of Jack and Shannon, an evil smile slowly formed on his face. He grabbed the other man by the shoulder and led him back inside the bridge, where they could be seen going below.

Activity on the yacht slowly came to a halt, as one by one, the crew finished their assigned tasks and went inside. Soon the yacht appeared deserted.

Half an hour passed slowly, and Shannon and Jack were on their second beer, and wondering if they should return to their boat or to Capt'n Pete's room, when all of a sudden, a flurry of activity erupted on the yacht. Four crewmen, followed closely by the old man and the blond man, strode purposefully off the boat and took up strategic positions at the foot of the only two staircases leading up to the Pelican Bar. The old man followed the blond man up the outer staircase and both converged on their table. The blond man pulled out a chair at the table for the old man who asked politely, "You don't mind if we join you, do you?"

Jack hesitated for a moment, and then shrugged his shoulders and held out his hand, palm upward to indicate approval. He figured that not much could happen in the crowd of people present on the sun deck.

The two of them sat down and without preamble, the old man asked, "I am trying to locate Captain Pete Olsen-Smith, who I believe brought your boat here from the Keys last Sunday. Can you help me?"

"I'm sorry, I don't believe we've been introduced. I'm Jack Elliott and this is Shannon O'Loughlin. To whom am I speaking?"

Somewhat taken aback, the old man replied, "I am Senator Shamus O'Malley of Boston, Massachusetts and this is my captain, Horst Keller. Perhaps you've heard of me?"

"Sorry, I'm afraid not. I don't follow politics. Is there any reason I should have?"

"I guess not. Can you help me?"

"I am afraid not, sir. Capt'n Pete left the boat on Sunday night after we docked and checked in at the Harbor Motor Inn across the road. To the best of my knowledge, he went back to the Keys on Monday. Maybe you'd have better luck locating him down there. Why do you want to find him so badly, anyway?"

"Cause the son of a bitch owes me ten thousand bucks, that's why! When he was employed on my boat, he stole it out of the ship's safe and took it with him when I fired him."

"Really? Well, obviously I don't know him very well, having only spent one day in his presence, but he didn't seem to me to be the kind of person who would steal from his employer."

"I didn't think so either, until I found the money missing the day after he left the boat, and now I want it back."

"Are you certain he stole the money? It couldn't have been someone else?"

"He and Horst were the only ones with the combination to the safe, besides me, of course, and neither of us took the money. So it had to be him."

"Yes, I can see your point. But if that were the case, I would have thought that it was a matter for the police, if you are so certain of his guilt. Don't you?"

"Unfortunately, I can't prove it."

"So this man is guilty until proven innocent, is that it? And you are going to beat the truth out of him and attempt to drown him if he doesn't cooperate. I didn't think that that was the way the law worked in the United States, Senator."

The Senator didn't answer. They sat in silence for a few minutes, each man watching the other's face, until the Senator abruptly stood up and left, throwing over his shoulder, "Well, if you won't help me voluntarily, I guess I'll have to try something else."

They watched his receding back as he descended the stairway, and then noticed that Keller had not moved. Jack turned to him and said, "If there is nothing else to discuss, why don't you trot after your boss like a good little boy."

An ugly expression transformed the man's handsome face into a hideous mask and in a low, threatening voice, he hissed, "You better watch your ass, Elliott. Accidents do happen, you know. I'd hate to see your pretty girlfriend or your boat damaged beyond repair, you know what I mean?"

Jack clenched his fists, stood up quickly and moved very close to the other man's face, and deliberately lowered his voice for emphasis. "You listen to me, you slimy Kraut son of a bitch. You're in my territory now, and I can make things tough on you. If you or your friends come anywhere near us again, I'll see that they lock you up and throw away the key. You read me, asshole?"

Keller just grinned, and as he stood up, bumping his head on the umbrella because of his unusual height, he issued a warning, "We know the Captain is here somewhere, and we're going to find him. If you help us, you'll be O.K. If not, we can make your life miserable from now on, in ways you couldn't even conceive of, and none of them pleasant."

With a final sneer, he turned and left, following his boss down the stairs. He had a few words with the men at the base of the stairs and then went back aboard the yacht. The two men stayed where they were, looking threateningly up at the couple.

"That wasn't Senator O'Malley I saw you with just now, was it?"

The voice caught Jack by surprise and he turned to see his mother walking towards them.

"Yes, it was, Mother," he replied, inwardly groaning. He had not yet wanted to explain Shannon to his parents, and especially not here in a public place. "Why don't you join us?"

When she was seated, he introduced the two women to each other, and then asked, "What brings you down here? This is the first time you've been down here at the marina to see me."

His mother smiled primly and answered, "I heard this ugly rumor that you were shacking up with some bimbo on your boat. May I assume that that is you, my dear?"

At that moment, Jack just wanted to slide under the table and die of embarrassment, but Shannon jumped right in there to rescue him. "Yes, that's correct," she said.

"Well, just what are your intentions with my son? He *is* married, you know."

Jack was amazed at the transformation Shannon underwent as those soft, deep blue eyes which had looked lovingly at him for the better part of a week now suddenly, dramatically, went steel hard, and glinted in the sunlight as she sat up rigidly straight and looked his mother directly in her eyes. Her voice was soft and measured, but her words were full of emotion.

"Mrs. Elliott, with all due respect, you are wrong. You may, if you wish, think of me as a bimbo, but your son is no longer married and is free to do as he pleases without asking your or anyone else's permission. That woman he was married to no longer has any claim on him no matter how much she sucks up to you to try and get him back."

"When I first met Rain, she was the town slut and would sleep with anything in pants. I'm glad Jack finally found out and divorced her, and I sincerely believe that she and that sleazy P.I. she hangs out with deserve one another."

"I've been in love with your son for years now, but I've kept quiet because I didn't want him on the rebound. You can come here out of the blue and make your snide remarks and insults, but until Jack himself tells me I'm no longer wanted, I'm going to stay right here by his side."

Anne Elliott was taken aback, and it showed. She had not expected this young woman to be so feisty and she wasn't used to people disagreeing with her assessment of the situation. Most people she encountered grudgingly went along with what she said just to keep the peace. And all those awful things she said about Rain. They simply couldn't be true, could they?

Jack saw the expression on his mother's face and guessed at her consternation, and decided to break all the bad news, from her point of view, at once, and said, "By the way, while you are here, you may as well know everything. Shannon and I are going to take the boat across the Atlantic and cruise in Europe for a while."

"What? ... Why? ... When? ... How long are you going to be gone?" she managed to stammer.

"Probably a couple of years. Maybe three," he said, watching her carefully for a sign of how she was taking the news.

"Just the two of you?"

"There is one other person coming along. Someone with a lot of experience," he said, heading off that objection.

She sat totally stunned for a while at this blow to her plans, and then, surprising them both, said, "Well, I can see you've made up your mind to go, and I know I can't change it once it's made up so I'll bow out gracefully. But I want you to come to dinner at least once before you go, if only to introduce Shannon to your father. He should get quite a kick out of her attitude."

"O.K. Mother, that I can promise you," Jack said, happy to get off so lightly. His mother was notorious for the scenes she could cause if she put her mind to it.

"Well, I'm going to go now and leave you two to your planning. Call me later for a date for dinner." She got up and started to leave, but said over her shoulder, "And say hello to Shamus, Senator O'Malley, from me next time you see him."

"O.K. Mom."

She disappeared down the stairs and they stared at one another, dumbfounded.

"What just happened?" asked Shannon.

"Heaven only knows," replied Jack, already switching his attention from the confrontation with his mother to the two men at the bottom of the stairs. Just at that moment, a movement on 'B' Dock caught his eye and he watched unbelievingly as the Senator and Keller walked up and down the finger pier by his boat, trying to look into the portholes in the hull and the windows in the superstructure, which were covered by closed miniblinds and curtains.

Jack grabbed his camera, selected the furthest setting on the optical zoom lens and started taking shots of the two men as they tried to investigate his boat from the dock. Eventually, of course, since they had been unchallenged, Keller swung down to the swim platform and was starting to think about proceeding up to the aft deck to investigate further than they could from the dock. Jack took two more photos and then used his cell phone to call marina security to inform them that someone was breaking into his boat.

It was only a minute later when the security guards arrived on the scene, and although the words could not be heard, it was quite obvious from the actions that Keller took that they had told him in no uncertain terms to get off the boat. He obviously started to argue with them because their hands dropped to their holsters before he reluctantly returned to the dock where he was severely chastised before he was allowed to join the Senator and the two of them walked off 'B' Dock. Jack finished shooting both digital stills and 1080 HD video as they left. One guard followed the pair back to their boat while the other waved at Jack and came walking over.

The two guards, Tom and Jerry (honestly, no joking) were like twins, both over 250 pounds and all solid muscle, except that Tom was Jamaican black and Jerry was New England white, but they could have changed places on the NFL teams they had both played for and nobody would have noticed the difference, they were that good. They were a fixture at Pier 66, always around when you needed them, friendly, courteous, helpful and a pleasure to talk to. They generally faded into the background until you really needed them, and then they were there with a vengeance. They were the great American, over-worked, under-appreciated, wage-earning class; the people who got the job done while it was the white collar executives who gave the orders, made the big bucks, never got their hands dirty, and who looked down their noses at the very people who made everything tick.

"You know, you could charge them with trespassing if you wanted to. I'd testify for you." Tom said as he leaned on their table.

"No. That's O.K, Tom. I don't want to get tied up in a legal battle right now. It could postpone the trip to Europe and that's of primary importance. Thanks anyway, though," said Jack. "But there is something you can do for me, if you've a mind to."

"Anything you want, Jack, just name it."

"From now until we leave, keep a special eye on my boat for me, and give us an escort home."

"O.K."

"You'd better keep your hand on your gun. Those two characters down there don't look too friendly and I know they are looking for us."

Tom led the way down the stairs, one hand resting on the butt of his gun, and he was followed closely by

Shannon and Jack. When he reached the bottom, instead of continuing on, he stopped and fixed in place with his stare the two crewmen who were clearly intimidated by Tom's sheer size, as well as his uniform and gun. Stepping past Tom, Shannon and Jack made their way down 'A' Dock towards the hotel.

Once inside, they made a series of diversionary moves, going up a flight of stairs and down the elevators and a couple of zigzags through the corridors of the main building of the hotel to foil anyone following them until even Shannon was confused as to where they were. One final turn and Jack led them straight to Capt'n Pete's room, where, after proper identification was established, they were let in.

As soon as they were settled, Jack turned to Capt'n Pete and said, "We have to talk. Get things out in the open because, quite frankly, I'm confused as hell."

"What seems to be the problem?" asked Capt'n Pete.

Jack's voice was very quiet as he posed his dilemma, "Shannon and I have just had a short and quite unpleasant conversation with Senator Shamus O'Malley and he told me that you used to work for him on that yacht out there and that you stole ten thousand bucks from him. Was he telling the truth?"

Capt'n Pete hesitated for a moment, obviously shocked at the revelation and considering his options, which were limited, and then answered, "Well, yes and no. It's true that I used to work on his yacht for him; in fact, I was her captain until that backstabbing first mate came along. But I never stole any money from him, despite what he told you. I suspect it was the new captain of the yacht, Horst Keller."

"But wait a minute, you told us a bunch of bullshit about not knowing the two people who attacked you. Now I find out different from the person who probably ordered the attack, even if he didn't participate. And besides that, there has got to be more to this story than I've heard so far. Someone as rich as Senator O'Malley would not go to this much trouble over a measly ten thousand bucks." Jack was mad. He was not used to being lied to and he was mad at himself for being taken in so easily by this man whom he had trusted with his boat and its occupants, and for whom he had formed a genuine respect and perhaps even friendship.

They sat in awkward silence for a while, neither man trusting himself to speak for fear of putting more strain on their rapidly deteriorating relationship than there already was. Neither man could meet the other's eyes and the atmosphere grew increasingly tense, until finally it was Shannon who broke the anxiety, when she got up, walked to the fridge, got a beer for herself and one for Jack, and a root beer for Capt'n Pete and as she sat down, said, "Why don't you tell us all about it, Capt'n Pete. Everything from the beginning and don't leave anything out. If we have to spend a couple of years together on our boat, and travel all the way to Europe, we have to trust each other. I think that we deserve that much, don't you agree?"

"Yes, I do," said Capt'n Pete, "but I want you to hear me out before you pass judgment. Is that agreed?"

"O.K."

They all sat back with their drinks and listened to the fascinating tale as spun by Capt'n Pete.

"Firstly, I was not born in England as I told you, but in Bremen, Germany, in the height of the depression. If you Americans thought you had it bad, you should have spent a few months in Germany during that time between the wars. My mother *was* Swedish, as I told you before, but my father was obviously not English, but German, going by the name of Schmidt. He was a U-boat captain during the Second World War and quite a successful one, but his last voyage was the one where he lost his command and his men when his sub sank under his feet somewhere off the Bahamas. He alone survived the sinking and made it to shore, where he spent the rest of the war in the brig in Nassau. After the war ended, he didn't bother coming home to his wife and child. My mother died shortly after the war when it became obvious that he wasn't coming back. I guess I can't really blame him for that, under the circumstances."

"I made a vow to her on her deathbed that if he was alive I would locate him and find out why he didn't return."

"It was only five years ago, before your divorce, Jack, when I was finally able to track him down. He had been living a dirt poor existence just outside a small town called Rock Sound on Eleuthera Island in the Bahamas. He had apparently spent the intervening years since the war's end trying to find his submarine so he could salvage her. For someone his age, he was pretty well wasted away, suffering from malnutrition and, I guess, a touch of Alzheimer's, because much of the short time we had together was spent in a series of incoherent ramblings which, at the time, didn't make any sense. When he died a few months after I found him, I was expecting some sort of legacy, but what I got was totally unexpected. All he left me were his few meager possessions, an old sea trunk, a few sketchy memoirs, and a deathbed request to continue his search. It had taken me so long to find him that I felt sorry for myself and really started drinking, thinking that I had wasted my life searching for him and then didn't even have time to get to know him before he was gone."

"When I finally got his legacy, I was pretty well soaked with alcohol and it was months before I finally realized what he had been searching for all those years and what he had been trying so hard to tell me."

"I have tried to find his submarine several times over the years since he passed away but it has always eluded me. It had also left me penniless to the point that I had to find employment to sustain my search. In those days only a few years ago, I was still able to remain sober much of the time. Somehow I impressed Senator O'Malley enough to land the position of Captain on the 'Shillelagh'. After several years as his Captain, I felt comfortable with him and because of that comfort, unfortunately, I made the mistake of telling Shamus about my search for the sub. For some inexplicable reason my story had a strange and unpleasant effect on him. He got extremely upset and started ranting at me that I was spying on him and that's when things turned nasty between us. I have never to this day understood the reason my story has affected him the way it has."

"Forgive me for asking, but why the hell is this sub so important to everyone anyway? Apart from your sentimental value in locating it, I mean," interrupted Jack.

"Because of the cargo it was carrying. That is the one thing my father was very clear about. I can still hear him now, rambling on about 297 wooden boxes. In today's dollars, it had on board about two hundred million dollars worth of gold bars and it is still out there somewhere." said Capt'n Pete.

"WHAT!!!"

"Funny, that was the reaction I got from Shamus, too."

"So he knows about the gold?" Shannon asked.

"Yes, of course, I told him about it. But what I don't understand is, why the anger, the vindictiveness, and the attempt on my life? I can't believe it's just greed. There has to be more to it than that. Something I'm not seeing or understanding."

There was total silence for a few minutes while Jack and Shannon digested this latest revelation for truth and content. Given the convincing way this man could bend the history to suit himself, Jack decided to take this story with a grain of salt.

"So how come I've never heard of this lost treasure ship. I've studied with great interest and intensity all the recorded shipwrecks in this part of the world, you know, and I've never even heard a rumor of a lost treasure laden U-boat." asked Jack.

"Mainly because it was World War II and it was a secret mission, not written up in the logs of the day and not recorded in the history books. The only reference I've been able to find in the official archives, both in the Library of Congress and various maritime departments in Germany, is that U362 was lost at sea on a mission in the Atlantic. Probably fewer than a dozen people knew about the gold back then, and who knows how many of them are still alive today? But I know better because I have my father's account of what really happened to the submarine in the diary he left me."

"But, if you know where it is, why haven't you gone and gotten it by now?" asked Shannon.

"Because I, like my father, only have a rough idea of where it is, really just a general area which needs to be thoroughly searched. My father never found it. To finally locate and salvage it, I would need a boat, a lot of specialized equipment and a lot of time and money. None of which I have."

"So what are you doing on 'Final Option' with us." asked Jack.

"Hey, I figure it beats the hell out of living in a trailer and getting drunk every night and it sure pays better than odd jobs, and I can tell you honestly that I do not for one moment enjoy being roughed up and thrown in the harbor. Besides, the name of this boat might just be prophetic." Capt'n Pete replied honestly, the levity in his voice helping to calm the atmosphere, which had grown quite tense.

"Were you planning to tell us the truth at all if we hadn't forced the issue?" asked Shannon.

Capt'n Pete hesitated, "I honestly don't know. I got burned badly the first time I told someone and I hadn't foreseen that the Senator would come looking for me. For all he knew it could just have been the drunken ramblings of an old man. Obviously, I didn't want to endanger any of you for something between the Senator and me, but probably I would have, eventually."

They fell silent again and the silence lengthened and became quite palpable before it was finally broken by Jack, who asked the question on everyone's mind, "So, where do we go from here?"

This time Capt'n Pete was the one who jumped in, "Look, I'm sorry that I had to lie to you, but I'm sure you can understand why due to the circumstances. I promise that it won't happen again. I still want to go on this trip to Europe, how about you?"

Both Jack and Shannon answered yes simultaneously and Capt'n Pete continued, "Then forgive me and let us continue with our plans."

The matter was set aside for further discussion at a later date as the enormous amount of work still to be done on all the fine details of the trip surfaced and were tackled one by one as they cropped up.

The tentative target date for the departure was set at April first and they knew they'd have to hustle to make it.

When the weekend finally arrived, things seemed to settle down. The 'Shillelagh' was still berthed on 'A' dock and, indeed, they saw various members of her crew around Pier 66, including Horst Keller, but no one accosted them, or even acknowledged their presence.

Surprisingly, they ran into no problems with all of the embassies that they contacted on Friday, they all cooperated very well, and promised to expedite the issuance of visas and cruising permits. They also managed to locate all the items that they required locally, and would begin picking them up, starting on Monday. They had also arranged for a marine mechanic to come down the following Wednesday to look over and tune up the engines and generators, a task Jack could have accomplished had he had the time.

On Sunday, Sean and Katie came over in the Cary and Jack and Shannon joined them for a day of bar hopping, a Florida tradition, aboard the sleek vessel. Being already at Pier 66, they went out the Port Everglades entrance and ran north along the coastal beaches. Sean really opened the boat up in the flat calm seas and Jack watched with amusement as the gas gauge appeared to be dropping as fast as the speedometer was rising. The mirror-like smoothness of the water's surface perfectly reflected the boat as they ran a half-mile offshore and before they knew it they were making that long smooth turn into the Boca Raton inlet.

"We are going inside?" Jack asked.

"Yes," replied Sean. "I would have taken you to Bimini in the Bahamas on a day like this, under normal circumstances, but since the Bahamian government has seen fit to extort a $300 cruising permit fee on this size boat, I'll do my cruising in American waters from now on."

"$300 a year doesn't seem so much," exclaimed Shannon, thinking back to the fees for some of the cruising permits they were at this time trying to get from some of the European nations.

"No, not $300 per year. $300 per visit. You know that I can afford it, but I'll be damned if I'll stand still for their extortion. Damned highway robbery it is. I'll just do my cruising in the Keys and Florida's East and West coast." Sean was hot under the collar about this subject.

As they negotiated the narrow entrance and passed under the A1A bridge, they threaded their way through the sport fishing boats waiting for the bridge to open so they could exit the inlet into the open ocean for a day in the Gulfstream, hauling in the big ones.

They turned south on the Intracoastal Waterway and made for the Beachview Hotel, the logical first stop for brunch. The Beachview was typical of the many watering holes for boaters in South Florida, which consisted almost exclusively of a length of dock, size depending on the size of the hotel, which usually had one or more swimming pools, one or more outdoor bars, a finger food restaurant, and huge amounts of sundeck, liberally strewn with tables, chairs and loungers. More often than not, the latter were covered with scantily clad young women and the rich old geezers who provided for them.

After brunch, which consisted of a Bloody Mary each, they got back into the boat and continued south until they got to the Shooters complex where the boats of the many patrons were rafted together four or more deep out from the dock. Shooters' own boat tenders on the dock saw the big Cary coming and quickly carved out a niche for Sean, for he was well known as a big tipper. They managed, by untying the entire raft of boats and for a few seconds allowing them to float freely in the canal, to get Sean directly alongside the dock.

This was convenient for the people on the Cary, but also inconvenient because it meant that the owners and guests on the outboard boats had to cross the foredeck or enter the cockpit of the Cary in order to get to their own boats. However those were the rules. Don't come here expecting an exclusive spot for your boat and not expect strangers to cross your boat to get to theirs, but this was a perfect way to meet new people with, obviously, the same interests as your own.

They had a pleasant lunch of smoked salmon, fresh vegetables and dip, while watching the World Famous 'Hot Bod' Bikini Contest beside the pool. Sean, of course, had managed, by contacting the bar's owner and invoking executive privilege, to get a front row center table with an exclusive view of the action. Judging by the eyes of the crowd, either Shannon or Katie could have won the contest hands down, had they chosen to enter but they declined to compete in the contest and so lost by default. The food, the drinks and the company were excellent and everyone was enjoying themselves.

When they finally decided to leave, the extrication of the Cary went smoothly and they set off southward once again. Cruising serenely past the million dollar homes and high rise condominiums lining the waterway, they relaxed and enjoyed the warm, sunny weather that Florida is world famous for, and which, unfortunately, half of New York and Canada come south to experience during those winter months when Mother Nature tries to extract the price for the other seasons' glorious sights and sounds up North, and whitewashes the world above the Tropic of Cancer with snow so she can paint her new palette once again in the springtime. They left to starboard the Las Olas Isles and to port, the resort of Bahia Mar, home port to 'Leprechaun', the fifty foot Cary upon which they traveled. They discussed briefly the possibility of stopping at a particular place near Bahia Mar, but decided to give it a miss. As they turned the corner into the channel that had originally been the bed of the New River, they passed between Harbor Beach and the southern Las Olas Islands, with multi-million dollar mansions on either side. They thought of continuing up the New River, but decided against it because it was too far out of the way. One of the nicer things about cruising in Fort Lauderdale's many waterways was that there were always plenty of choices.

A half mile further south, the Marriott Hotel and Pier 66 faced each other across the waterway at the 17th Street Bridge and as they approached Jack's home base, they noticed something different about the marina. Because of the large amount of water-borne traffic all around them, they didn't at first comprehend how that change would affect them. It was Shannon who finally put her finger on it.

"The 'Shillelagh'! She's gone!" she shouted with glee.

Jack looked and saw that she was right. The Senator's yacht was nowhere to be seen. "Perhaps they've just taken her out for a cruise." Not daring to believe his eyes, he was trying to find a logical explanation to what, for them, would be a godsend.

They had now completed the circle they had started that morning, and they once more sailed through the bridge opening into Port Everglades. This time, instead of exiting out into the ocean as they had done that morning, they continued south on the Intracoastal Waterway past all the cruise ship berths and the container ship terminal to the Dania Cutoff Canal, where they proceeded on up the canal to Skylines Bar and Grill.

Once again, as Sean expertly guided the boat to the dock, Jack noticed the looks of appreciation the two women were drawing from the crowd and vowed silently to stay close to Shannon for the duration of their stay. After the boat had been secured, they claimed a table near the outdoor stage where a reggae band was working up a storm, ordering drinks and nachos as soon as they were seated.

Shannon induced Jack onto the dance floor with a series of lascivious promises for the upcoming evening, and although dancing was not one of his strong suits, Shannon more than made up for his lack of grace. All he basically had to do was to stand in one spot and move his hips and shoulders somewhat to the rhythm, while admiring the way her body moved to the frenzied Jamaican beat. She flowed with the fluidity of a cat, and drew many longing glances, and even outright stares, from the mesmerized audience. When the set wound to a finish, she received an enthusiastic standing ovation from the crowd, women as well as men, which she accepted with a large smile and a small curtsy.

Jack was feeling very proud of her as he led her back to the table where Sean and Katie sat, also applauding enthusiastically.

They sat and talked together until the next set began, and Sean took Katie onto the dance floor. Katie turned out to be just as good at dancing as Shannon was and Sean was much better than Jack could ever hope to be, and by the time the set ended, the crowd had found a new set of heroes to worship.

They spent the rest of the afternoon relaxing and getting Sean and Katie's opinions of various options in their plans to tour Europe. Sometime during the afternoon, Sean called for a berth and dinner reservations at Claudia's. While still tied firmly to the dock, the two women availed themselves of the relative calm to go below to shower and change for the evening because the restaurant they were going to was a class place.

When they emerged an hour later, to allow the men below to get themselves spruced up, they were dressed to the nines and immediately elected to remain in the cockpit of the boat due to the unruly segment of the inebriated crowd, who were whistling and cat-calling at the visions before them.

A short while later, casually but neatly attired, Sean and Jack joined the two women in the cockpit. Preparations were made to get underway for the short, protected trip to Claudia's and many willing hands on the dock assisted them.

Fifteen minutes later, having passed under the Dania Beach Boulevard Bridge, they were nosing up to the dock at Claudia's helped by the dock crew from the establishment. They were shown to a table on the second floor deck and enjoyed a remarkably prepared dinner for which Claudia's was renowned. They wined, they dined, and they danced the night away until around midnight, when they all piled into the boat for the slow, protected trip back to Pier 66, and for Sean and Katie, back to Bahia Mar.

Chapter 4

It took almost a week for the realization to sink in, but it seemed that the 'Shillelagh' had finally left for parts unknown. No one, but especially the crew of 'Final Option', was sad to see it leave for its crew had caused no end of trouble while they were in port. In many ways it was like lifting a dark cloud from everyone's enjoyment of their environment.

Capt'n Pete was finally able to escape from his room, which had become a prison cell for him while that obnoxious crew were still around. He was finally able to help with the outfitting of the boat and he set to work with a vengeance, making up for lost time in order to bring their plans back on schedule.

The day being the beginning of another glorious weekend and the end of their preparations being firmly in sight, Jack suggested that they all take the weekend off. Shannon readily agreed but Capt'n Pete, aware of how he had been forced to neglect his share of the work due to his incarceration in his room during the early part of the preparations, decided to continue the assignments he had set himself.

Jack and Shannon decided to spend some time on the beach and quickly assembled an assortment of towels, swimsuits and suntan lotions into a carrying bag and set out for the short walk to the beach, hand in hand. As they walked, they discussed the upcoming trip and the implications of the unexpected complications that their decision to include Capt'n Pete in their plans had brought to them. They agreed that it was still the best thing for the safety of the journey that he was coming. But they conjectured that the crew of the 'Shillelagh' may still cause trouble for all of them in the future, and even though they had left for the moment, that complication was still a very real worry. The possibility of running into them in another port could not be discounted, and the mystery of what the Senator really wanted was baffling. They finally decided that, at least for now, they would leave things as they stood and let the future develop as it might.

They spent a couple of hours sunbathing and swimming in the still cool waters off the beach and then decided to go to lunch at Hooters at Beach Place. Secretly, Jack was hoping to see Janine Beaumont one last time before they left for Europe and he wanted his two favorite women in the entire world to meet and he hoped that they would approve of one another. When they got to the establishment, it was Lisa who brought them their menus and Jack inquired about Janine. He was told that she was in the back but that her shift didn't start until a little later. They ordered beers and hot wings and Jack asked Lisa to tell Janine that he was out front and would like to see her if she had time.

They held hands while they engaged in Jack's favorite pastime, people watching. Well, second favorite, anyway. Their beers arrived without any sign of Janine, but when their hot wings came, there were three orders instead of two, and they were brought over by the one and only, the delectable Miss Hooters 1997, Janine Beaumont.

She arrived in her street clothes, as opposed to the tight little uniform that is the trademark of Hooters establishments the world over, and wearing a large welcoming smile that outshone the sun on the balcony where they were sitting. She placed the wings in front of each of them and put her food down between them, wrapped both arms around Jack's neck and gave him a huge, and terribly exaggerated, kiss on the lips that brought a smile to Shannon's face and stares of disbelief to the faces of those men present who had already been eying Shannon ever since they got there. One man, somewhat handsome in a rugged sort of a way, got up and moved to the other side of the room, shaking his head and muttering to himself, "It ain't fair, it just ain't fair."

"Jack," said Janine, "every time I convince myself that the devil has finally taken you from the face of the earth, and I'll never see you again, you show up out of the blue with another little surprise for me. What have you brought me this time?"

"Good to see you, too." said Jack, "I want you to meet a very special lady in my life, this is Shannon. Shannon, this is Janine."

Janine smiled and said, "I wondered what you would look like. I have heard a lot about you, from Sean amongst others, and I have pictured you in my mind, but I must say that the reality is much better than the imagination. I am very pleased to meet the one who finally caught Jack. I hope the two of you will be very happy together."

Shannon smiled, too, and replied, "I have heard of you, too, from Sean and I am pleased to finally meet you, too, but I must say that you could have put a strain on our relationship if I wasn't so confident of how Jack felt about me."

"You know, I remember, when Jack was still married to what's her name..."

Jack interjected, "Hello, you two, remember me, I'm still here, and don't you be talking about me as if I were a thousand miles away."

Both women looked sheepishly at him, realizing that he had been completely ignored in the conversation, and then they both pouted at him to tell him to grow up, that this was a woman to woman talk, and he was to eat his wings and drink his beer and shut up.

This gave him the chance to sit back, relax and glance around the large room at the delightful young ladies who made up the majority of the staff in this restaurant, and at the mostly male clientele. Almost all were engaged in their own conversations, and concerned with their own well being, except for one man sitting by himself in the far corner, who seemed vaguely familiar to Jack, and who was gazing intently in their direction. Jack almost came to the conclusion that the man was infatuated with one of the women at the table and was still daydreaming about one or the other, or both, of them, but the man did a very strange thing. He saw Jack watching him and immediately looked down at his food, and then got up abruptly, spilling his beer, threw a couple of twenties on the table and quickly left the restaurant. Jack thought for a second about following him, but by the time he decided to do it, the man had already disappeared.

His attention was jerked suddenly back to his own table as he heard his name being called. Both women were staring at him as if they had revealed all the secrets of the world and he had slept through them, but he quickly recovered with, "I *am* sorry, I missed that last part. Could you repeat it?"

Shannon said, "I was just explaining to Janine about Capt'n Pete coming with us, explaining to her about the things that have been happening to us since that night in the Keys and I asked her if she had heard of a place called Rock Sound. And guess what?"

"What?"

"Turns out that that is where she is from."

"What????"

Janine answered, "Yes, that's right. Born and raised there. In fact, my father still lives there, and has been there all his life."

Jokingly, Jack asked, "I don't suppose that he rescued any German sailors during the war, did he?"

It was the first time that Jack had seen Janine at a loss for words, and she sat there for a good ten seconds before answering, "I don't know how you knew but, yes, he did rescue a German sailor during the war. He was the captain of a submarine and his boat was lost during a hurricane."

"Where?"

"Off the coast of Eleuthera, somewhere around Rock Sound, I presume. My father has never left the island, so it had to be somewhere close. My father hasn't even been to Nassau. He says that he has paradise right there, so why should he go anywhere else?"

"So what happened to the German Captain?" asked Jack.

"Even though the German was arrested and interned on New Providence Island for the duration of the war, he came back to Eleuthera after the war to live in Rock Sound."

"When does your shift end?" Jack asked suddenly.

"I'm off at ten thirty p.m.," she said. "Why?"

"Do you think that you could come around to the boat when your shift is over? There's someone I'd like you to meet."

"Sure, I can do that. I've got my car so you don't have to pick me up."

"All right."

"Anyway, I've got to start my shift now, and you know how Lisa hates to be kept waiting. I'll see you tonight."

"O.K."

Just before eleven that night, Janine's fire engine red Porsche 911, part of the prize she had won in the Miss Hooters Contest, eased its way past the guard gate at the entrance to the Pier 66 parking lot. Although the area was well lit and there were other people around, she felt unaccountably apprehensive. She kept swiveling her head, scanning the immediate area for unusual activity but found none. Even the two security guards were more than conspicuous, being stationed within sight of each other at the head of, respectively, 'A' dock and 'D' dock.

Even though she had been to Jack's boat countless times, and the boat had had the same slip number since he'd first got there, for some unaccountable reason, she started down the wrong dock, choosing 'C' instead of 'B' dock. She was halfway down the pier before she looked across the narrow expanse of water between the docks at the stern of Jack's boat. Realizing her mistake, she had started to turn back toward the shore when she noticed something amiss.

A black lump was hard up against the stern under the swim platform of Jack's boat, and try as she might, she could not identify it. It was moving but it didn't have any definite shape, being just a dark lump. She hurried back to terra firma and her abrupt movements drew the attention of both Tom and Jerry. She motioned for both of them to follow her and they all arrived at 'B' dock simultaneously.

As they raced down the dock, a distinct splash was heard behind 'Final Option' and when they screeched to a halt beside the boat, ripples could still be seen radiating out from the stern. Mindful of the anxiety felt by Jack and his request to keep an eye on the boat, Tom drew his gun and started prowling around, while Janine and Jerry stared out at the water.

They were both startled and confused when suddenly Tom started laughing uproariously, the sound echoing off the closer boats. They rushed to where he was standing at the end of the pier finger, grinning from ear to ear. Their eyes followed his outstretched arm as he quietly informed them, "It's only a manatee."

Jerry asked, "A what?"

"A manatee, a dugong, you know, a sea cow, what the old time sailors mistook for a mermaid. They are around here all the time, you must have seen that one." Tom explained, pointing to the dark shape.

"To tell you the truth, I don't have the time or the inclination to look at the water. I'm too busy looking for bad guys." Jerry's life was simple. Work and football was all he wanted to know about.

The dark lump in the water looked for all the world like a small sandbar in the subdued moonlight until it moved. It dove under the water, surfacing a short time later further down the canal, at the stern of another boat.

"It's probably feeding on the accumulated vegetation around the waterline of the boats. Some of them haven't moved for months," commented Tom, "you might want to suggest to Jack that he have his bottom cleaned before he leaves for his trip."

Janine smirked, "His bottom or his boat's?"

"You know what I mean."

The two guards walked off down the dock laughing as Janine boarded 'Final Option' and was greeted warmly at the aft saloon door by Jack and Shannon. She was explaining what had happened with the manatee as she entered, and didn't at first see the other man in the room, who turned out to be a stranger to her. Jack introduced him as Captain Pete Olsen-Smith and she found him to be a little shy but well mannered and hesitant to step out of the shadows.

"Do you want a drink?" asked Shannon.

"Yes, please, a Dark and Stormy if you don't mind."

"Sounds good to me. Jack?"

"One for me, too, please"

"Capt'n?"

"Nothing, thanks."

Shannon went to the galley to mix the drinks as Jack and Janine sat down on the saloon couch and Jack said, "Capt'n Pete is the person I wanted you to meet. But first a question: do you remember the name of the German captain your father rescued on Eleuthera in 1944?"

"Yes, of course I do. My father told me his name was Schmidt."

Jack had been watching Capt'n Pete, and the reaction was sudden and unpredictable. At the mention of the name, the old man sat bolt upright and his eyes went as wide as saucers. He stood up quickly and with two mighty strides, he was towering over the young woman, who shied away in alarm.

"What do you know of my father?" he demanded.

The situation was tense for a few moments until Shannon, who must have been aware of what had happened, cheerfully carried the drinks into the saloon and placed them on the table, bending between Capt'n Pete and Janine. She stood up tall and looked Capt'n Pete squarely in the eyes, and almost immediately the old man wilted before her gaze. He sagged visibly, and then sat down on the couch next to Janine and, eyes downcast, apologized profusely for frightening her.

"I'm sorry, young lady. Please tell me what you know of my father," he asked quietly.

She looked at Jack, who with a nod bade her to go on. "I really don't know all that much," she explained nervously. "My father has only mentioned parts of the story in passing, and only when he is reminiscing about the 'good old days'"

"What ever you can remember will help," said Capt'n Pete.

"Well, from what I gather, it was the morning after a terrible late season hurricane. They didn't have names for them back then, but I remember him telling me it was late

1944, and my father was walking on the beach at dawn trying to see what damage had been done and what had washed up on the shore. With the reefs just offshore, there was usually something worthwhile salvaging along the shoreline and he definitely needed any money it would bring. He told me that at first he was disappointed because, apart from driftwood, coconuts and an empty crate, the only thing he found was a half drowned German sailor. He had almost decided to let him lay where he was because he looked dead. He would report the body to the authorities later. But when the man started spluttering and coughing up seawater, my father was quickly at his side to help him."

"The German put up no resistance when he was helped to my house, years before I was born, of course, and eventually the authorities came, took him away and put him in prison in Nassau for the duration of the war."

"You can imagine my father's surprise when the German captain came back after the war was over and thanked him for saving his life. The white man then surprised everyone when he settled down in Rock Sound, which was and still is primarily a black township, and started fishing with the rest of the men from the village. He eventually bought some land and built a house near ours and didn't seem at all inclined to move on, and so was eventually accepted as a member of the community."

"It was years before he got around to telling my father about the U-boat and its mission, even I heard some of the stories, and I guess because he took my father into his confidence, a firm friendship developed between them."

"I can even remember myself seeing the 'great white German U-boat captain' when I was very young, but even then he looked so old and worn out."

At this point, Capt'n Pete interjected, "He died a couple of years ago without telling me of your father. In fact, I never met anyone who had known him during all those intervening years. Do you suppose that your father might know something about what he was up to and where he was searching?" he asked.

"There is always that possibility. He is very old, but he still has all his faculties. In fact, he's quite spry for his age."

"Do you think we could call him, and let me ask him some questions?" Capt'n Pete asked.

"He doesn't have a phone. Never has and, he insists, never will. Calls it 'one of those new fangled inventions' and refuses to have one or to use one. Even though he has made the concession to drive a car, he still prefers his kids and kin come by if they want to talk."

She lapsed into silence, and everyone being at a loss for words, the silence lingered. The tension had dissipated from the atmosphere but had left in its place a feeling of confusion and even contemplation. Everyone was looking at each other as if expecting them to say something.

Finally, Shannon rose from her seat and, unbidden, went to make more drinks for everyone, Capt'n Pete included.

When she returned, Jack was the first to find his tongue, "In light of what we've just heard, I think I can safely say that our trip to Europe has been postponed indefinitely. I don't think Capt'n Pete's heart would be in it and if we don't help him find out about his father and the submarine, I personally would probably go crazy wondering if he had ever found it. Therefore, I propose that we go to the Bahamas, to Rock Sound, to talk to Janine's father and find that submarine."

"But first we have to loose the Senator for good," added Capt'n Pete.

"Yes, we will," said Jack. "We have to come up with a plan to make him think that we are going to one place when we are really going to another."

"Janine, I know you gave me a great many reasons why you couldn't come to Europe with me," Jack said, "but could you take some time off and come with us to Rock Sound to talk to your father?"

"For you, Jack, of course I could," she replied, and then, turning to Capt'n Pete, added, "and for you, too, Captain."

Chapter 5

The Senator slammed the phone back into its cradle, absolutely disgusted.

"God damn it! That stupid idiot! I am surrounded by fools and imbeciles!" he yelled across the saloon of the 'Shillelagh'. "Why can't anyone accomplish just one of the simple tasks I set them?"

Keller was sitting comfortably in an easy chair in the expansive, richly furnished (at the taxpayer's expense) saloon of the luxury yacht. He was startled by this outburst, dropped the Playboy magazine he was looking at and lowered his head in embarrassment under the wrath of his superior. Despite his size and strength, this man who was his boss still had the power to intimidate him.

"What now?" he inquired softly.

"That private-eye jackass, Stevenson, who YOU hired to keep an eye on the people on 'Final Option', and who nearly got himself caught by Elliot at Hooters, has once again failed to get the correct information to me on time."

"What has he done now?" Keller felt his temper rising for he was always anxious to placate his boss, and the thought of someone else's stupid mistakes causing ripples on the water to his detriment gave him cause for anger.

"It seems that the 'Final Option' left her slip several days ago for parts unknown and all his feeble attempts to find her have come up empty. Damn it!" He hurled the heavy, cut crystal rocks glass he was holding across the saloon into the fake fireplace at the other end, where it hit with a resounding crash and shattered into a thousand pieces.

"Let me go back to Fort Lauderdale and I'll find out where that boat is now." Horst promised.

"Go! Get out of here!" screamed the Senator, now turning red in the face, "and don't come back here until you can tell me where those people are. I want to know what they are doing, where they are going, and what they intend to do next. And while you're at it, take that stupid jackass out and teach him not to screw around with me. I don't ever want to hear from him or about him again, do you understand me?" He added as an afterthought, stalking over to the bar to mix himself another tall drink.

"Yes, sir!"

Horst hurriedly escaped the hostile confines of the saloon and, after reluctantly turning responsibility for the Feadship over to the first mate, grabbed his emergency bag and quickly left the ship. He had never before witnessed his boss, normally a cool, calm, and collected man in control of himself and his surroundings in such a foul mood. It shook him to his core to finally realize that, for whatever reasons, the Senator had his shortcomings, too. The whole support structure upon which he had been leaning seemed to be crumbling away. In fact, it had been crumbling since that day at Holiday Isle and his first contact with Jack Elliott.

He rented a car and left the private Ocean Reef Club on Key Largo, where the ship was tied up, and took Card Sound Road to the Florida Turnpike and within a couple of hours arrived in Fort Lauderdale.

His first stop was Pier 66 where he confirmed that 'Final Option' had indeed terminated her lease on the slip she had occupied for many years. Those slips, he knew, were extremely difficult to come by, so hard in fact that only those who knew that they would be away for a long time, or those who died, would allow their leases to expire. It seemed reasonable to assume that the 'Final Option' would not be returning soon.

Amongst the marina staff he interviewed, those who could be intimidated into talking, opinions ranged far and wide as to where the boat was headed. The majority favored Europe for that was common knowledge but there were holdouts for the Keys, or the Bahamas, and all the various getaway and tourist islands in the Caribbean were mentioned, but no one could say for sure.

After securing and settling into his room at Pier 66, he mixed himself a drink from the in-room wet bar, and arranged himself in a comfortable position on the lounge, laying out the phone, the local phone book, his personal phonebook and his notebook within easy reach and started dialing. His list of contacts, both private and official government sources, was extensive and he felt that this was the best way to find the missing boat.

Several hours and numerous phone calls later he had been able to ascertain that 'Final Option' and its crew had cruising permits and visas for the Bahamas, Bermuda, the Azores, Spain and Portugal, France, Belgium, Holland and Germany, as well as the British Isles, Ireland, Denmark, Norway and Sweden. In the Mediterranean, Italy, Croatia, Turkey and Greece were there, too. It was beginning to look like quite a long cruise, and it looked like they intended to go to Europe.

As if to further enhance his theory, Horst eventually located and spoke to, by phone, a marina owner in Stuart, Florida, who confirmed that 'Final Option' had indeed spent the night there and had left only that morning outbound for Savannah, Georgia, with a crew of four; owner, girlfriend, Captain, and a black girl who was described as a real looker. It was that man's understanding that the boat was heading for Europe and that after Savannah they would head for Wilmington, North Carolina at the mouth of the Cape Fear River, where they would refuel and reprovision before heading across the Atlantic for Bermuda, the Azores and Cadiz in the south of Spain.

The blabbermouth also said that they spoke about a grand cruise in the Baltic before winter drove them south into the Mediterranean. After that they didn't mention anything, at least not in his presence.

Horst was a difficult man to understand, for although his size, strength and cruelty made him a man whom most people feared because of his physical attributes, he was also smart. What most people didn't even suspect was that a first rate mind also resided in that body. Although the papers that Elliott had obtained included the Bahamas, which was out of the way if they actually intended to go to Europe, he was certain that this was a false trail and was therefore satisfied that he had finally found the illusive vessel. Horst placed a call to the Senator at the Ocean Reef Club, who took his report with calm satisfaction and ordered him to return to the 'Shillelagh' after taking care of the other little matter he had been assigned.

So before leaving Fort Lauderdale, and following the Senator's instructions to the letter, he paid a surprise visit to the incompetent fool he had hired to spy on Elliott and his crew. The private eye was even glad to see him, for the first few moments at least, but shortly thereafter, in the man's sleazy, run down office, behind locked doors, Horst methodically beat the man to within an inch of his life and left him bleeding and broken on the threadbare carpet covering the floor. Horst had not even had the need to remind the man that if he said anything to anybody his life would be over. He felt much better when he left, admitting to himself that he had even enjoyed the physical abuse that he had meted out on another human being because it had been a long time since he had been able to vent the fury that had been building up inside him since the incident at Holiday Isle. He left the PI's office whistling a happy tune.

Despite driving like a maniac on a mission, and endangering countless unfortunate motorists on the Turnpike who were slightly tardy in getting out of his way, Horst returned to Key Largo barely in the nick of time. As he pulled into the parking space, the big Feadship was already slipping her lines in preparation of moving out to sea. He only just had time to grab his overnight bag, rush onto the dock and leap across the ever widening gap between the ship and the shore before it was too late. He landed on the side deck awkwardly, twisting his ankle and landing in a tangle of arms and legs up against the side of the superstructure. Ignoring the pain from his already swelling injury, he raised himself and hobbled his way up the stairway to the bridge.

"So nice that you could join us, Mr. Keller." The Senator smiled at him. At least his lips were smiling but the humor and warmth never touched his eyes. As he was turning to leave, he added, "Please take over from me, and make all possible speed for Miami."

Horst took particular care executing the extrication of the vessel from the harbor, while favoring his damaged appendage, but as soon as they had cleared the marked channel, he turned the yacht over to the first mate along with specific instructions as to course and speed. He then gingerly hobbled below to the aft deck where the Senator was lounging, already halfway through the large Martini he had ordered after leaving the bridge.

"What the hell happened to you," asked the Senator as he watched Horst hobbling towards him. "Don't tell me that that wiry little P.I. got a few licks of his own in?"

"Not likely," he replied, "I just misjudged the distance to the boarding ladder, that's all."

"Ah, I see. Do try to be more careful in the future, I'd hate to loose another Captain so soon. Sit down and take the weight off that leg."

"So where are we going in such a hell of a hurry?" Horst asked when he was seated.

"Bermuda," was the Senator's reply, "but first we have to stop in Miami to refuel, and I want to get there as soon as possible, because I have arranged for a tanker to meet us at Miami Beach Marina to give us a full load of fuel. I don't want to have to wait until tomorrow morning before starting the crossing to Bermuda."

Horst was thoughtful for a moment, and then he nodded. "I can understand why you want to go there, but if all you want to do is beat them to Bermuda, why not just fly over in your long range Learjet?"

"Because I want the boat and this crew close by when we catch up with them." The Senator's eyes narrowed and a look of eager anticipation came over his face. "We have information to gather and it may just be that we will have to be a little more persuasive than we have been in the past in order to obtain it. Personally, I'd just as soon be well away from the prying eyes of the U.S. authorities when we employ some of that persuasion. Besides that, according to my calculations, if they want to make it to Bermuda, they will have to slow down to 10 or

11 knots based on the amount of fuel they can carry. We, on the other hand, can maintain 18 knots all the way across. Therefore, since we have more speed and greater range than they do, we will be able to beat them there, refuel and reprovision and then we will stay out of sight and watch them from the time they arrive until they leave for the Azores. I know for a fact that their boat only carries a 36 mile radar, so it'll be easy to keep tabs on them and follow them at a distance, unobserved by them, but keeping them within range of our 72 mile radar until it is time to intercept their little boat."

"And then?"

His only answer was a triumphant smirk from the Senator, who raised his Martini and downed the remainder in one swallow. His mind dancing with the euphoria of sweet revenge against Jack, Horst returned the grin tenfold.

Chapter 6

As they cruised serenely northward five miles offshore of St. Augustine, Florida, which was the first city founded by the Spanish on the mainland of America, they were headed for Savannah, Georgia, where Jack had arranged to have the boat hauled out, scraped clean and have new antifouling paint applied at the Palmer Johnson Yard in Thunderbolt. He had announced that morning an all hands meeting on the flybridge of the 'Final Option' to discuss the task before them. On board were Jack and Shannon, Capt'n Pete and Janine, who had taken a leave of absence from Hooters in order to come with them on this circuitous route to their eventual destination in the Bahamas. Jack felt that a formally convened meeting would produce a more serious discussion of their goals, options and the difficulties that lay before them. As soon as they were all settled with full coffee cups in their hands, including Capt'n Pete, who was on watch, Jack opened the discussion.

"Firstly, I firmly believe we have to assume that Senator O'Malley knows exactly where we are at this very moment, and is preparing some sort of nasty surprise for us in the near future," he started, "so what we have to do, with planning and not a small measure of luck, is to foil their attempts by loosing them."

"We are going to proceed to Savannah as planned and, when we get there, we are going to spend some time in that city playing tourist while the boat is hauled and the bottom painted. We will all have to keep a close eye on our surroundings specifically to try to spot any familiar faces in the crowds around us. I doubt if even the Senator will be stupid enough to try to detain any of us before he ascertains what our objectives are, so I don't believe we will be in any danger. However, I do believe we should always travel in pairs, especially since I don't trust that snake-in-the-grass Horst Keller to do even what his own boss wants him to do. He is too much of an out of control hothead."

"After a certain amount of time we will leave and continue northward to Wilmington on the Cape Fear River in North Carolina to refuel and reprovision. We will again play tourist to see if we can spot anyone who has more than a passing interest in us, and when we determine an opportune time, we will leave Wilmington. We will go through Customs and Immigration and declare our next port of call to be Bermuda en route to the Azores and, ultimately, Europe. We are going to leave late one afternoon and continue on course for Bermuda until we are out of range of any surveillance from ships or the shore, probably a couple of hundred miles or so should do it, then we will turn 90 degrees to starboard and run south outside the Gulf Stream down to the Bahamas. Once we clear Customs in the Bahamas, we will find a hidden anchorage near Rock Sound, and it will be quite a while before anyone realizes that we won't be showing up in Bermuda. Once in Rock Sound, we will gather all the information we can to help us locate the U-boat, before we actually start searching for it. Are there any questions so far?"

"What sort of information are we looking for?" asked Janine.

"Anything that might help us pinpoint the final resting place of the wrecked sub. Your father will help us, I hope."

"Of course he will. Although his memory isn't what it used to be, he is an honest and decent man and besides, from what I remember, the German captain was a great friend of his, and he will be tickled pink to meet his friend's son. And you know that he will do anything for me."

At this point, Capt'n Pete interrupted, "Even if by some remote chance we get the information which helps us pinpoint the location of the sub after so many years, what are we going to do with it. We sure as hell can't raise it all by ourselves."

Jack smiled ruefully, "Well," he said, "if we get some information which eventually leads us to the location of the sub, and we do indeed locate the wreckage, the plan gets a little sketchy from there. We could declare our find to the Bahamian authorities, who will claim possession because the wreck lies in their waters, or the U.S. Department of Marine Administration, who will find the owners of the cargo and allow us to negotiate a percentage of everything that is recovered. Then there is the War Risk Insurance Office of the British Government, who insured all vessels during the war, and who would also want to investigate to insure their claims to the gold. And you know that the German officials would claim the U-boat and its contents as their property."

"Are there any alternatives?" asked Capt'n Pete.

"It depends on how honest you want to be. If we could bring up the gold before we announce our discovery to the world, there are any number of Cayman Island or Jamaican banks who would deposit our loot without any questions being asked."

"But first we have to find it." Capt'n Pete interjected.

At this point Shannon interrupted the two-way conversation with some questions of her own. "Even assuming that we find something worth salvaging, how are we going to bring it up from the sub to the surface? I would imagine that that much gold must weigh tons."

This time Jack actually smiled before answering, "Believe it or not, we have aboard this boat at this very moment everything necessary to locate and salvage the U-boat. Sometime ago I bought and had installed a lot of equipment in the foolish hope of finding a Spanish galleon somewhere in my travels. I have side scan sonar to show the contours of the ocean bottom which will aid in the identification of underwater objects, and a remotely operated video camera to check out any anomalies we find without the necessity of diving on every target we find, as well as a Fisher Photon magnetometer, which is used to locate large ferrous metal objects on the ocean bottom. I was all set to go on my adventure when someone correctly pointed out that Spanish galleons were made of wood and wouldn't show up on the magnetometer, but I would think that a steel 770 foot submarine qualifies as a large ferrous object, don't you?"

"I would think so. How reliable is the equipment, anyway?"

"The equipment is new but it hasn't even been turned on for the past year. I guess we would have to find something to test it out on."

"Now say hypothetically that we have found it, how do we bring it up? Shannon asked.

"If we are lucky enough to locate the wreck, I have several sets of scuba gear on board and a compressor in the lazarette as well as two K10 Hydrospeeders."

"What in the blue blazes is a Hydrospeeder?" asked Capt'n Pete.

"It's a diver propulsion system built by a company in Fort Lauderdale. It's kind of like an underwater mini jet fighter, and because it provides the diver with breathing air and propulsion for almost five hours at speeds of up to seven knots, it is an ideal search vehicle."

"Sounds to me like something straight out of James Bond," complained Capt'n Pete. "I'm afraid it wouldn't do me any good, though, I never did have the time or the inclination to learn scuba diving."

"That's not a problem." Jack replied, "Someone has to hold down the fort aboard the boat, and I can't thing of a more qualified person than you. Shannon, Janine and I can take turns doing the diving."

"What about hauling the gold to the surface?" asked Janine, who up until this point had been remarkably quiet, allowing the speculation to evolve without her input.

"That is a simple problem. The davit for the tender will provide more than enough lifting power to get the gold up from the sub. The only real problem we might encounter would be getting into the sub in order to remove the gold, but I guess we'll solve that one if and when we get to that point."

Numerous other concerns were addressed and some solved that afternoon, and by nightfall they were abeam of Jacksonville, and the lights of the city loomed off to port as they continued on their way towards Savannah.

Savannah, queen city of the south, greeted them early the next morning as they steamed boldly up the river to a dock behind the controversial hotel which had been built on the waterfront despite being in the historical district of downtown Savannah. Beside the hotel stood the renovated cotton warehouses of a by gone era which now housed chic boutiques, trendy restaurants, lawyer's and dentist's offices, and a few local government offices. Recent laid cobblestone streets reflected the past and wound in front of, behind and through the varied ex-warehouses before climbing the steep hill to the main street.

After securing the boat to the public dock east of the modern reproduction of a pirate ship, which took tourists on scenic cruises of the picturesque, historic Savannah harbor, Jack contacted the harbor master to make arrangements to dock there overnight, since they were not due in Thunderbolt for the service to the "Final Option" until the next morning.

"What a beautiful city," exclaimed Shannon as they sat finishing brunch on the flybridge.

"Yes, it is," agreed Jack. Impulsively taking her hand, he said, "Come with me, there is something I want you to see."

He led her down the aft stairs and onto the dock explaining, "I have been here before, and there is a symbol of the city down here a little way that really impressed me the last time I was here."

Walking hand in hand with Shannon felt so good on this warm morning that Jack felt that he was walking on a cloud. As they proceeded down East River Street, a large, empty container ship sounded its horn, proceeding down the Savannah River to the sea. Jack pointed out the many old warehouses that had been turned into boutiques, restaurants and novelty shops along this historic stretch of the river, the cobblestone streets and the disused tram tracks which recalled an earlier age, and the ramparts which ensured the main downtown parts of the city were not flooded in times of heavy weather.

Presently they came to Morrell Park, and the Waving Girl statue of Florence Martus, still welcoming inbound river traffic and cheering outbound ships as she had done for so many years while she was alive. It was a beautiful and restful spot and Jack and Shanon sat and watched the river traffic go by.

"So what is this all about?" Shannon asked.

"What do you mean?"

"What are we doing here, really?"

"I'm sorry. I thought we all agreed that we would help Capt'n Pete to find out what really happened to his father and see if there was any truth to his obsession about the gold supposedly being aboard that sub."

"Yes, well, how much chance do you think we have, firstly finding the sub, secondly, being able to get into it, and thirdly, doing it while we are being watched and harassed by the Senator's people?"

"I know what you mean, but I've been thinking. There is something here that doesn't fit. Stop and think about it. Why is the Senator going after us so aggressively? I mean, the thought of a couple of hundred million dollars worth of gold is tempting in anyone's language, but the Senator has more money than most people in the world, and more influence and power than one person should have, but what could it be that was so important to him to make him go to these illegal lengths to try to stop us from finding and discovering the truth about this sub? There has to be something about this sub that the Senator doesn't want us and the world at large to know about. But for now, I have no idea about what that might be."

"Do you think Capt'n Pete knows why the Senator is so persistent?"

"I don't know but if he does, he hasn't shared the information with me."

That afternoon, having toured some of the impressive squares in the historic downtown district of Savannah, they locked up the boat and the four members of the crew adjourned to a nearby restaurant for dinner. Despite their heightened sense of paranoia, they had noticed no one suspicious during their ramblings through the historic part of the city. After an enjoyable Southern down home meal of chicken and dumplings, chitlins, and locally grown vegetables, consumed in an old fashioned, family-style restaurant, they walked arm in arm through the now quiet streets back to their boat and retired for the night.

Early the next morning, they slipped the lines of the yacht and proceeded back down the river to the channel which would take them to the shipyard at Thunderbolt. The morning was spent hauling the boat out of the water in order to renew the anti-fouling paint on the ship's bottom. Several shipyard workers came aboard to change the oil and check over both engines and both generators. The crew found a nearby hotel and checked in since they could not stay on the boat while it was hauled out and standing on the hard.

Two days later, during which time all the necessary work had been completed, including the installation of a hidden compartment to Jack's specifications, designed to hide the firearms which they were bringing, the 'Final Option' was returned to its natural element and, leaving Savannah astern, began its journey north to Wilmington at the mouth of the Cape Fear River in North Carolina.

Blessed with pleasant weather and a favorable forecast and encountering no obstructions on their course, and with the Gulf Stream still giving them a favorable push, it turned out to be a pleasant cruise totally without any incidents. At this point, Jack was beginning to wonder if the Senator had any idea where they were, but surmised that it was better to be safe than sorry.

Immediately after passing under the bridge at the entrance to the Cape Fear River, 'Final Option' turned starboard into the city docks and tied up within sight of the majestic downtown church steeple, which had been rebuilt not long after being toppled by a hurricane in 1996. As it turned out, they were fortunate enough to be right across the street from a very special restaurant that Jack remembered from his last trip to this part of the country.

While Jack and Capt'n Pete refuelled the boat and arranged for a slip for the night and the next day, Shannon and Janine walked across the street to the nearby supermarket and bought those things that had been forgotten or consumed since they had left Savannah. Once they returned, the boat was motored to its assigned slip, tied up for the night and locked securely. They spent the rest of the afternoon relaxing, walking the streets of the historic downtown area, and window shopping the quaint little shops before going to dinner at Joshua's Crab Shack on the Riverwalk, just a little east of Market Street on Water

Street, which was Jack's favorite restaurant in this part of the world. They were shown to a table on the deck overlooking the river. Across the river behind a line of trees which obscured the hull but left the superstructure and the huge gun turrets clearly visible, was the permanently moored WW II battleship USS *North Carolina,* and several other vessels of the era, that made up what was now a maritime museum.

After a delicious and delightful dinner of just molted soft shell crabs over baby greens and perfectly cooked Maine lobster over linguine, consumed in a charming and comfortable setting, the crew made their way back to the boat at a leisurely pace. All of them decided that, after a long day, a decadent meal and an appropriate nightcap, an early night and a good sleep was called for. Since they would not be leaving until nearly nightfall the following day, it was also decided that sleeping in late was the best course to follow.

They cleared Customs, Immigration and Homeland Security in the late afternoon, after a day of sightseeing and just after sunset, 'Final Option' left the Cape Fear River astern. At 6 a.m. the following morning, having run 120 miles from Wilmington, Capt'n Pete executed a 90 degree turn to starboard away from their stated destination of Bermuda and headed due south towards their rendezvous at Harbour Island, in the northeast corner of Eleuthera in the Bahamas.

Chapter 7

"So, where the hell are they?"

The question, yelled at the top of his voice and with considerable menace in it, came from the Senator and was directed at Horst Keller and two crew members who had been keeping watch for the 'Final Option" which should have been in Bermuda by this time.

The 'Shillelagh', having arrived in Bermuda several days before, was anchored in a secluded cove well away from the Customs Dock and the capital city of Hamilton. They had already refueled and re- provisioned and were ready to follow 'Final Option' when she left for the second leg of her Atlantic crossing.

"I don't know, sir. By my calculations, they should have been here early this morning, unless I overestimated the speed they could travel. They may have had to travel slower than I guessed in order to conserve fuel, or they may just be dawdling along." Horst replied, trying to sound confident.

The Senator turned quickly and snarled, "I know that! Stop taking me for a fool! And I don't care how you do it, find them. Now get out!!"

Quickly turning and exiting the main salon, glad to escape the Senator's firing line, Horst and the two crew members climbed the stairs to the wheelhouse and seated themselves on the settee behind the captain's chair.

"Joe, are you certain that 'Final Option' has not slipped by you somehow?" Horst had left the surveillance of the points of entry to his men operating the Donzis.

"Not a chance. One of our crew has been watching the main entrance and the Customs House 24/7 ever since we got here." The first mate replied. "And I have paid people to ensure that she is not at any marina that can hold a boat that size, and I have had both tenders checking all the anchorages every day. She is not here!!"

"All right, all right. I believe you. But we have got to find her. You keep doing what you're doing and I will make some phone calls, and, if you come up with some bright ideas, let me know."

"I have one idea you might want to consider."

"I'm listening."

"We know where she's coming from, and we know there's only one entrance which she has to use in order to clear Customs into Bermuda. Why don't we rent a plane or use the helicopter to fly a reciprocal course back towards the U.S. mainland. Might just find them loafing along since they don't seem to be in any kind of a hurry."

"Good idea! Get the helicopter pilot up here and get him going as soon as possible. We still have six hours of daylight left today, that's three hours out and three back, so he could cover about 200 miles back towards the States. And if he fails to spot them this afternoon, tomorrow we could rent a long range plane and, if necessary, fly all the way back to Wilmington until we find them."

"Aye, aye, sir!"

Having received their orders, the two crew members left on their assigned tasks, and Horst immediately got on to the ship's Sat phone, and called back to the many contacts he had in the States. After a period of about 15 minutes, he was interrupted by the noise of the helicopter on the aft deck starting up and leaving on its search mission. Only after the racket abated was he able to resume his calling.

Some 4 hours and many phone calls later, Horst, with a sense of dismay, once again reluctantly reported to the Senator in the main salon.

"I have found them, sir." Horst announced hesitantly.

The Senator looked up from his drink and said, "About bloody time! So where are they, and when can we go see them?"

"They cleared Customs in Wilmington, North Carolina, stating to the authorities that their destination was Bermuda. It turns out that that was a ploy. They are actually in the Bahamas. They cleared customs this morning in Harbour Island on the island of Eleuthera."

The Senator's eyes grew wide and his jaw dropped, his obvious anger mounting by the second. "I thought that you had determined that they would be coming here to Bermuda?"

Horst's eyes dropped to the floor, his shoulders sagged, and a nervous tremor ran down his spine before he replied. "That's what they told the customs officials in Wilmington. It seems to me that they lied. I think the Bahamas was going to be their destination all along. They were probably trying to give us the slip but they underestimated just how long a time it would take for me to locate them, and just didn't think we would find them so soon."

Angry now instead of incredulous, the Senator snarled, "Don't you realize how much it costs to run this boat all the way to Bermuda?" Inserting a short hesitation for added emphasis, the Senator put the fear of God into

Horst. "Well of course you do. You *are* still the captain, at least for the time being."

Horst paled at the thought of losing his job and maybe even something much more valuable, like his ability to breathe, for he had seen many times in the past the inhumane ways the Senator most of the time took care of his problems.

"Now, get the helicopter, the tenders and the crew back on board, and prepare to leave immediately. We will go to the Bahamas, and this time your information had better be right! ... OR ELSE!!!!"

Chapter 8

Having cleared customs, re-provisioned and refueled at Harbour Island, or Briland as the locals call it, 'Final Option' then continued, with the guidance of a locally hired pilot, through the 'Devil's Backbone', a particularly difficult passage through the northern reefs of Eleuthera, past Spanish Wells, where they dropped off the pilot, and traveled inside, west of the main island and across the flats, also known to the locals as 'the skinny water'. They sailed down the coast to Rock Sound, once called Wreck Sound because of the past inhabitants' propensity for luring unsuspecting ships onto the sharp reefs with false lights, and anchored out just off the town pier since there was no marina in Rock Sound and extremely shallow water close by the shore.

Arriving in the late afternoon, they quickly and securely locked up the boat, launched the Novurania tender and motored in to the single pier which had The Rock Bar restaurant at the end of it. They met the owner and his staff, childhood friends of Janine's, and arranged for a watch to be kept on the 'Final Option'. This was one of their many expenditures, but Jack reasoned that it was worth the expense.

Leaving the restaurant, they crossed the Meridian Highway and walked the few blocks to Janine's father's home, a modest, clean but somewhat neglected single story house built of CBS block.

Anxious to see her father, Janine walked right in without knocking, as if she had just been to the corner store

145

instead of having been gone for two years, leaving her companions standing at the front door.

"Hello, Papa," she called as she crossed the living room towards her father, Moses, who looked as if he has seen a ghost, but he immediately flashed the largest gap tooth smile you have ever seen.

"Janine, baby, welcome home, it's been so long."

"I know, Papa, but I'm here now," she says, bending down, kissing and hugging the old man. "It is so good to see you. Come, I want you to meet some friends of mine."

Jack, Shannon and, finally, Capt'n Pete shuffled into the room like people in a police lineup and stood uncomfortably just inside the door.

"Papa, I want you to meet my good friends, Jack Elliott, the owner of the boat that brought me here, his girlfriend, Shannon O'Loughlin and Captain Pete Olsen-Smith."

The old man fairly jumped out of the settee, walked quickly to the trio, and shook hands all around, saying, "I'm Moses Beaumont, and I'm pleased to meet you all. Thank you for bringing my little girl home to me. I've missed her so much." Looking around, he cleared a few books and newspapers off the sofa and chairs, saying, "Please sit down. Have you eaten? Would you like a drink?"

It was Jack who answered as he walked to the sofa, "Thank you, no and yes, please, in that order," as a large smile creased his face.

"All I have is Scotch, Jameson's, I believe."

Janine moved towards the kitchen as her father retook his seat on the settee, already slipping into her role as hostess, as she had been since the death of her mother many years before.

This time, Capt'n Pete answered with a big grin, knowing that 'Final Option' would not be going anywhere tonight, "I believe that would do quite nicely."

Janine was chuckling as she went to fetch drinks for everyone.

"Mr. Beaumont," began Jack.

The old man interrupted, "Firstly, my name is Moses, Mr. Beaumont was my father, dead these many years, and any friend of my daughter's deserves the right to call me by my given name."

"Thank you, Moses," said Jack, "and that goes for us as well. But I wanted to let you know why we have brought your daughter home."

"I don't care why, I'm just glad you did." said Moses. "But if you feel you must, go ahead."

"Thanks. It is my understanding from Janine that during the war, you rescued a German sailor from drowning, a Captain named Schmidt."

"Oh my God, I haven't heard that name in years. But he is dead, you know." A look of sorrow came across the old man's face. "I still miss our adventures together."

"Yes, we know he is dead, but we came here to continue his search, because of Capt'n Pete, who is Schmidt's son."

Momentarily taken aback, Moses stared openly at Capt'n Pete and muttered, "I knew that I remembered those features from somewhere, you know, you look just like him."

As Janine walked back into the room with drinks and snacks on a tray for everyone, Capt'n Pete said, "Any

147

help you could give me, I mean, us, would be greatly appreciated."

The old man sat there for a while, sipping his drink, and everyone joined him. Then, without a word, he got up and walked into the back bedroom and was heard rummaging around his closet.

After about 10 minutes, he returned, bearing a small book, bound in leather which was salt stained and dirty. Handing the book to Capt'n Pete, he said, "Then this rightly belongs to you. It's your father's journal, where he kept all his information on his searches and thoughts. When he felt his mind going, he asked me to keep it safe for whoever came searching for his sub, for he knew someone would come."

"Thank you. I never knew that this journal existed, and he didn't mention it when I was here. Although, he was pretty far gone by then and maybe he just forgot he had made a journal." Tears appeared in Capt'n Pete's eyes and with his sleeve, he wiped them away.

"When were you here?" Moses asked.

"About five years ago, but I only stayed a few weeks, until he died and I spent most of that time in his little shack up on Gregory Street. Afterward, I went to Nassau until his possessions reached me and then I went back to the States."

Moses seemed taken aback, "I seem to remember something about him having a visitor about that time but I didn't think anything of it. If I had found you then, it would have saved you a lot of grief in the last five years. I'm so sorry."

"That's OK. I understand. But I hope you can help me now."

"Anything I can do, I will. What did you have in mind?"

"I want to take this journal back to the boat tonight to study it and then in the morning, if you would, you can show us where you found him washed ashore. That will give us a better idea of where to start looking."

"Certainly, and I can also tell you of all the places that he and I searched over the years and found nothing. Although, I guess they have more sophisticated equipment nowadays, so you will be able to go places we couldn't."

"And, on that note, I think it would be a good idea to get back to the boat, have dinner and get an early night so we can be fresh in the morning. Thanks for the drinks, Moses, we will see you in the morning." Jack said.

They stood up and headed for the door, leaving Janine on the settee with her father.

"I'll be staying here tonight," she said.

"I figured as much. We'll see you in the morning, too."

It was just getting dark as the trio made their way back to the tender and motored out to the yacht, which appeared undisturbed. Shannon went to the galley to make dinner, whilst Jack made drinks and settled down in the main salon with Capt'n Pete, who was already studying his father's journal.

Jack sat in awe about what they had already accomplished in the short time since arriving. Glancing at Capt'n Pete, he saw not the whiskey-soaked drunk that they had pulled from the harbor at Holiday Isle, but a seemingly younger, stronger and certainly better fed man with his new clothes, clean shaven and sporting a short haircut, it seemed a few years had been rolled back.

'Even if nothing comes of this search and we do not find the sub, at least we have given this man a new lease on life, if he chooses take it,' thought Jack.

Early the next morning, they all met up at Moses' house and saw an old, battered but serviceable Mercedes parked outside. Just as they arrived, Janine came out of the house, twirling the keys on her first finger, with Moses following close behind.

"Papa got us some transportation, so we don't have to walk. It's about 12 miles." she said.

"Nice," said Jack.

With Janine driving and Moses navigating, the trio in the back seat took this opportunity to discuss what Capt'n Pete found in the journal, since he had been up until 2 a.m. studying it.

"So what have you found in the journal?" Jack asked. "Something that can help us, I hope."

"It's absolutely fascinating. He describes the whole journey from Brest in France to the sinking of the sub here. The most pertinent parts, as they relate to us and our search, are about halfway through and the rest is the part where he and Moses were searching for the sub after the war. He says that he was in the conning tower with two lookouts when the boat struck the reef and he was thrown clear when the conning tower broke away from the body of the sub. He distinctly remembers seeing the tower separating from the body. Naturally, he doesn't recall anything else until he was found and taken to the hospital."

"So how does that help us?" asked Shannon.

"Since it broke in two we now have two pieces to look for instead of one, both large enough to register on the magnetometer. And since the sub hit bottom while surfaced, it couldn't be more than twenty or thirty feet deep where it sank."

"OK, we're here," interrupted Janine from the front seat.

They had been traveling on a dirt road for the last 10 minutes and Janine had pulled into a small dirt parking lot. They exited the vehicle and walked in a group over the small dune at the shoreline. Standing at the top, Jack scanned his eyes left and right. The beach itself was only about 50 feet wide running the length of the 2 mile long bay but was at the foot of a series of 30 foot cliffs with a limited number of access points, one of which was a steep incline just to the left of where they stood. Offshore about half a mile away they could see the reef with, even on this calm day, many large waves breaking on it in spectacular fashion. There was not a house, person or even a boat to be seen anywhere.

"What a desolate place, beautiful but desolate." said Jack.

"Yes, I know what you mean. This is what the out islands of the Bahamas are like, for the most part, except where the big corporations have come in and spoiled the place." Moses said, his voice indicating vehemently that he didn't want it to change.

"So, do you think that perhaps that reef could be the one the sub struck? It looks pretty deadly, even from here." Jack speculated.

"It is always possible, but Ernst-Jurgen and I explored most of the reefs on this side of Eleuthera over the many years we were together, including this one and we never found a thing. If it was this one, then the wreck has slid off the reef into the deep water on the outer side. The water slopes down steeply to 300 or 400 feet deep out there very quickly. I have a chart at home which shows all the places that we have already looked." Moses sighed, remembering his friend and the myriad times they had together, drinking, partying and exploring. Perhaps not surprisingly, his thoughts of that time together brought a tear to his eye.

"OK. There is nothing to be gained by standing here and looking at this place. Let's go back to your place and look at this chart you have got and see if we can come up with a plan to locate the sub."

On their way back, Jack casually mentioned how comfortable the car was and Moses blurted out, "Yes, it is. It belongs to a friend of Ernst-Jurgen's and mine, another German who owns land around here, and when I mentioned to him about looking for the sub again, he was very excited about the prospect and was happy to lend us his car for as long as we need it."

"Moses, I thank you for getting us transportation, but I think that it might not be a good idea to be telling anyone else about what we are doing here. In a small community like this, gossip abounds and the walls have ears, if you know what I mean."

"Oh, yes, sorry about that, I didn't think," Moses said sheepishly.

Back at Rock Sound they formulated a plan for using the town as a home base and, using the much newer and more accurate charts from the boat, and the marked up ones that Moses had accumulated over the years, to start a systematic search offshore.

Hours turned into days and then into weeks, as they are wont to do, with no discernible progress. Running lanes was not much fun. It was like mowing a lawn, each time going north or south overlapped the last lane so the magnetometer could cover the whole bottom. Unfortunately, while they did get some spikes on the magnetometer, they proved to be false strikes caused by various pieces of debris on the floor of the ocean, and therefore each day they returned to Rock Sound empty handed.

After several weeks they finally took a day off to explore Eleuthera. Jack and Shannon visited the Ocean Hole in Rock Sound and, using the Mercedes, drove north to picnic at the Glass Window in northern Eleuthera. Jack, seeing the erosion the waves from the Atlantic had wrought on the limestone, began to formulate an idea that the sub may have been driven inshore. When they visited the Preacher's Cave, the idea came to fruition. It was not difficult to imagine that the sub may have ended up in a cave. When they returned, he started to search the charts more closely for any indication of such a cave on the island's eastern and much wilder coastline facing the Atlantic Ocean, but without any success. Naturally, it stood to reason that if there was a cave marked on the map, someone before him would have searched it and found the submarine.

Later, while having dinner once again at Moses' house, Jack was told of a big new boat in Briland and people asking questions about them.

"Somehow the Senator has found where we are, which I guess is not surprising, seeing the resources that man has. We need a faster way to search, and I know just the man to help us."

Jack picked up his cell phone and punched in the numbers from memory. The phone on the other end of the call was picked up on the second ring.

"It's your quarter; start talking." The voice sounded a little harried, but friendly.

"Birdman, it's Jack."

"Hey, man, how've you been keepin'?"

"So, so. Do you have a few moments to spare? I have a proposition for you."

"For you, Jack, all the time in the world, you know that." Jack was one of the few people who didn't call him Birdbrain to his face.

"Do you still have that beautiful helicopter you built?"

"Do you seriously think I would sell it?"

"No, but these days, who knows what might have happened since the last time I saw you."

"Well, rest assured, it's sitting right here next to me and, as always, it's in perfect flying condition." Birdman lived in a small efficiency attached to the back of his hangar at Fort Lauderdale's Executive airport, and spent all his free time between charters, maintaining and upgrading his three Bell Jet Ranger helicopters and the love of his life, a Rotorway Exec 162F two seater helicopter, which he had built by himself from scratch.

"Would you have the time to help me out on a special project, which I think would be right up your alley?" Jack suddenly realized that he had his fingers crossed in hope that Birdman would be free to help.

"I don't know, Jack, I'm right up to my eyeballs just now. Julie and Pierre, my two best pilots, are out on week long charters right now and I'm supposed to be leaving in the morning for Mobile, Alabama to do a series of crew transfers to the Gulf oil rigs. That'll leave only John to mind the office."

"Birdman, listen carefully. Can John take your oil rig transfers for you and can you get a temp in to mind the office? It is really important to me that you come personally and bring the Exec with you. I am willing to pay you top dollar for your time."

Sensing the urgency in Jack's voice, Birdman replied, "You don't have to bribe me, Jack, I'll do anything you want. Just tell me where and when, and I'll be there. And at my normal charter fee."

A sigh of relief preceded Jack's next request. "Great, I appreciate this. Now, if I recall correctly , you have the ability to mount a Helipod between the skids on the Exec. Correct?"

"That's correct."

"Do you think that there is a possibility that we could mount a magnetometer inside the pod to where it would give still you any kind of a decent reading while you were airborne?"

"Now that is something that I couldn't tell you. As far as I know, it has never been done before. However, if you have a substantial reason for doing it, there is no harm in trying, I guess."

"O.K. Call DK Electronics in Miami and buy the magnetometer on my account; they put in the one I have mounted in my boat. Have their techs deliver it and have them mount it in the helipod. Then you need to get yourself and the equipment to Rock Sound Airport in Eleuthera."

"Sounds to me like you already knew what my answer would be before you called me."

"I was counting on you. Do you foresee any problems being here by Tuesday?"

"I don't think so. With the limited range I have in the Exec, I'll have to stop to refuel in both Bimini and Nassau but I shouldn't have any problems. Just make sure that Rock Sound has enough fuel for me to do whatever it is that you want me to do and then get back to Nassau."

"You can count on that. I wish I could tell you what's going on, but I'm hesitant to discuss the job over an open line. I promise to fill you in completely when you get here. Your job will not be hard or dangerous, that I can promise you. Boring maybe, but not hard or dangerous."

"Rats, just when I thought this was sounding interesting, you go and take the wind out of my sails. But if you say it's important, I'll take your word for it."

"Anyway, I appreciate you dropping everything to help me out."

"Jack, you helped me with your sound advice in the stock market when I was almost broke. You were the one who enabled me to get the capital to start this business. I haven't forgotten and you shouldn't, either."

"Thank you for that. I'll see you Tuesday."

"I'll be there, Jack. Count on it."

Chapter 9

After breakfast Tuesday morning, they secured the boat for the day. Once again, Jack paid for a watch to be kept on it. They adjourned to Moses' house where Capt'n Pete and Moses settled down at the kitchen table to correlate the words that Ernst-Jurgen had written in his journal with the still sharp memories in the brain of Moses.

Jack and Shannon once again borrowed the Mercedes and arrived at the Rock Sound Airport, which consisted of a single, haphazardly maintained runway and only one thoroughly rusted hangar, which was securely padlocked.

A short while later, Birdman arrived in his Rotorway helicopter from the mainland with the second magnetometer and they spent the remainder of the day fitting it into the helipod between the helicopter's skids. DK's techs had informed Birdman, after being shown where it would be mounted, that there was no way that it would work. He listened to what they had to say, but had bought it anyway and had brought it along, reasoning that if it didn't work, Jack could always return it or sell it on Ebay or Amazon.

Birdman and Shannon seemed to hit it off and get along well together, much to Jack' chagrin, who felt threatened by her interest in the younger, more handsome chopper pilot.

In order to test the magnetometer, they flew out the next morning, with Birdman at the controls and Jack as co-pilot and observer, again under a cloudless blue sky to the train wreck. The location of this wreck, where a barge carrying a civil war locomotive had sunk in fifty feet of water, was well known because it was a popular dive site. As it was still early morning when they arrived, they were able to run directly over the top of the large iron object, and the magnetometer showed them a satisfying spike on its screen, proving to them that it would indeed work correctly.

They were now comforted by the fact that, if indeed there was something metallic on the bottom, the instrument would show them its approximate location. With the assurance of the reliability of their equipment, they spent several more days running the offshore reefs with the helicopter, returning each day to Rock Sound without any results. Frustration was growing, and boredom was setting in until late one afternoon, when an abnormally large spike registered on the instrument and set the plans for the following day.

With a great deal of anticipation, they arrived at the indicated spot on the reef early the next morning, anchored the boat securely and the two divers, Jack and Shannon, methodically checked their SCUBA equipment. The other two, Birdman and Janine, remained aboard the boat as safety backups in case of problems, both fully suited up and ready to go. Capt'n Pete, the only non diver aboard, stayed on the flybridge, scanning the horizon with Jack's powerful Nikon binoculars, patiently searching for other boats in the vicinity.

After several unsuccessful dives, they finally came upon a large steel object jammed into a cleft in the coral reef beside a clean break in the reef, through which a strong current swept, carrying everything not firmly planted along with it. Jack's suspicion that it was the conning tower of the

U-boat was confirmed when they found, barely readable after so many years immersion, the legend U-362 on the side facing away from the strong flow of water. The side facing the constant onslaught of the current had been scoured clean, right down to bare metal, by the sandblasting effect of the moving water.

Upon surfacing and after a group consultation, their joy of discovery was, however, tempered by the obvious fact that it was only the conning tower and not the entire sub that they had found. The U-362 legend on the tower was upside down as it lay on the bottom, and the metal sides ended abruptly in a crushed and torn edge where normally it would have joined the main hull of the U-boat. It was pointedly obvious that the rest of the sub lay elsewhere and was as yet undiscovered.

Their elation, though slightly subdued, was dealt a further blow upon their return to Rock Sound, for there was a reception committee awaiting their arrival. A familiar looking Donzi Runabout was tied to the concrete dock opposite the usual berth for the Novurania, and a quick glance around revealed Horst Keller and two of his rough, tough crewmembers were seated on the verandah at the Rock Bar, one of the two waterfront bars on each side of the end of the dock. The three were all wearing identical evil grins and came instantly alert at the appearance of 'Final Option' entering the bay. When they didn't move during the anchoring and shutdown of the boat, Jack hoped that there will be no trouble.

"Ignore them," he whispered. "Maybe they will go away."

"Not bloody likely," replied Capt'n Pete. "They look like they're here to stay."

Leaving Birdman behind on the boat, because Jack did not want to put him into any danger or let Horst know that they had an extra crew member, they gathered their things and conscientiously locked up the boat. The remaining members of the party lowered the dinghy and carefully made their way to the pier, remaining on the opposite side from the Donzi. Three sets of eyes watched their every move, but their owners made no move to interfere or impede the progress of the group. Immediately Jack turned to the right, away from Horst and his two crew members, where Uncle Joe's Bar and Grill welcomed the weary treasure hunters with open arms and comfortable seats.

"Why did we come here?" asked Shannon.

"I don't think it's a good idea to show them where we are going," explained Jack. "I don't want to put Moses in any danger."

Uncle Joe himself (Janine's real uncle) came over, and after introductions by Janine, he took their drink orders. He was then asked by Jack, "Can you get one of your lads to slip out the back way and go warn Moses to stay put for a while?"

"Sure, no problem," said Joe. "But what should I tell him if he asks why?"

"Because I don't want those three shady characters over there to know where we are staying, and unfortunately it looks as if they'll be hanging around for a while longer." replied Jack.

"Do you want them gone, Boss?" asked Joe.

"Gone how?"

"Outa here and away in their boat."

"Yes, of course I do. But how are you going to manage that?"

"You jest watch, Boss."

Half an hour later, Jack was just starting his second Kalik and thinking that this Bahamian beer compared favorably with Killian Red, when a disturbance at the bar opposite them caught his attention. He witnessed a sudden influx of very large, young and extremely fit looking Bahamian men entering from all directions and quickly occupying every last available seat on the verandah.

The last to arrive, without a doubt the tallest and largest of them all, stood at least six foot seven and two hundred and fifty pounds of whipcord sinew and muscle, strode in and looked about him with undisguised disgust.

"You know what the trouble with dis place is?" he proclaimed for all to hear, his voice booming across the quiet afternoon water. "Too many whities taking up space where dey don't belong," he added, looking directly at Horst Keller and his two companions.

He turned slowly to face the Rock Bar's owner, who was standing in the open doorway.

"I thought you told me that my table would always be available for me," he said, indicating the table occupied by Horst and company.

"Hey, mon, if you want it, you go right ahead and take it." With that he turned and walked inside the bar, indicating that he wanted no further part in the discussion.

Horst looked around nervously at the sea of dark faces as the huge black man, glowering at them, slowly approached their table. Deciding that discretion was indeed the better part of valor, he stood up slowly and, motioning to his two henchmen, started to move away from their table on the verandah.

As the three men backed uncertainly down the dock toward their boat, the Bahamian, standing tall at the rail around the verandah, called after them, "Whitey don't belong in Rock Sound, you hear? Catch you here again, me and the boys gonna whup your ass. Understand?"

Horst, almost at his means of escape, finally screwed up the courage to yell back, "What about those white boys over there?" indicating Jack and his group, who up until now had been enjoying the show.

The powerful figure took his time looking in all directions, including at Jack's small group, before declaring, "I don't see no Whitey around here 'ceptin you three. Now git!"

Grudgingly, the three men boarded their boat, and with an all too familiar volume of unnecessary engine noise, left the harbor in haste and headed north, skirting the poorly marked sand flats on the west side of the narrow island of Eleuthera. They appeared to be heading for either Spanish Wells or Briland, which was not a recommended night journey for anyone, let alone someone without local knowledge.

"With any luck, they'll run up on a sand bank and have to spend the night on their boat." someone observed behind them.

As all his attention had been focused on the rapidly disappearing speedboat, Jack turned toward the source of the voice and came face to face with the big Bahamian, who had approached unseen from the other bar.

"In any event, I doubt if they'll be back, at least not tonight." The large powerful body, clad in torn jeans and a once white T-shirt, which had definitely seen better days, was the same one that had been taunting Horst at the other bar, but instead of gutter talk, he spoke with the rich Harvard accent of a New England barrister. "I'm Courtland Williams, and I'm really pleased to finally make your acquaintance, Jack. I've heard a lot about you these last few days."

"I don't know where you came from, but I am very pleased you showed up when you did and took care of our little problem," said Jack. "Please thank your friends for me, too. Their drinks are on me tonight."

When questioned about his abrupt change of accent, Courtland explained that he had thought that the Senator's men would be more likely to react to gutter talk than the quiet reasoning of an attorney on vacation.

After Capt'n Pete had returned to 'Final Option' to pick up Birdman, by mutual consent, Courtland accompanied them back to Moses' house, paying a lot of attention to Janine as they walked the short distance to her father's place.

"I don't think you remember me, Janine," Courtland said, "but I remember you from school, and I must say, you have certainly grown up from the skinny little girl whose pig tails I used to pull."

"I do remember you, but you were a skinny little runt before you and your parents moved to Nassau. When did this change happen?"

"Isn't it amazing what a growth spurt and five years of working out in the gym during college can achieve? Once I bulked up I found I was interested in all kinds of sports, so it wasn't hard to keep it up, and it has come in handy several times in the past, like this afternoon."

Jack was naturally relieved at the outcome of the confrontation, but understandably concerned at its implications. It seemed that the Senator had unknown resources in this area, even if it had taken a long time for him to track them down. Some planning and some deviousness was definitely called for in the future.

That evening, over dinner at Moses' house, Jack explained to Courtland the situation into which he had stumbled. Surprisingly, he immediately offered his help in any way necessary. He, too, remembered the German U-boat captain who came to live in their community, and the hopes he (Courtland) had had as a child of finding lost treasures.

The next morning, Capt'n Pete decided that now was as good a time as any to do some much needed maintenance on the boat, and was soon incommunicado in the engine room, changing the fluids in the engines and generators.

Janine and Courtland, at Jack' suggestion, traveled up to Briland in the borrowed Mercedes to snoop on the Senator's boat, having been given the photos from Ft. Lauderdale to identify the other people involved, besides the ones they had seen the day before.

That evening, when Capt'n Pete had completed the oil changes and finished all his inspections and declared the boat seaworthy once again, they all gathered at Moses' house for dinner. Shannon, who had spent the afternoon provisioning the boat from the local supermarket, utilizing a Jeep belonging to a neighbor of Moses', joined them as they sat down for their before dinner cocktails.

Janine and Courtland had returned from Briland with a report on 'Shillelagh'. "We found the Senator's boat. It is too big to moor alongside anywhere in Briland, so they anchored out of the fairway about 350 yards off Valentine's Marina." Courtland said.

"They are using the Donzis as shuttle craft. Unfortunately, it looks as if Horst made it back last night, because both Donzis are there. We saw the Senator and that horrible captain of his, but not the two crewmen." Janine added.

From the way they were finishing each others thoughts and the closeness of their seating arrangements, it was immediately obvious that a strong romance was developing between them.

Over another of Moses' excellent dinners, they discussed their plans and strategies for the upcoming search.

Chapter 10

Another glorious, cloudless morning greeted the crew of 'Final Option' as they were just leaving port when the Exec 162F roared overhead on its way to the search area. Birdman, who had spent the better part of the previous evening convincing Moses to act as copilot and observer, quickly flew to the area of the conning tower and laid out a search pattern centered on that location.

Moses, grinning from ear to ear, commented, "First time in a helicopter. Kind of fun, but noisy."

"You OK?"

"Oh, yeah, just tell me what to do."

"I'll do the flying, you just need to watch this screen and tell me if it has a spike on it."

After a couple of hours searching the adjacent section of the grid next to the conning tower, Birdman was turning inland for another northward run when Moses said, "Is that a spike?"

"Oh, yes, WHOA!!" Looking down, Birdman was momentarily confused, for below them was a rocky hill well away from the shoreline.

A jubilant, but coded, radio call from Birdman to the 'Final Option' sent them scurrying south down the coast a short distance to where Moses had found the large return on the magnetometer, not under the water where they were expecting it but under the ground a couple of hundred yards inshore.

After giving them his location in the cryptic language they had worked out and adopted the previous evening, Birdman landed the helicopter on a secluded beach and Jack and Shannon joined him via the Novurania, leaving Capt'n Pete, Janine and Courtland cruising around offshore on 'Final Option'. Jack told them of his theory that the sub is in an underwater cavern under the island, having been driven there by the force of the storm, and that is the reason it has been undiscovered for so long.

Now that they had a likely target, Birdman and Moses were reassigned the task of surveillance, keeping an eye on the Senator's boat and its crew. To this end, they flew the helicopter north to the airport on the mainland near Briland, took the ferry across with a bunch of tourists and secured accommodation at Valentine's Marina. They were lucky enough just to get into the resort on such short notice, and they even managed to get a junior suite on the second floor facing the water. When they stepped onto their balcony, the Senator's boat was right there, front and center, only a short distance out from shore and easily observable.

In the meantime, Jack and Shannon returned to 'Final Option' and secured the Novurania to the aft swim platform. A strategy session was then held in the main salon. Laying out a chart of the area on the dining table, Jack marked several positions while explaining their importance.

"This is the position of the conning tower on the reef. And here is the break in the reef. And here is the position of the spike Moses got from the helicopter. As you can see, if there is a cavern large enough to take the sub, the opening has to be underwater. There is nothing but cliffs on the surface, but it is a straight line from the conning tower, through the break in the reef to the spike."

"Could we get this boat through the break, and is there enough water on the other side?" Courtland wanted to know.

"If we send the tender in ahead of us, yes and yes, I think so because this big boat only draws 5 feet of water." Jack replied.

"Then let's get to it." Capt'n Pete said excitedly.

Jack and Shannon took the tender through the gap in the reef, which turned out to be a little narrow but a straight shot through, and found that most of the water inside the reef was 50 to 70 feet deep, plenty enough for 'Final Option', even at low tide. Capt'n Pete manned the helm of the big boat and, utilizing both engines and the bow and stern thrusters, brought her slowly through the gap without any problems.

After anchoring 'Final Option' as close to shore as possible in a spot that seemed the most likely location for the entrance to the cavern, Jack and Shannon, along with Courtland and Janine, all scuba divers, formed two teams in preparation to start the search. Capt'n Pete, being the oldest member of the crew and also the least fit, elected to stay aboard the boat to maintain radio contact with Birdman and to ensure that they would have a place to return to when their tanks were exhausted. Both teams of two made several dives that afternoon, high on enthusiasm but without any success. With evening coming, they moved the boat to a more secure position behind the protection of the offshore reef and laid out a fore and aft, Bahamian style mooring, anchoring the boat for the night.

After an exhausting day, Shannon prepared a simple meal and, shortly afterward and by mutual consent, led Jack to the master stateroom for the night. He, of course, would be up at 2 a.m. to stand the watch after Capt'n Pete finished the early watch.

Janine and Courtland retired to her cabin immediately after dinner, intent on further exploring their budding romance.

Another bright morning dawned without incident and they moved the boat back in toward the shore to continue their diving to try to find the entrance to the cave they knew must be there. The day before they had thought that finding the spot would be easy, an admitted mistake. But this day would be different. With a definite area to search, Jack revealed another of his secret weapons purchased from a company in Fort Lauderdale, packed away and almost forgotten.

"Today we do things the smart way." said Jack, smiling in an thoroughly embarrassed way.

From the commodious lazarette of the boat he unveiled two K10 Hydrospeeders, twin-engine diver's propulsion vehicles that act like a cross between a Gran Prix motorcycle and a jet fighter, except they operated underwater. Barely 82 inches long, the machines become hydrodynamic shapes when the diver is seated in the normal operating position, as on a racing motorcycle. With an average speed of seven knots and the ability to dive to 200 feet, the vehicles have an endurance of five hours, allowing the operators to search a much wider area with considerably less effort than by traditional SCUBA tank and flippers. They had been plugged in and charging all night since, halfway through his watch, Jack had finally remembered that they were on board.

The first dive of the day belonged to the marginally more rested of the teams. Janine and Courtland needed only a few minutes orientation on the Speeders to feel comfortable with them, and then set off for the first hour's search. Jack and Shannon lingered in the shade of the aft deck overhang, for the day, as always in the Bahamas, was already getting very warm.

After an hour, the pair surfaced and reported no success. The area that they had covered in that one hour was greater than the area covered by both teams the whole afternoon of the day before. Jack and Shannon donned their scuba gear and resumed the search after a few minutes getting used to the Speeders. After their hour of searching on the Speeders revealed nothing of interest, they returned to 'Final Option' and Janine and Courtland took over.

As it happened, it was on Jack's second dive of the day that the entrance finally revealed itself. He was turning away from what looked for all the world like the cliff face which rose above the water to become the island of Eleuthera, when the 170 pounds of thrust the little vehicle exerted on the surrounding water parted an overhanging curtain of seaweed to reveal a gaping black hole behind it. It was only by sheer chance that Jack chose that moment to turn around to check the clearance between the wall and his Speeder, and he gazed with wonder at the yawning cavern behind him. He eased off on the throttle and instantly noticed that he was being drawn slowly backwards toward the curtain of grasses which obscured his goal. It didn't take an overactive imagination to see that this gentle current could easily become a raging torrent during a hurricane, one that was impossible to fight against.

He punched the waypoint button on the vehicle's GPS locator, fixing in its memory his current position to within ten feet, before once again throttling on the power to move away from the wall. Although the water was only about seventy feet deep, the entrance's position on the dangerous lee shore of the island and the perfect camouflage of the hanging curtains of sea grasses, left no doubt about why it had not been spotted until now.

Having completed his mission, he was the first to return to the boat. Amid high fives and much whooping from Janine and Courtland, he warmed himself with a cup of coffee provided by Capt'n Pete, who spiked it with a little Jameson's. He wondered about what, if anything, lay hidden in the darkness beyond that veil of seaweed.

Shannon finally returned, having found nothing in her assigned search area and, as she boarded the boat, was greeted with a high five by Jack, who told her of his success. She accepted a cup of coffee, similarly spiked, as they made their plans to explore the hidden entrance. Without orders to the contrary, Capt'n Pete, with Courtland's help, brought in the anchor and moved the boat closer to the GPS coordinates from Jack's Speeder marking the entrance to the cavern.

As owner of the boat and acknowledged leader of the expedition, Jack nominated himself to be the first diver to penetrate the living curtain and enter the unknown, taking Shannon with him. Both used the Hydrospeeders, reasoning that the extra air and power might become necessary. They found the entrance easily enough, relying on the GPS position to get them close enough to visually spot the hanging curtain of vegetation. Nosing their way into the darkness beyond, they switched the Speeders' spotlights on simultaneously to reveal a reasonably smooth tunnel leading inland under the island's cliffs.

They followed the dead straight tunnel perhaps a little over a quarter of a mile until the water overhead began to perceptibly brighten. As the ceiling of the tunnel began to slope upwards, they followed, Shannon behind Jack in single file, and seconds after the roof of the tunnel broke the surface, they did as well, only to be confronted with a truly awesome spectacle. The cathedral-like cavern lay open before them, several shafts of pure, brilliant sunlight streaming in at them from the heights and illuminating the pure white limestone walls which sparkled like diamonds before their eyes. Removing the regulator from her mouth, Shannon let out a tiny squeak of delight as they cruised slowly to the beach inside the magnificent hall. Cruising slowly into the beach that lay at the foot of those limestone walls, they both unmounted their Speeders and floated them to shore. With little effort, for they were quite light, they carried their Speeders up beyond the high water mark after dropping their tanks and weight belts and removing their flippers, and then stood together in awestruck silence gazing at the wonder before them.

"This is so awesome," whispered Shannon, "I've never seen anything like it."

"Neither have I. Just look how the shafts of light play on the white limestone and reflect off the water. It's so bright in here." Jack was amazed at the incredible beauty that this cavern was showing them.

After many minutes of standing and gazing, and turning in slow circles to take it all in, Jack noticed something awry with the symmetry of the cavern, and as his eyes grew accustomed to the unusual, flickering lighting conditions, he saw for the first time what was causing the anomaly. With a sudden start, he realized just what he was looking at with such intensity. He recognized that it was the ugly steel nose of the very submarine they were looking for, barely visible in the darkness at the opposite end of the cave. With a twinge of alarm, quickly shrugged off, he saw that it was the front of the U-boat with its four forward facing torpedo tubes pointed directly at them. He grasped Shannon's hand and, pointing it out to her, they started to walk down the beach towards it.

They hadn't traveled but a dozen yards from where their Speeders were beached when they glimpsed, from their altered perspective and within a niche in the wall, a glitter of bright metal which reflect a shaft of the brilliant light to their new position.

A totally unexpected and thoroughly spine chilling sight met their eyes.

A skeleton sat upon a golden throne.

Chapter 11

Horst hurried into the saloon with what he hoped would be good news for the Senator who was, as usual, mixing himself another drink. The man's capacity for hard liquor was incredible, even his most ardent detractors agreed.

"I've just gotten word from one of our friend on the island. From what he told me, Elliott's boat is anchored in a cove about forty miles north of Rock Sound, on the Atlantic side. And, it looks as if he's found something of interest."

The Senator put down his drink and smiled. "Now, that IS interesting. Show me on the chart," he said, and when Horst finally located the spot on the chart and pointed to it, the Senator let out a groan. Frowning intensely, he muttered, more to himself than Horst, "that's inside the reef. I'll be damned if I know how they managed to get that far inside amongst all those coral heads. We won't be able to get 'Shillelagh' in there, the entrance is too narrow, it's too shallow and, with those coral heads, much too dangerous."

"If we station the big boat off the reef and use both Donzi speedboats and the helicopter, we shouldn't have any trouble boxing him in effectively." Horst offered as a plan. He was already getting excited at the prospect of finally being able to meter out suitable physical punishment to his nemesis for all the embarrassment he had suffered because of Jack Elliott.

"And then what?" asked the Senator, regarding his Captain with a look of utter contempt. "Use what little brains you have been given and think, man. We don't know if he's actually found anything, or if he's just faking to see how close an eye we're been keeping on him. And besides, even if he has found it, why not let him and his peons do the heavy work of bringing it to the surface? We can always take it off him once it's on his boat."

"Yes, that makes a lot of sense, but it's not very satisfying, is it?" grumbled Horst.

"Don't you worry, my friend, once we have secured the gold, you can personally deal with Mr. Elliott and his crew anyway you please. In the meantime, have our friend ashore find a way to keep a close watch on them without being spotted. He will need to give us enough notice for us to get down there before they are able to clear out of the bay."

"Now, that might be difficult. It's a pretty remote area and with that chopper of theirs hovering above them, anyone coming close is sure to be noticed." Horst protested.

"Find a way!" ordered the Senator, returning to his drink.

Chapter 12

Jack and Shannon stood dumbfounded, staring at the apparition before them. Except for the fact that he was a skeleton, the man, for that much was evident, seemed quite relaxed, with both of his elbows resting on the arms of the chair, hands clasped in his lap and his head laid back upon the high back of the throne. While some of the bones had probably been displaced over the intervening years, he looked remarkably like the skeletons you would expect to see in a high school science classroom.

Jack felt the hairs on the back of his neck rise as he struggled to comprehend the strange vision before him. He turned slowly towards Shannon, who stood in shocked silence, seemingly staring into empty space with a glazed look in her eyes. He reached out and touched her bare shoulder and suddenly the spell was broken.

"What …? Who is that …?" she managed to stammer, seemingly incoherent.

He took her by both shoulders and turned her away from the awful scene, for it was not every day one came upon a skeleton, and as he drew her close to him, she shuddered violently, closed her eyes, folded herself into his arms and started sobbing. He understood what she was feeling for he also felt a sadness come over him as he looked at what had once been a living, breathing human being.

After some time, she managed to bring herself under control once more and with a great effort, and some caution, they started toward the seated figure. They approached from the front, hand in hand, appraising the figure and the throne further. It took only half a circumference to discover that, hidden behind the throne, a chest lay half buried in the sand. With great trepidation they crept closer, just enough to see that, although closed, the chest was not sealed. It was not your proverbial 'treasure chest' but appeared to be someone's travel chest from long ago.

Jack released Shannon and, leaning forward, opened the lid, which resisted his actions slightly before swinging upward with a screech. With bated breath they gazed upon the contents, and even in the half-light of the cavern behind the throne they marveled at the jewelry; dozens of emeralds and rubies set in delicately filigreed pure gold, glistened and sparkled with a fiery brilliance, dazzling their eyes and quickening their heartbeats.

"There must be a king's ransom here," said Shannon. "But where did it come from?"

"I don't know, but I intend to find out." replied Jack.

Hidden amongst this wealth, Jack found something which captured his attention more than the riches of the stones and precious metals. It was a book, or more correctly, a journal which, as it turned out later, belonged to the long deceased occupant of the golden throne.

Carefully lifting it from the chest and gently opening the cover and reading the opening passages, Jack decided that it was in too delicate a condition to be further manhandled here in the cave. He retrieved from his Speeder the waterproof bag he had brought and carefully inserted the volume along with several exquisite necklaces and rings, and sealed the bag tightly, stowing it back into its niche on the Speeder.

"We can get the information from the journal a lot more easily if we are in the comfortable, dry environment of the boat, so let's wait until we are back on board to find out what is in this journal," said Jack. "But since we are obviously running out of time, lets see what other surprises this place has in store for us. After all, this jewelery did not come from that sub."

"Just as long as they are not as unexpected as this last one," Shannon said, shivering slightly as she glanced toward the skeleton. "This one surprise is enough for one day."

Hand in hand, they wandered further down the beach, going back into the gloomy recesses at the end of the cave where the natural light from the ceiling had a hard time penetrating. The roof of the cave was gradually getting lower and Jack started wondering if there was anything else to be discovered before it reached the surface of the water. They could see the bow of the sub pointing its torpedo tubes menacingly at them.

"I don't believe this! We have found the wreck!" shouted Shannon, suddenly realizing that they had achieved their goal and grinning from ear to ear, her voice echoing off the walls of the cave. She dropped Jack's hand and broke into a run which carried her right up to the steel hull of the sub and then gave it a good smack with her open hand.

"That's for wasting all that time we spent looking for you," she cried, rubbing her hand from the blow. "Why couldn't you have been simple to find?"

"Because then someone else would have found it years ago, and we wouldn't have had anything to search for." Jack remarked, having walked up behind her. "Well, we found her, but we still have to find a way inside. As you have just proven with your exuberance, steel is a mighty hard substance."

"But with the conning tower ripped off, shouldn't there be a great big hole in the top of the hull?" Shannon reasoned.

"You would think so, but we still have to get up there and look. We may just find that the hole is blocked with bent metal and debris, but who knows, some of the airlocks might still be operable. At least she is still sitting upright on her keel."

They decided to explore further and walked toward the stern of the submarine, where they made an unexpected discovery. Large, broken wooden beams were laying scattered around the beach like matchsticks or the aftermath of a Jenga game, and also leaning against the steel hull of the Uboat in a random, haphazard fashion.

"Now where the hell did these come from?" asked Jack. "They look like the longitudinals and decking off an old wooden sailing ship."

"You mean like that one back there that the sub has crashed into," said Shannon, pointing backwards into the cave toward the remains of what appeared to be an old Spanish galleon in the dim recesses at the very end of the cave. The wreck appeared to still be in remarkably good condition considering its age and despite the fact that it had a steel WW2 submarine sticking into its side.

"Now that has got to be where the jewels and the golden throne came from." Jack speculated.

With a smirk, Shannon dug one in, the elation of their find finally sinking in, "I doubt very much if the sub was the one carrying the golden throne, don't you?"

Jack looked her way, and with a slight shake of his head, said, "OK, you are right about that. But at least it gives us a way up onto the deck of the sub"

"What do you mean?"

"Stack these pieces of wood together against the hull and make a rough ladder going up or down." Jack was already trying to figure out the simplest way to accomplish this task.

"That'll work, but not today." Shannon said, pointing at the water.

Noticing that the tide was starting to recede, and knowing that they had to leave the cave on an outgoing, falling tide, they reluctantly retraced their steps to the golden throne and after another quick look around, prepared their equipment for the outward journey. Jack double checked the waterproof pack containing the journal and as many precious stones as it would hold to make sure it was secured properly to the luggage rack on top of the Hydrospeeder and after all the necessary safety checks, Jack preceded Shannon out of the cave through the tunnel.

Chapter 13

That evening, having successfully returned from the cavern and celebrated their amazing find in the appropriate manner, everyone gathered in the main salon and made themselves comfortable. Jack carefully opened the journal and started reading the century old words of the condemned man on the throne.

The first part of the journal was a detailed description of many and varied caves, all being located somewhere in the islands of the Bahamas and all with almost scientific technical discourse on the dimensions and characteristics of each cave or system of caves. More than halfway through the book they finally came to that part which was of immediate interest.

The beginning of the section was dated August 8th, 1904.

"This is an accounting of the circumstances which have led to my incarceration in this godforsaken place. Be it known that I, John Jefferson Beaumont, Governor of the Bahamas, and my faithful friend and companion, Stanley Gresham, have become trapped in this cavern by a rockfall which, unfortunately, has sealed the tunnel through which we gained entry into this grotto which holds the wreck of a Spanish galleon."

Hearing a sudden gasp, Jack looked up from the journal and into Janine's eyes. "Beaumont?"

"My great Grandfather," her eyes misted over. "He and his adjutant disappeared in 1904."

"Do you know what happened?"

181

"My father told me that they were both amateur spelunkers, you know, cave explorers, and were very secretive about where they went on their many trips. It was generally assumed that something like this had happened to them. Although there were those that thought they had disappeared on purpose."

"Why?"

"There was quite an amount of money missing from the treasury around that time and the assumption was that they had made off with it. It was never recovered, as far as I know. The other theory is that my Grandmother had something to do with it, but they could never explain why Gresham had disappeared, too. Apparently she was ostracized by the suspicions for the rest of her life."

An awkward silence followed the pronouncement, and it was only broken when Jack started reading from the journal again.

"After an extensive search of the cave, we have concluded that there is no other way out and have resigned ourselves to our fate. We have explored the wreck of the galleon and found to our amazement, a solid gold throne carved in the most intricate manner and designed in a most ingenious way. It is not one solid piece, but a number of interlocking pieces small enough to be carried by a single man, albeit a strong one, and assembled to form a single seat fit for a king. On a whim, we decided to remove it from the ship and reassemble it here on the beach along with as many pieces of jewelry as we could find. We may have missed some, but we searched pretty thoroughly."

Jack paused once again and looked into Shannon's eyes. "That explains why we found him sitting there. He was protecting his last accomplishment."

"Yes, poor man. But what happened to his friend, this Gresham fellow?"

"Let's find out," Jack said as he continued reading.

"It has now been six days since the cave in, and our food and fresh water has been exhausted. Gresham has come up with a theory that there must be a large underwater opening somewhere in this cave in order to get the galleon inside. For the last two days he has been diving around the perimeter of the lagoon in hopes of finding it. Unfortunately, I have not been able to help as I cannot swim, but he was on his university swim team and is quite accomplished."

Jack looked up and asked Shannon, "How long was that underwater tunnel from the cave to the open sea, would you estimate?"

"Somewhere between a quarter and a half mile, maybe more."

"You are a strong swimmer. Could you have held your breath long enough to swim through it?"

"I doubt it very much." Shannon replied, shaking her head.

Returning to the journal, Jack continued.

"Gresham has found a large tunnel out of here and has swum a short way down it. He says it has to lead to the open sea because he can feel the currents in it. He says he is going to wait for high tide and then ride the outgoing tide back to the ocean. He is also going to take our two empty water skins, fill them with air and with that extra air, he believes he can make it through to the surface of the open ocean."

Jack smiled, "That man was still thinking straight." The journal continued on the next page, despite the fact that the last passage ended only halfway down.

"Unfortunately, it has been two days since Gresham left on his outbound journey through the tunnel. I remain hopeful that he is even now on his way here with a rescue party, but I fear for his safety. It was a foolish hope that he could get through, but a hope nonetheless. This will probably be my last entry in this journal because the last of the fuel for the last lantern is being consumed. I am surprised it has lasted this long. I will seat myself on the seat of a king and await whatever comes after this, if anything.

To whoever finds these words, please if you can, convey my love and thanks to my wife and son for a wonderful and fulfilling life and my fervent wish that they do not suffer too much at my demise."

A heavy silence fell over the boat. It was broken by Janine getting up and going into the galley, getting glasses and a bottle of champagne, coming back and filling everyone's glasses.

Janine raised her glass and said, "I propose a toast. To my great Grandfather, may he rest in peace. At the very least, we can now lay all the rumors to rest and let history record what really happened."

Later that night, Jack retrieved his satellite phone from the pilothouse and placed a call to Sean in Fort Lauderdale.

"How's my favorite leprechaun doing?"

"Jack?"

"The one and only."

"Where are you, you old bugger?"

"We are, at the moment, anchored in a little cove just off Eleuthera. We are sitting here drinking champagne, and feeling very mellow."

"Does that mean......?" Sean, having been in on the start of the expedition, and knowing the reason behind it, sounded positively radiant.

"It sure does. And with added bonuses, too."

"What does that mean?"

"I'll tell you when you get here."

"I'm coming there?"

"You are. No arguments, and bring Katie, too. I need all the divers I can get, within our circle."

"Earliest I can make it is Saturday."

"That will work. Now, here are the coordinates of where we are and a list of stuff you need to bring with you. You got a pen?"

After dictating a long list of requirements, Jack hung up looking forward to the weekend. He double checked the security of the boat, and left Capt'n Pete on anchor watch, then retired to the master stateroom, joining an already sleeping Shannon. After the exhausting day, he was asleep as soon as his head hit the pillow. That was a good thing, for tomorrow was going to be a long day.

Chapter 14

The next morning they all rose with the sun. They hurried through breakfast, knowing that a full day of diving lay ahead.

On the first dive, Jack took one Speeder while Courtland took the other. Using the GPS coordinates obtained the previous day, Jack had no trouble finding the entrance to the cavern, and Courtland punched them into the second Speeder. They transited the tunnel and, after beaching, Courtland had his first view of the skeleton on the golden throne. It had been described to him in great detail, but it still shocked him into silence as they approached.

"This is totally unexpected," Courtland said as he examined the throne. "How can we possibly get this onto the boat? It must weigh tons."

"You were there last night. According to the journal, it breaks down into pieces light enough for an individual to carry. The two of them carried it from the galleon to here, and I don't think that we are any weaker than they were. So we just have to transport it, as they did, one piece at a time. But first, we have to solve the mystery of the submarine."

"So where do we start?"

"We need to move those baulks of timber up against the pressure hull of the submarine, so we can get inside and make sure the gold is still there."

"Any reason it shouldn't be?"

"No, but who knows? Remember, the sub was not there when the governor found the galleon, so we need to find out if it is still there, sooner rather than later."

"Then let's get to it."

Having warned the people remaining on the boat beforehand that they would be working in the cave to try to gain entry into the sub's interior, it was several hours before Courtland and Jack were satisfied with the progress they had made.

The baulks of timber that the submarine had sheared from the side of the galleon as the heavy steel vessel, moving backwards, struck the deteriorating wooden hull of the older ship with its hull and propellers, lay scattered across the beach and needed to be cut and organized to form a stairway up to the deck of the sub.

Through sheer effort and the few hand tools they had brought with them, an acceptable ladder and slide arrangement had been fabricated after a couple of hours. If they did find gold bars on the sub, as they expected to, the slide was the easiest way of getting them down to the beach with the least amount of damage. As they stood on top of the sub's deck peering into the hole left when the conning tower broke off, and seeing only water inside the sub, they mutually agreed that enough was enough for one day.

They returned to the "Final Option" and, turning the Hydrospeeders over to Shannon and Janine to allow the two women the opportunity to experience the pristine cavern for themselves, they agreed to 'do' lunch. Capt'n Pete had already prepared lunch for the female half of the crew and now pulled out leftovers for the men, much to the protests of the hard worked and hungry males.

"This is what you get if you're not here on time," he said.

"We were working, hard. And now we need sustenance, big time." Jack said, trying not to show his annoyance, but barely succeeding.

"Too bad. If you want something more, you can always make it yourself." Capt'n Pete was smiling when he said this, obviously enjoying Jack's consternation.

"Seriously?" Jack was beginning to see the light.

"You know I'm just kidding, right? I've got burgers and fries coming right up."

During this bantering, Courtland, sitting silently on the settee on the aft deck, was staring vacantly out toward the reef. It was not too distant, but his gaze was far beyond anything which could be seen.

"Penny for them." Jack said.

"Huh, what?"

"Your thoughts. I'll give you a penny for them."

"Oh. Yeah. Well, I was just contemplating the forces necessary to drive that Spanish galleon and also a WW2 submarine through that tunnel into the cavern. They must have been tremendous."

"I should imagine. Like a hurricane, maybe?"

"And then I was thinking about an old wives tale I heard as a kid growing up in Rock Sound about Eleuthera. The old men of the settlement used to scare us kids with stories of this part of the coast. About how, during the big storms, what you call hurricanes these days, this bay would form a giant whirlpool and suck all small children down to hell, if they had been bad."

"Really?"

"Some even embellished the tales to include a phenomenon known locally as 'the boils'. It is an area directly across the island from here where, during really bad storms, the water literally boils like a steaming cauldron, not from heat but from pressure."

"Across from here?"

"Yes, almost as if the whirlpool and the boils are connected beneath the island."

"But you saw for yourself that the end of the cavern was solid rock."

"Above the surface, yes. But underneath the water there are probably a series of vents channeling the water under the island and exiting in the unstable sands of 'the boils' on the other side."

"That would explain why both the galleon and the sub stopped where they are now and went no further."

"I am willing to bet that during those times when big hurricanes come this way from the Caribbean, the storm surge coming through the only opening into this bay, it being deep but not very wide, sets up a circular motion in the bay forming the whirlpool and over the millenniums, have bored the tunnel and the cavern and will eventually work its way right through the island to 'the boils'."

"Well, I am not a geologist, but it sounds like it might be a reasonable assumption. But, regardless of how it got here, our job now is to recover what we can before the next big storm, don't you agree?"

Courtland smiled, "That would seem to be a prudent plan. Even if we have discovered a lot more than we ever imagined."

After several hours, Shannon and Janine returned to "Final Option" bearing gifts. They had taken waterproof bags with them and had loaded some more of the gems from the chest and brought them to the surface.

"We completed a pretty thorough search of the beaches on either side of the cavern, looking for any more 'surprises'." Shannon said. "Didn't find anything we didn't already know about."

"That ladder and slide arrangement you guys built looks great. It should work perfectly." said Janine. "Are you going down again?"

"No," said Jack. "Too late in the day, and we deserve a rest. Sean and Katie will be here the day after tomorrow with a boatload of equipment that will make our task easier, so I propose taking tomorrow off and relaxing so we will be ready for Saturday."

"Second the motion," Courtland agreed. "We still have a lot of hard work ahead of us."

Saturday lunchtime arrived with a roar. The roar of the big turbo-charged engines of Sean's green 50 foot Cary, "Leprechaun."

"Ahoy, mate, permission to tie up?" shouted Sean when he was 5 feet from the side of the "Final Option".

Jack and Courtland grabbed the thrown lines and held the Cary off until Sean and Katie had hung the fenders between the two boats, then made the raft up complete by cleating the bow, stern and spring lines securely.

Sean jumped the small gap between the two boats, then came over and enveloped Jack in a huge bear hug. "So good to see you, buddy." he said, punching Jack on the shoulder.

By this time, Katie had made her way aboard and literally launched herself at Jack, hugging him around the neck and planting a huge kiss on his lips.

Courtland's eyes went huge at this display, seeing Katie was wearing nothing but the tiny bikini from the Keys trip. He turned and his eyes went instinctively to Shannon, fearing the worst, thinking that 'this can't be good', only to find her laughing and hugging Sean.

"Hey, buddy, I think introductions are in order," said Sean, gazing wide-eyed at the huge black man standing before him.

"Oh, yes, of course, you haven't met. Sean this is Courtland, my new bodyguard. Courtland, Sean, the biggest pirate in the whole Caribbean. That do?" Jack was, of course, smiling when he said this.

Courtland held out his very large hand, saying, "Good thing Jack is vouching for you, I don't like the Pirates, I prefer the Boston Red Socks." He, too was smiling when he said this.

Sean shook the hand, wincing a little when the pressure came on, saying, "I can see why Jack hired you as a bodyguard."

"Actually, I am a New England solicitor, not a bodyguard."

"I bet you don't lose many cases. I'd hate to get you mad at me."

"All right, enough pleasantries, let's grab some lunch and then get Sean's boat unloaded." Jack said, leading the way to the flybridge where Capt'n Pete had a spread laid out for them.

After lunch, they all spent the afternoon unloading the equipment Jack had asked Sean to bring with him from Florida. There was a small diesel generator, impulse start and shrink wrapped in plastic so as to make it completely waterproof. A crash pump as used by the Coast Guard on sinking vessels, electric, also shrink wrapped in plastic, with a capacity of 10,000 gallons per hour was accompanied by several spools of hoses and boxes of filters. Three waterproof sleds, which were essentially waterproof boxes with buoyancy control bladders attached to them, had been quickly fabricated to Jack's specifications and several 5,000 foot spools of 30,000 lb. tensile strength polypropylene line. An underwater cutting torch was included, in case it was necessary to cut their way into the sub, and 2 extra Hydrospeeders as well as many assorted bits and pieces. Sean and Katie had also brought their own personal scuba gear and all hands pitched in to transfer everything to 'Final Option', with the exception of the two Speeders, which stayed on 'Leprechaun'.

At the end of the day, over well deserved drinks, Jack explained his future plans to the gathered company, all of whom were listening intently.

"I have tried to think of as many problems as I could and anticipate an answer to that problem. After I explain my plan, I want input from everyone about anything I've missed." Jack started.

"Firstly, we need to use the sleds to transfer the generator and the pump, hoses and filters down to the cave to get the sub pumped dry. We will tow the sleds down with the Speeders and set the generator and pump up on the beach and start pumping ASAP. We will also use the sleds to bring down fuel for the generator. Once the sub is dry, we will search it for the gold, and assuming we find it, use the sleds and the polypropylene line attached to the boat davit to bring it to the surface and onto the boat. A spool of polypropylene line will also be attached to the generator in the cave to pull the carriers back into the cave. Any questions?"

"I have got one. Why not simply use the speeders to tow the gold out?" Shannon asked.

"It's a question of weight. I know the gold is going to weigh a lot less underwater but the Speeders simply don't have the power to move the sleds except on a favorable tide. We do have to move the genny and pump into the cave on an ingoing tide, because of the weight, but by using the line to move the gold, we don't have to wait for the tide to change. Does that make sense?"

"Yes, it does. But how do we ensure that the sled doesn't get hung up on something?"

"We will have a person behind each sled. The sleds are fitted with handles, air tanks and bladders which work as a buoyancy compensator, same as the BC you use when diving, you can put in air to rise, let it out to dive."

"What about communications? I mean, the guy on the boat has to know when to start or stop pulling, right?" This came from Courtland.

"I thought about that for a long time," admitted Jack. "Best I could come up with was a speaker wire attached to a simple on/off switch. On for go, off for stop. Attached to the polypropylene line pulling each sled. With a bit of slack at the end so it can be operated by the person behind the sled."

"That might just work." said Sean.

"Anything else?"

"What is it we are doing and why are we doing it?" Katie had been sitting behind the group the whole time, looking mystified and lost, as if she was supposed to know what was going on and didn't.

Jack threw an annoyed glance at Sean and asked. "You haven't told Katie about what we are doing here?"

"Thought I'd give you that pleasure. I'm not privy to the whole story, either, you know."

Jack was thoughtful for a moment, then said, "You are right of course, so I'll start at the beginning...." and proceeded to lay out the whole adventure up to that point.

Early the next morning, they were discussing the plans for the day when they interrupted by the ringing of Courtland's cell phone. Excusing himself from the table, he went to the aft deck to take the call, returning a few minutes later with some bad news.

"That was my partner in the law firm up in Boston. Seems that they still think that I work for them, and have given me an assignment." he said, smiling. "Apparently, one of the firm's largest clients got himself into a spot of bother in South Beach last night and spent the night in the slammer. So, I need to be in court in Miami first thing Monday morning, which means I need to leave right now if I'm going to catch the flight from Nassau."

Sean spoke up right away. "Katie and I can run you over to Nassau in the Cary, you catch your flight and then we will stay in Nassau for the night, since she has never been there. I'll show her the town and then come back tomorrow."

Janine said, "I'll come with you."

"No, that's not necessary. I'll only be gone a couple of days and since it's Sunday, why don't you all relax here until Sean and Katie get back?"

"I think that's a good idea." Jack said. "We have all been working hard and a day off sure appeals to me."

It didn't take Courtland long to pack a suitcase, and after delivering a long and tender farewell kiss to Janine, he joined Sean and Katie on the Cary, which soon disappeared into the morning sunlight with a self satisfied roar.

Shortly after their second cup of coffee, Janine announced that she wanted to go for a dive. For pleasure, of course, not to work. Shannon begged off saying that she just wanted to stretch out on deck and catch some rays. Reluctantly, Jack volunteered to go down with her, since, in the interest of safety, she needed a partner.

Thirty minutes later, they were both suited up and ready to go on the aft swim platform. Shannon, who had changed into the skimpiest bikini Jack had ever seen, held up the progress into the water by swiveling in front of Jack, pouting.

"See what you are missing?"

"Damn, woman, you're going to give an old man a heart attack, wearing something like that. Ain't enough material there to make a decent handkerchief," muttered Capt'n Pete.

Jack was already regretting his decision to go diving, but managed a weak, "Really?"

Shannon laughed, "Hey, minimum coverage, maximum exposure, right?" she said, winking at Janine, who was laughing right along with her.

With an exaggerated Marilyn Munroe curtsy, Shannon teased Capt'n Pete, "What's the matter, Pete, haven't you ever seen a *girl* before?"

Standing a little straighter, he replied, "Sure, even chased a few a long time ago, problem is, I've forgotten why." A big grin followed this announcement. "You just go ahead, Jack. Take care of Janine and I'll take care of Shannon."

They all stood around laughing, until Janine said, "Come on, Jack, Let's go."

With Shannon and Capt'n Pete watching, the two of them goose stepped off the platform into the water. After completing their safety checks and mounting their respective Hydrospeeder, they started their dive without noticing the two Donzi speedboats creeping slowly into the bay through the break in the reef.

With the help of the Speeders, they were soon exploring the southern portion of the unspoiled coral reef, almost to the shore line, marveling at the colors and textures surrounding them. Even with the regulator in her mouth, Jack could see that Janine had an ear to ear grin on her face. The squadrons of tarpon, some five feet long, cruised in formation just off the reef, while angelfish, snappers and grunts played among the soft corals and the lobsters and moray eels poked their faces out of their respective holes in the hard coral. The bathtub warmth and gin clarity of the water induced them many times to stop and just hover above the reef or settle softly onto one of the many sandy patches between the corals and simply enjoy nature at its most spectacular.

Although both wished to stay longer, all too soon it was time to return to the surface. As they slowly cruised along the reef toward their boat, the high pitched whine of high speed propellers was clearly audible causing Jack to wonder if Sean and Katie had, for some obscure reason, come back to the boat. But then he noticed that the sound was receding and was soon lost as whatever boat it was cleared the gap in the reef.

They reached the swim platform, stripped off their dive gear and, as Jack was lifting the Speeders onto the platform, Janine excused herself to use the bathroom.

She had not been gone ten seconds when she screamed, "Jack, get up here, NOW!!!"

Jack raced up the aft stairs, across the deck and through the salon doors, and came to a screeching halt beside Janine, who was pointing to Capt'n Pete duct taped to one of the dining room chairs, unconscious and bleeding.

Grabbing a paring knife from the galley, Jack sliced through the duct tape and layed the victim on the floor and instructed Janine to get the first aid kit from the pilothouse. When she returned, his only instruction to her was, "Find Shannon."

Just as Jack was starting the triage process, Capt'n Pete awoke, sat up groggily and started cursing in German. He barely stopped himself from taking a swing at Jack, recognition registering at the last moment. Janine came up from below and seeing Capt'n Pete sitting up on the floor, sobbed, "I can't find Shannon on the boat, anywhere."

"The bastards kidnapped her!!" Capt'n Pete was now trying to stand up, but finally collapsed into the chair to which he had been tied. "I tried to stop them, honest I did. Jack, I tried, but I wasn't strong enough, and they had guns."

"All right, it's all right. Tell us what happened." Jack calmed him down.

"Right after you guys left, me and Shannon were still on the swim platform, when the two Donzis came creeping up on either side of the boat and caught us there. They had at least a half dozen guns trained on us and we would have been shot down if we had tried for the stairs. That jackass Keller, big grin on his face, got onto the swim platform with us and I smacked him a good one, but he just shrugged it off. Then he hit me, and the stars came out. We were dragged up to the main salon, where I was tied up while they searched the boat." All this came out of Capt'n Pete's mouth in a rush.

"Did they say what they were searching for?"

"No. But they didn't find the hidden compartment where we left the journal and the jewels, because they left with nothing. Except Shannon. They took her! There was nothing I could do!"

"OK! Is there anything else?"

"They left that. Told me to draw your attention to it, before they took Shannon away and beat me up and knocked me out." Capt'n Pete was pointing to a cell phone laying atop of a piece of paper with a typed note on it, which graced the dining room table. Jack retrieved the phone and paper and read the note, which said.

Please call as soon as you receive this, we have much to discuss.

Chapter 15

Jack read the short note, then picked up the cell phone. It was a cheap throwaway prepaid phone that anyone could buy anywhere. He powered it up and searched the contacts list. It was a short search. Only one number appeared.

"I would venture to guess that this is the number he wants me to call." Jack muttered sarcastically to himself.

Jack was confused. '*Why now? Why would the Senator want to expose himself to this kind of official scrutiny unnecessarily? Why would he take such an irrational step as a kidnapping?*' he thought to himself. '*Unless Horst Keller saw an opportunity to get back at me, and acted on his own. That kraut would probably do something that stupid, I'm sure.*'

"I guess it's time to find out who is at the other end of this phone." Jack said, dialing the number in the list automatically, and putting it on speaker.

The phone on the other end rang, rang again, then again and was finally picked up.

"Good afternoon, Mr. Elliott," the Senator's gleeful voice came through the tinny speaker of the throwaway, "so nice of you to call me so promptly."

"Senator, I haven't called to exchange pleasantries. I want to know where Shannon is and when you'll be letting her go. I can't believe *you* would do something this stupid, so it must have been Keller acting on his own." Jack was determined not to let his frustration and anxiety show in his voice, but was having a hard time achieving it.

"Actually, I had hoped you would all be there on the boat, so Horst could have brought everyone here at the same time. However, this will do just as well."

"What will do just as well?"

"I had thought to invite you all to dinner on my yacht so we could discuss what is going to happen here, but you would have refused to come. Now, however, you *will* both come to the boat and we *will* come to an agreement. In the meantime, Ms. O'Loughlin will be my pampered guest."

"By both, who do you mean?" Jack picked up on the Senator's slip of the tongue, realizing that the Senator had no idea how many people were involved in the search for the sub and, obviously, had no clue about the galleon. He fervently hoped that Shannon had not let anything slip.

"Why, you and Capt'n Pete, of course. Horst will come by at six this evening in the Donzi to pick you up, and bring you here. Oh, and by the way, do bring a change of clothing for Shannon, she wasn't wearing very much when we picked her up."

"And if we refuse?"

"Well, Jack, in that case, this boat would set sail for Ft. Lauderdale tonight but when we arrived there tomorrow morning, Shannon would no longer be aboard. Do I have your attention now?"

"Yes, you do. Send your boat tonight." Jack was desperately trying to think of a way to rescue Shannon before Horst arrived, but, given the time constraints, could not come up with anything that even looked like a plan.

"And, Jack, no funny business. No firearms, no knives in your boots, no explosives. You will both be searched. Do you understand me?"

"Yes, I do."

Both parties hung up at the same time, one gleefully looking forward to the night's entertainment, the other dreading it. On their separate boats, both men sat down with a stiff drink in their hands, but for totally different reasons. Jack realized just how deadly the situation had suddenly become, and again wondered what the Senator's motivation could be. It certainly wasn't the $10,000 that Capt'n Pete had allegedly stolen, and it might not even be about the gold on the sub, but there was just something about the sub itself that seemed to stink to high heaven.

Jack called Sean in Nassau to explain the situation to him.

"I'll skip the night on the town and come right back." Sean said. "We'll take care of those bastards." He sounded furious, and rightly so, since Shannon was a good friend of his, too.

"No," said Jack. "I want you to stay there in Nassau tonight, and in the morning, I want you to go to Briland, get a slip at Valentine's and join Janine's dad, Moses, and Birdman, who are already there, Room 12. Hook up with them and together keep an eye on the Senator and his crew."

"OK. But won't they recognize my boat?"

"As far as I know, they have never seen us together, unless they remember you from the Keys. But it would be you and not your boat. Just wear some of your Raybans and a ball cap."

"OK. Call me if you need me."

Jack then called Birdman to explain what was going on and to coordinate with him.

"Shannon has been kidnapped by the Senator's men and is being held on the 'Shillelagh'. You will be getting company tomorrow in the form of Sean and Katie."

"You know, I thought that that was Shannon I saw getting on the Senator's boat, but I talked myself out of it because I didn't think Shannon would wear anything *that* skimpy." Birdman's voice was full of admiration and envy. "They were practically manhandling her up the steps from the swim platform."

Jack made a mental note to be sure to bring Shannon something decent to wear.

"We will be going to the Senator's boat tonight to negotiate for Shannon's release. I want you two to keep an eye on what is happening on the Senator's boat and call the police if something doesn't seem right, got it?"

"Got it, Jack. Be careful, you can't trust snakes like that."

Jack turned to Janine, who had been sitting silently listening to the disturbing conversation and who was, understandably, badly shaken up by this turn of events.

"Janine, here is what I want you to do," said Jack. "When they come by to pick us up this afternoon, I want you to be in the anchor locker, hidden away. I doubt if they will search the boat, since they don't know you are here, but if they do, I hope they won't think to look in there. Once we leave, you can come out and move about the boat, but try to stay unobtrusive, just in case someone is watching the boat. You will have a cell phone, so you can talk to your dad, Birdman or Sean if there are any problems. Just make yourself comfortable and wait for our return. If we don't turn up in 24 hours, by 6 pm tomorrow, call the police and the Bahamas Air Sea Rescue Association and tell them everything. Can you do that?"

"Yes, of course, but why do you want me to wait 24 hours?"

"The police would have to wait 24 hours on a missing persons case, anyway. So if you don't hear from us by 6, make the calls."

"OK."

That afternoon, the Donzi bearing Horst Keller and several other crewmembers of the 'Shillelagh' appeared at the break in the reef at precisely six p.m. and proceeded slowly over to 'Final Option's position. They tied up to the aft swim platform and Horst stepped triumphantly aboard.

"So, Jack, how does it feel to lose?" he said as he swaggered about.

"Depends upon what you consider loosing." Jack, carrying a duffel bag with Shannon's clothes, was careful not to antagonize the powerfully built German, but still felt the need to insert small barbs into the conversation. "Can we just go and get this over with? I don't think that this conversation is part of the deal and I'd just as soon not have it. I'll talk to your boss when we get there."

Horst shrugged his shoulders, took the duffel bag from Jack and after a quick inspection, he handed it back and indicated the way he wanted his two passengers to proceed. "It'll keep, Jack, but I will make you sorry that you interfered, believe me, you *will* be sorry."

As soon as the pair had boarded but before they a chance to sit down, the throttles were firewalled causing both Jack and Capt'n Pete to fall to their knees. They found their seats rather unceremoniously, much to the amusement and laughter from Horst and his men.

The Donzi was every bit as fast as the Cary, although at 28 feet long and sporting turbocharged engines it should have been faster. This was due, no doubt, to a lack of maintenance and care, unlike the kind Sean lavished on his beloved Cary. Still the Donzi had no trouble maintaining top speed in the flat calm of the late afternoon.

Less than an hour later, they were entering the harbor behind the barrier island where the town of Harbour Island stood. Before them, riding at anchor, was the gin palace named 'Shillelagh', easily the largest vessel in the harbor. Judiciously cutting the power so as not to attract attention, something he was not known for, Horst skilfully brought the speedboat to the lowered boarding ladder on the port side of the big boat and tied up. Jack noted with interest that the big boat was between them and the town, and therefore they were going aboard unobserved by anyone on shore.

Horst preceded everyone up the boarding ladder, a gorgeous teak and stainless steel custom creation which must have cost tens of thousands of dollars to build, followed by Jack and Capt'n Pete with the two guards bringing up the rear. As they stepped aboard the opulent vessel, they were met on the side deck by the Senator himself.

"Welcome to my little slice of heaven, Jack, and welcome back, Pete. I have decided that I'll dispense with the Captain, since you no longer are one." Shamus laughed at his own joke, followed by nervous laughter from the crewmen who surrounded them.

"I beg to differ, sir, for Capt'n Pete is in command of my boat." Jack said defensively.

"Yes, well, I wouldn't let that get around if I were you. Anyway, enough pleasantries, to business. Follow me." He turned and stalked aft.

With, seemingly, the whole of the 'Shillelagh's' crew crowding them, Jack and Capt'n Pete had little choice but to do just that. Walking behind the Senator, Jack observed that he was an overweight, out-of-shape stump of a man with wispy white hair, but well groomed and impeccably dressed in a custom-fitted suit undoubtedly from Saville Row, peering at the world through coke bottle glasses.

As they entered the main salon, Jack took in the luxurious compartment in a single glance, but he noticed immediately the cadaverous man standing at the bar. He was well dressed in formal clothes, not as well as the Senator, but impressive, none the less. He turned when the door opened and glared at them as they entered.

"Ah, Otto, our friends have arrived. Be a good fellow and bring us drinks." The Senator said, proceeding to the sofa in the middle of the salon. "Please, gentlemen, have a seat."

As they seated themselves in the club seats across from the sofa, Jack said, "I don't understand why you would describe us as friends to Otto, is that your name? I've never met the man."

"Oh, but I consider you my friend, Mr. Elliott." Otto replied in a quiet voice, a smirk on his face, "After all, you've been driving my Mercedes for over a month now."

"Ah, you are Moses' German friend."

"Yes I am, but so much more than that." Otto admitted, cryptically. "What would you and your Captain care to drink?"

"Water would be nice." Jack said. "We are hoping that this will not take long."

"On that note," interrupted the Senator, "Since I am afraid I will have to insist that you stay for dinner, you might as well indulge in something more substantial. I can afford it, you know. My chef has gone to so much trouble preparing his specialty dish, I would hate for you to miss out."

Jack looked at Capt'n Pete, who shrugged his shoulders and asked, "You don't happen to have Jameson's, do you?"

"Yes, of course, but tell me, does that duffel you are carrying contain Shannon's appropriate clothing? I would very much prefer that she join us before the discussion gets too serious." The Senator waved to one of the crewmen standing by. "Take this, I do presume it has been searched, to Ms. O'Loughlin, allow her to get dressed, *in private*, and then ask her to join us."

The young man, clearly disappointed, nodded, took the duffel and disappeared below decks.

Otto brought the drinks, Jameson's for Jack and Capt'n Pete, a large Dark and Stormy for the Senator and a Bushmill's for himself, and sat down in a third club chair off to the side. They all sat in silence, Otto and the Senator sipping their drinks. Jack and Capt'n Pete's drinks sat on the table, while they eyed each other, attempting to gain some insight of what was about to transpire.

A noise from below made all their heads turn toward the stairs where they observed the regal entrance of Shannon, who was, as well as a kidnap victim, one thoroughly pissed off woman. No one dared approach her, the crew having retreated to the far corners of the salon. She was dressed to kill in the sparkling electric blue, short sleeved top from the Keys trip over white linen slacks and gold sandals, and she walked, as if on a royal visit, slowly and directly over to Jack, sat down on the arm of the club chair and delivered a long and tender kiss to his upturned face.

"Could someone please tell me what is going on here?" she inquired.

The Senator stood up, his drink in hand and said, "I have asked.... no, coerced you all here tonight to try to come to an agreement about the situation in which we find ourselves." He sagged a little. "I have no wish to harm anyone, and so far I haven't, but I find myself in a position where I realize I will have to make compromises and ....accomodations." He sat back down, put his elbows on his knees and his head in his hands, and, in a low voice which everyone strained to hear, said, "I need your help."

Chapter 16

Jack, Shannon and Capt'n Pete sat in stunned silence and stared at the Senator unbelievingly. Even the effervescent Otto had lost some of his sparkle. Horst and the rest of the crew stood about looking lost and bewildered. The Senator's eyes took on a moist sheen and he looked down to avoid their scrutiny.

'Either the Senator is the world's greatest actor, or this is for real,' thought Jack.

"Jack, Shannon, Capt'n Pete, I want to tell you a story." started the Senator. "This is probably what I should have done in the first place. Horst and Otto, you two stay, everyone else give us some privacy and close the door behind you."

He waited until all the crewmembers had shuffled out closing the door behind them, and indicated for Horst to take a seat in the other club chair.

The Senator took a deep breath, picked up his drink and began his tale.

"Way back in World War 2, my father was also a U.S. Senator, as I am. He was the head of a committee whose task it was to regulate and oversee the War Department. He wielded a lot of power in that position, had many important contacts, both at home and abroad, and had a lot of powerful friends, both in politics and industry." He paused to take a sip from his drink, a lot less than usual, Horst noted. "In 1944, he was handed an assignment by the Secretary of Defense. He was put in charge of overseeing the team of OSS agents who handled the security of a large shipment of gold from the States to England, which would ultimately be trans-shipped to Russia. Since he was a staunch anti-communist, he didn't think that Russia should get any help from the U.S., especially in an untraceable form such as gold, and therefore, he made arrangements for this gold to disappear along the way. Unfortunately, like so many people in the States in those days, he was also pro-Nazi, believed in what Hitler was trying to achieve, and was willing to do what he could to help."

He again sipped from his drink, noting that Otto was drinking, too, and Horst was looking around for a drink. "The names of the people involved have long ago disappeared from my memory, but the scheme was brilliant. He bribed the captain and certain other crewmembers of the Liberty Ship which was carrying the gold to England to have engine trouble and to have to make an emergency stop in Ireland. It was in Belfast Harbor, at a deserted wharf, that the exchange took place. The gold, packed in wooden boxes, was offloaded and an equal number of identical wooden boxes filled with lead were loaded in their place. The ship then went on to Liverpool, its original destination. Through his many connections, my father insured that the switch was never noticed, or at least, never acknowledged, in England. I imagine the Russians were a little miffed when they received a shipment of lead from the U.S., though. Even though 1944 was still in the middle of the war, communication was a lot better than it had been before between allies, but somehow the report of the gold turning to lead never made it back to the States."

"Before the war, my father was a member of the Diplomatic Corps, and served in many foreign countries. Germany, Great Britain, Ireland and the Bahamas among them. He met a great many people during this time, people who would prove useful to him during the war. It was one of these contacts who provided the trucks and necessary papers for him personally, for he had crossed the Atlantic on the Liberty Ship, to transport the gold from Belfast to the Dingle Peninsula, where it was loaded onto a Nazi submarine. After the sub sailed, he went back to Belfast and caught the next transport plane home."

"He then went to the island of San Salvador in the Bahamas, chosen as the transfer point because of its height of 140 feet above sea level, which made it an excellent navigation mark, to await the arrival of the submarine, which, as we all know, failed to show up. He actually waited almost a month, just in case the boat had only been delayed, but eventually he had to concede the fact that it was not coming. It was a devastating blow to his plans and he spent the rest of the war doing menial tasks and was extremely bitter that his only consolation was that he had kept the gold out of Russian hands."

"After the war, my father heard about the survivors of a German U-boat from a contact in the Bahamian government. Apparently, they were being held in prison in Nassau, so he immediately flew there to arrange their repatriation. It took some doing, but eventually they were released. But, of course, we know that they didn't go home to Germany, but went back to Eleuthera." The Senator paused, finished his drink in one long swallow, and signaled to Horst for a refill.

Capt'n Pete interrupted, seemingly interested in the developments for the first time since they had left 'Final Option'. "But my father always thought that he was the only survivor from the sub. You distinctly said survivor_s_. Plural. Were there others?"

"Actually, there were only two."

Otto, who had been sitting silently to the side during the Senator's story, spoke up. "I was the other survivor, Capt'n Pete. I was one of the lookouts up in the Wintergarten when the conning tower broke off. I was only 18 at the time and a much better swimmer than your father, but even I had a very hard time getting ashore. I was surprised he made it. Surprised but not disappointed, because he was a fair man and a great captain. It had been a pleasure to be on his crew."

"Ernst-Jurgen, your father, and Otto were both helped by my father, financially and otherwise, to start a new life in Eleuthera. He helped them both equally, but kept them separated. Otto was placed on a pineapple plantation, which, after many years, he eventually owned, and your father went to work fishing, eventually building his house with the help of his friend, Moses, the man who had rescued him and his new friend, Otto. He didn't recognize Otto because at the time Otto was just an ordinary seaman newly assigned to the boat and had not had much contact with the captain. Of course, their time in prison had also changed their appearances. He accepted my father's explanation that Otto was a German immigrant from before the war. Otto also reported back to my father from time to time on the progress in the search for the sub." The Senator accepted the drink offered by Horst, who had also made one for himself. "So you see, Capt'n Pete, your father and my father were the greatest of friends going back to the Diplomatic service before the war when they were both serving, partying together in Berlin, and continuing when they met in Dingle Bay for the transfer of the gold, and then after the war when he settled here in Eleuthera to attempt to find the sub."

"But I don't understand why you were so surprised and angry when I told you about my father and the gold on the sub." Capt'n Pete said.

"It wasn't the gold or the sub, but the fact that I hadn't realized that you were his son. You look remarkably like him, and I was mad at myself for not noticing. My biggest mistake, of course, was firing you. Sometimes my temper gets the best of me and I do things that I regret, if not immediately, then later when I have calmed down. I did try to find you to apologize but you had already disappeared. When I heard you were in the Keys, I searched for you and when we located you in Islamorada, I sent Horst to bring you to the boat. Unfortunately, I had not stressed to him that it was a request, not an order, so things got physical. He has a tendency to resort to violence when he can't have his own way."

Jack spoke up, "Shannon's kidnapping, your idea, or his? And throwing Shannon overboard on the way back to Ft. Lauderdale, your idea, or his?"

The Senator looked very much embarrassed. "On the first count of this indictment, his idea. He felt we should be dealing from a position of strength, his long suit, but I admit, I did go along with him. On the second count, during our phone conversation, my temper just got the better of me. It just seemed to me such a simple request, to come and have dinner with me on my boat. But I am all talk and no action. I never would have hurt her, believe me." The look of sincerity on the Senator's face seemed genuine.

"OK. This had been an interesting and enlightening story, but just what is it you want from us?" Jack wanted this to be over and made no effort to hide his frustration.

"I wish to propose a truce, an end to hostilities. I wish to sit down with you, negotiate and work out a plan which is mutually beneficial to all of us." The Senator sat back, joined his hands and placed them in his lap, and smiled agreeably.

Once again, stunned silence filled the salon. Even Horst and Otto had not been expecting this statement, for the look on their faces was as bewildered as the one on Jack's.

Jack glanced quickly at both Capt'n Pete and Shannon before asking, "What exactly do you mean by that pronouncement?"

The Senator smiled benevolently, "Since we first met, Jack, we have been adversaries and I simply want that to stop. Now that you know of my father's involvement in this affair, you can see how I would want to keep it quiet in order to preserve his good name. Over the intervening years the evidence of his...." he hesitated momentarily, "crime has been found and systematically destroyed. All records of his travels to Ireland and here to the Bahamas have been destroyed, all except the evidence locked into the sub's safe, put there by that SS pig OberGruppenFuehrer Hans Kessler. All the photographs, negatives, the ship's log and other incriminating evidence is still there. I can even give you the combination to the safe, which your father entrusted to my father, who passed it to me."

Jack was incredulous, "So you want us to destroy evidence for you?"

"No, simply hand it over to a representative of the government, which I still am, and not follow its trail too closely." The Senator leaned forward toward the group, and a pleading look emerged upon his face, "Look, Jack, my father has been dead for a number of years now, so there is nothing anyone can do to him except destroy his good name, which is what I am trying to prevent. I don't have the slightest interest in the gold. God knows, I have more money than I could possibly spend for the rest of my life. I just want to preserve my father's good name and reputation. Despite his one lapse in good judgment, he did a lot of important, and brave, work for our country during the war, and then afterward, he dedicated his life to public service, becoming a Senator, a philanthropist, and chairman of many charities and other organizations which helped those in need."

"So you are saying that we can keep all the gold, as long as we turn over to you all the evidence which is in the sub's safe." Jack stated somewhat incredulously, fully aware that he was speaking for the whole group now.

"Most certainly not," the Senator raised his voice only slightly but very emphatically, "the gold will be turned over to the U.S. Treasury Department. I have already contacted them and two Treasury Agents will be here in the morning."

"But you don't know where the sub is."

"Jack, I am sure that you will acknowledge that the U.S. Navy has the best divers in the world. If you found it, they can, too. But then my secret will be out and my father will be vilified. Which is why I want your group to salvage the gold, and the documents, from the sub. I have already gotten an agreement from the Treasury Department for a finder's fee of twenty percent of all gold recovered to be paid to you. Plus a charter fee of $5000 per day for the use of your boat and personnel, from the day Capt'n Pete set foot on your boat to the end of the salvage operations, plus all of your expenses. That's over forty million dollars, Jack. Don't you think that's fair compensation for your troubles?" The Senator leaned back on the couch, crossing his arms over his chest.

"Honestly, I am a little overwhelmed to think of anything right now, and you know I will have to talk it over with all the members of our group."

"I understand. If I may, I suggest that we have a pleasant dinner together, not mention this subject again, you can stay on this boat tonight, and we will meet with the Treasury Agents in the morning."

"And if we would prefer not to stay on this boat?"

"Then, after dinner, since it is too late, too dark and impossible to find that small opening in the reef at night, we would put you ashore at Valentine's. I'm sure they would have rooms at this time of the year."

"All of us, Shannon, too?"

"Of course, Jack, I hardly see the need to keep a hostage now that you know the full story."

Upon hearing this guarantee, Jack was quick to make up his mind, "In that case, we would love to accept your kind invitation to dinner."

"Very well. Horst, would you let the chef know that we are ready when he is?"

"Of course, Senator."

As soon as Horst had left the salon, Jack asked, "I can understand Otto's involvement in all of this, but why was Horst allowed to stay when all the other crew were dismissed?"

"Ah, yes, Herr Keller. An interesting man. And not what he seems to be."

"So is he involved?"

"Indeed he is. He is the grandson of Herr Kessler, the SS presence on the sub, the man who took the incriminating photos of my father so long ago. He was recruited by my father when he came to the States, having changed his surname before he came. We had a little trouble locating him, but once we did and explained the situation to him, he became quite a valuable asset. He is the one primarily responsible for the location and destruction of the evidence against my father."

Horst returned and said, "Fifteen minutes, enough time for a drink."

Dinner, as it turned out, was superb. An appetizer of scallop bruschetta (seared scallops on top of red and yellow bell peppers, pine nuts, and wild mushrooms in olive oil on slices of Italian bread) was followed by Zuppa Di Tuscany, and an entree of grilled salmon with mango peach salsa and Mediterranean vegetables, followed by a dessert of chocolate chip waffle delight. Jack, Shannon and Capt'n Pete were stuffed when they were finished and especially appreciative of the fact that they didn't have to cook or clean up afterward. The Senator, Otto and Horst, being used to this kind of extravagant meal, were surprised at the gusto with which their guests attacked their food. Later, over coffee and brandy, the atmosphere actually became relaxed and somewhat friendly.

"Are you sure that I can't convince you to stay on the boat?" The Senator asked.

"I think we would prefer to stay ashore tonight," Jack spoke for the group.

"O.K., then. Horst will run you ashore. The Agents should be here around eleven tomorrow morning, you know how island time works, so if you want to ride over with them, hopefully we can come to an agreement and get some papers signed, sealed and delivered. I'll see you then." With that, the Senator turned on his heel and returned to the bar.

They made their way to the aft swim platform where one of the Donzis was tied up.

"After you," Horst said almost gentlemanly to Shannon and allowed the two men to follow her. It was a short, quiet trip over to the dock and shortly thereafter, they had two more rooms booked and were on their way to see Moses and Birdman.

As soon as they were all together, Jack called Janine, who was beginning to get somewhat worried all alone on the boat. After ascertaining that all was well on board, Jack filled her in on what had transpired on the Senator's boat and promised to call in the morning.

Since it was a little before eleven, Jack also called Sean in Nassau and filled him in. Together they arranged for Sean to be tied up to the dock in Briland by ten the next morning, and they would have a brainstorming session before going back with the Treasury Agents to the Senator's boat.

Chapter 17

"So, how far do we trust this guy, if at all?"

The question, voiced by Shannon at breakfast the next morning, hung in the air above the table like a dark, malevolent cloud. They were all sitting on the verandah of their suite at Valentine's, gazing out over the marina at the Senator's yacht anchored off shore in the deep harbor.

"I honestly don't know," said Jack. "I would like to believe him, because I think that this would work out best for everyone, but I still have a lot of reservations. I guess we'll have to wait and see what the Treasury Agents have to say for themselves."

"Personally, I'd like to shoot the bastard." Capt'n Pete was not mincing his words. "He, or at least, his father, is the cause of my father's death."

"Technically, that's not true. His father helped your father after the war in his search for the submarine. Albeit for his own personal reasons, he did help your father survive." Jack surprised himself for defending the Senator. He saw the wounded look on Capt'n Pete's face, and added, "of course, he did deprive you of your father's love and support for so many years. Support you needed during your formative years. But you still wound up a thoroughly good person."

"Oh, for God's sake, cut it out. Do you want me to start bawling or something? And why are you, all of a sudden, on the Senator's side?" The questions fired out staccato style, accusingly, totally unlike the man they had come to know, showed everyone the torment Capt'n Pete had to be going through.

An awkward silence followed that outburst, with all of them looking askance and embarrassed, sipping their coffee, and wondering what to do, what to say.

Jack rose and walked over, put his hands on Capt'n Pete's shoulders and shook him lightly, "Nobody, least of all me, is taking the Senator's side. But, he *has* presented us with a way to resolve all the questions I've had about what is to become of all of this. From what Moses said, your father had a good life here in the islands, with friends, co-workers and a healthy lifestyle, and enough money from the Senator's father to be able to build his own house and live comfortably. Despite him never having found the sub, I think he had a good life. You should be grateful for that, at least."

"Yeah, I know you're right, Jack. I just miss all those years we could have had together, and all because of this Godforsaken gold."

They were unpleasantly interrupted by the roar of large, turbo-charged engines entering the marina. Without even turning, Jack said, jokingly, "It must be ten o'clock, I'd know that sound anywhere." And, sure enough, Sean's big Cary, 'Leprechaun' was just tying up to the dock.

Shortly thereafter, Sean and Katie entered Moses' and Birdman's suite, where they had all congregated, and bear hugs and kisses were exchanged.

"Good to see you again so soon, old son," Sean said as he came in. "Tell me all about it."

"We were just about to start talking and planning, but we thought we would wait for your input, too. And to see if you had any news."

"One thing you don't know about. I've called some of my friends in the Powerboat Club and invited them on a poker run here to Valentine's and they are all coming. I told them to bring scuba gear for everyone, that there would be a treasure hunt. They should be here tomorrow afternoon. Four boats, two crew apiece and I've already made docking arrangements. The management was quite appreciative. That should give us a reserve of manpower for anything that might happen."

"Seriously? You got them here on false pretenses?"

"No, they have an idea of what is happening, but I didn't tell them everything, of course."

Jack was unsure of the need of the Powerboat Club members, but allowed Sean to have his way. "All right, we have some reserves. But first, I think that Capt'n Pete and I need to go to the Senator's boat to meet with the Treasury Agents to find out what is happening in the official and legal world. Wouldn't you agree? I mean, if we could settle all of this legally and above board, isn't that the most desirable outcome? Everybody wins, right?"

"Sure, *if* everybody wins."

With all the islanders operating on 'island time', it was almost noon before the airline passengers, including the two agents, arrived at the docks. Horst, in the Donzi, was there to greet them, and just then, the throwaway phone in Jack's pocket started warbling. He had forgotten that he still had it, but when it started ringing, he answered it.

"Jack, are you ready to come and negotiate? Horst will wait for you."

"We will be right down, but just me and Capt'n Pete."

"That's fine, as long as you speak for the entire group."

Twenty minutes later, Jack and Capt'n Pete boarded the Donzi and sat down on the opposite side of the boat from the two agents. No-one spoke as Horst slipped the lines and proceeded in a subdued fashion out to the 'Shillelagh'. The Senator was waiting on the aft deck and, as they emerged from the gangway, greeted and shook the hand of all four guests.

"Jack, these two men are the agents I told you about last night. Special Agents Jacob Smiley and Peter Sanchez. Gentlemen, Jack Elliott and Capt'n Pete Olsen-Smith. Shall we go inside?"

Smiley was pale, short and of slight build and carried a black, locked briefcase, while Sanchez was well over six feet, darkly tanned and heavily muscled and was obviously the more physical of the two. Neither smiled or offered a handshake before turning and proceeding into the main salon after the Senator, leaving Jack and Capt'n Pete to follow in their wake. A luncheon spread and drinks awaited them with the Senator handling the drink mixing duties himself. Horst and Otto joined the group and, as soon as everyone was settled, the Senator said, "Now let's get down to business. Mr. Smiley, I believe you have some papers for Mr. Elliott in that briefcase of yours."

Jack held up his hand, "Before we proceed, I would like to see some credentials."

Both men's hands went to their inside coat pockets and both produced Department of the Treasury identification packs, complete with gold badges. Jack read them carefully, handed them to Capt'n Pete, then both nodded their acceptance of the documents.

Smiley spoke for the first time, a high pi
reedy voice which matched his appearance. "Yes, wel
as long as you all realize that this wasn't my idea
proceeded to unlock the briefcase and pulled a thi
folder out, opened it and started reading.

"This agreement, signed by the Secretary (
Treasury, stipulates that you will receive, tax free, t
percent of the current value of all the U.S. gold b
recovered from the wreck which you are cur
salvaging. It also states that you will receive, as a c
fee, $5,000 per diem, commencing on March 22nd (
year and continuing until all the gold bullion has
recovered and the operation has been terminated. Tl
will, of course, be taxable. There are a few stipulatioi
if you will read it, and if you agree to all the terms,
sign one copy and keep the other for your records." S
dropped the two copies of the agreement on the
table, rose and walked to the galley to pour himself a
coffee, black with two sugars. He did not offer anytl
anyone else.

Jack leaned over and retrieved the document
the table and handed one to Capt'n Pete. They both re
agreement in silence, noting that the watermark in the
and the letterhead upon it were both from the
Department of the Treasury. The few stipulations in
in the document simply dealt with the timing, one
hence, and place, Ft. Lauderdale's Port Everglades,
exchange of the gold for the agreed upon fund
presented no problems, as far as Jack could see. He g
at Capt'n Pete to see if there were any objections fro
quarter, and received in return a shrug and a slight sl_____ __
the head.

"Capt'n Pete, do you see any problems with this agreement?"

"No, I don't. It seems straight forward to me."

"Then, I don't have any objections to signing it. Pen, please." Jack asked of the Senator, pleased to see a smile form on the old man's face.

Suspicions already aroused by the lack of formality and the speed by which the documents had been prepared, authorized and signed by the Secretary of the Treasury, Jack nevertheless signed the document with a flourish, and handed it to the Senator, who said, "I can lend you as much manpower as you like, Jack, let's get this gold to the surface."

"OK. Let me tell you exactly how this is going to go down. My crew, my people are going to do all the salvage work. Your people are going to keep out of our way and stay away from our boat. We are going to load all the gold on our boat and sail it to Ft. Lauderdale, where the exchange is going to take place. If you don't agree to this, no work is going to start."

The Senator's jaw dropped, and a glimmer of anger showed momentarily in his eyes, and then a smile formed on his face, "Of course, Jack, we will do it any way you say."

"Then if there is nothing else, perhaps Horst will run us back to Valentine's and we will take a water taxi back to our boat."

"Horst will be happy to pick up Shannon and take you all back to your boat, if you like." The Senator still seemed a little hesitant to allow everyone out of his sight.

"Actually," Jack said with a smile, "I would just as soon that Horst stay as far away as possible from our boat, and that goes for you and the rest of your crew, too. I still have your phone and I will contact you when *we* are ready to proceed."

"In that case, you will need this," The Senator said, handing Jack a slip of paper.

Jack looked at it and noted that it was the combination to a safe, presumably the ship's safe on the sub. He and Capt'n Pete stood up and proceeded to the Donzi which had brought them over, and after a reluctant wave of the Senator's hand, Horst followed them to the runabout and ferried them to shore.

"Remember, Horst. I don't want to see you or any of your crew anywhere near our boat. Understand?" When Jack stood up straight, he was an inch or so taller than Horst and that gave him a psychological advantage, at least.

As soon as the Donzi had left the dock after ferrying them ashore, Jack and Capt'n Pete turned and proceeded up to the hotel and into the room where the others were waiting.

"So, tell us what happened," Sean seemed to be really getting into the intrigue.

Jack handed him the copy of the agreement that he had signed, and Sean passed it around to everyone else. The reactions ranged from suspicion to disbelief, and they all started speaking at once.

"I don't believe him…"

"So much money…"

"What happens now??"

"Can we really do this??"

Jack held up his hands to silence them. "Someone once said, 'Trust but verify'. I believe that's what we must do now. Verify."

"How?"

"Leave that to me, I know just the person with the right government connections." Jack smiled, wondering if his mother really did have the access he needed.

Picking up his own cell phone, "Hello, Mum." he said as the line was answered. "This is Jack."

"Jack, it's wonderful to finally hear from you. I thought you had disappeared off the face of the earth. Where are you, and how are you?"

"We are in Harbor Island in the Bahamas."

"Bahamas? I thought you were going to Europe."

"We were, but we got sidetracked. Long story and we'll get into that later. Right now, I need some information from you. Do you know the Treasury Secretary, C. Bryant Palmer?"

"Charlie? Of course I know him, and you do, too. He is one of our oldest friends. Don't you remember, he used to live right next door to us, before he moved to Washington."

Jack let out the breath he didn't know he had been holding, "Could you contact him on my behalf and ask him to call me on my cell phone, at his convenience, of course?"

"Sure, Jack, I can do that, but let me give you his private home number and cell number just in case. Give me about an hour, and if he hasn't called you, call him tonight. Got a pencil?" A slight hesitation, then she said, "Why do you need to talk to him?"

"Like I said, it's a long story and I'll explain everything later. Enough to say, I need to speak to him

225

urgently. Please, Mum, make this a priority." Hanging up on your mother was just not done, so Jack tried diplomatically to get her moving on his request.

"You are not in any trouble, are you? I mean, if you need money….."

"No, Mum. I am not in any trouble, but it does involve money, a great deal of money, and I hope he has the right answers to the questions I have for him."

"Oh, all right. I can see I'm not going to get anything out of you right now, so I'll go. Here are his numbers." She read them out and then hung up. Jack copied them into his cell phone, then laid the instrument in the center of the coffee table. "And now we wait."

Mothers the world over will move heaven and earth to aid their offspring, and Jack's mother proved that she was not an exception to the rule. Less than an hour later, Jack's phone started its warbling and vibrating, and he answered it on the second ring and put it on speaker phone so everyone could hear and maybe contribute if Jack forgot any details.

"Hello, Jack? Charlie Palmer here. Your mother told me you needed to speak with me rather urgently. What can I do for you?"

"Secretary Palmer, you are on speaker phone with me and my team. I have a very delicate situation on my hands and I am hoping you can give me some clarification as to what to do."

"Firstly, Jack, let's set this scene properly. To you, I am Charlie, not Secretary Palmer. I've known you and your parents all my life, hell, I even bounced you on my knee back in Chicago when you were only a year old. I was Charlie then and I am still Charlie to you now. O.K?"

"O.K. Sorry." Jack paused awkwardly, unsure of where to start. "Anyway, the reason I wanted to talk to you was that we, my team and I, have found an old, wrecked German U-boat over here in the Bahamas, and we have reason to believe that it has aboard her about two hundred million dollars worth of U.S. Treasury gold bars from the end of World War II."

"WHAT?"

"Why does everyone have that reaction?" Jack mused, smiling.

"You had better tell me everything, from the beginning to right here, right now. And don't leave anything out." Charlie sounded not only interested, but intrigued.

Jack recounted the whole story starting with their fishing Capt'n Pete out of the harbor at Holiday Isle and finishing with the Senator's truce.

"Truth is, Charlie, I don't know if I believe that Senator O'Malley is being honest with us or if he is just getting us to do his work for him, and will just take the gold after we have recovered it."

"Believe me, Jack, Senator O'Malley is a swindler without an honest bone in his body. I've been trying to pin something on him for years. Unfortunately, nothing has stuck yet, despite all my efforts. He is just too good at covering his tracks. Maybe this will turn out to be the situation which will finally bring him down. He has been getting away with his excesses for far too long." At this point, Charlie seemed to be practically salivating over the phone, and anticipating a scenario where he could finally take the Senator down.

"Then can I take it that this document which I hold in my hand describing all the benefits to which we are entitled because of our discovery, all the millions in finder's fees and charter fees and which bears your signature isn't worth the paper it's written on."

"Unfortunately, Jack, I've never seen the document before and therefore I could not have signed it. In fact, until now, I was unaware that there was any gold missing from the Treasury during the war and I have not heard of any rumors of a sunken submarine carrying U.S Treasury gold, neither in the Bahamas or anywhere else for that matter."

"How about the two Treasury Agents, Jacob Smiley and Peter Sanchez? Their credentials seem to be genuine and the agreement is on Treasury watermarked letterhead."

"I will definitely find out about them. If they are genuine Treasury agents and have been seconded by the Senator, I guarantee they won't be agents for long. What I am going to suggest to you is to go back to your boat and secure the site. I will make inquiries and come up with a plan to catch O'Malley in the act and I will call you tomorrow to discuss it. And don't worry, I will make sure you and your crew are adequately compensated for all your efforts, you can trust me on that. I won't blow a lifetime of friendship with your parents and with you just to save the government a few bucks, believe me. I'll call you tomorrow."

With that assurance, he hung up, leaving everyone sitting around staring at one another in stunned silence. Jack reached over and retrieved his phone and placed it in his pocket.

"Sean, I need you to run me, Capt'n Pete and Shannon back to 'Final Option'. Birdman and Moses, you stay here tonight and keep watching the Senator's boat. We need to know where Horst and his crew are as much as possible. Sean will be back in the morning to meet his friends from the boating club. Then we will all rendezvous at my boat tomorrow afternoon to start the salvage operation. Are we all in agreement?"

Sean, ever the smart ass, said. "That goes without saying. For tomorrow is another day."

Nods of assent assured him that all were on board. Moses and Birdman settled down in their comfortable chairs, while everyone else stood, gathered their things and trooped out of the suite.

Chapter 18

Sean and Katie left early the next morning for Valentine's Marina, and Jack, Capt'n Pete, Shannon and Janine had a leisurely breakfast on the flybridge, keeping a watch out at the opening in the reef. Jack was worried that the Senator would have changed his mind once again and sent Horst to collect them or at least keep an eye on them. To his immense relief, they saw no-one lurking around.

Janine collected the plates as the last of the coffee was consumed, transporting them to the dishwasher in the galley. Jack, Shannon and Capt'n Pete divided up the work of getting the diving equipment ready for the salvage operation, checking and double checking that all was in working order. As they worked, Jack said, "What do you think about the people Sean has coming? How much do we tell them and how will we use them?"

"I would tell them that we have found something on the ocean floor, and we are bringing it up for further examination. No need to go into details. And I don't think we need any help, with you and Shannon, Sean and Katie, and Courtland and Janine diving and me topsides; about all the help we might need from Sean's friends would be security against you know who." Capt'n Pete was not under any illusions that their agreement with the Senator was written in stone, despite being back on the boat and, apparently, not under surveillance.

Shannon piped up, "Come on, Jack, Sean told me who was coming and they are all people we have known for years. You know we can trust them. Except Carl Leitner

230

and Max Fairfield, they are sketchy at the best of times, but we can keep them up top and not have to worry about them. And I for one am not adverse to having a couple of their strong backs helping with the weight of all that gold. It's heavy, you know."

Jack smiled, knowing Shannon's metabolism worked overtime and she had never had to do any working out to maintain her exquisite figure. "Yes, but here's the problem. If we have them dive with us, they will not only know where the entrance of the cave is, but also the existence of the galleon and the golden throne. That's something no-one knows except for the people on this boat, not the Senator, not even Sean, and I want to keep it that way. We will have to bring Sean and Katie in on the secret but that's all."

"But why not tell everyone who is helping?"

"Because we are only salvaging the gold from the sub at this time and we will have to come back later and get the rest. If someone else knows about the galleon, there is nothing to prevent them from claiming their own salvage rights."

"Don't forget about the documents the Senator wants you to retrieve for him." Capt'n Pete reminded him, a sour look on his face, "I sure as hell don't want that S.O.B. to get his grubby little hands on our discovery and claim it for himself, do you?"

"No, of course not, but now that they have made the trip over here, at their own expense, I might add, what do we tell them when they start asking questions?" Shannon was frustrated.

"I don't know. I'll talk with Sean and we will come up with something. Maybe they can just help out topside and keep a good security screen around the boat. We'll see."

Their conversation was interrupted by the insistent ringing of Jack's cell phone.

"Jack, this is Charlie. I got back to you as soon as I had things set up. Got a pen? You need to take these coordinates down."

Jack grabbed his Parker pen and notebook, and remained silent as he took down the instructions from Charlie. It took quite a while, but when he finally finished, he exchanged pleasantries with Charlie and promised to stick to the script as much as possible. He deliberately kept the plans to himself until all the people involved were present.

"Let's finish up here and wait for everyone to arrive. We might still have enough time this afternoon to dive down and set up the generator and pump and start getting the water pumped out of the sub."

A short time later, sitting comfortably on the flybridge, they observed an armada of small boats coming through the gap in the reef, led by 'Leprechaun." The operators of the boats quietly and expertly formed a raft of boats, honed by the skills learned at the annual Columbus Day regattas they all attended, tying together two boats on each side of 'Final Option' with 'Leprechaun' tied crosswise across the stern of Jack's boat, which was the largest. There was a 46 foot Skater catamaran, a Cigarette 38 foot Top Gun, a 44 foot Riva and a 50 foot Baia classic, in addition to Sean's 50 foot Cary. Jack was pleased to discover that, when Sean had mentioned two men per boat, he actually meant a man and a lady, except it the case of the Baia, which belonged jointly to Carl and Max. As usual, they preferred to come on these outings without women, so they could have the choice of the local beach bunnies to keep them entertained.

After all the boats were settled, the crews descended on 'Final Option' and Jack was pummeled and bear hugged by all the men and kissed by all the ladies. It was like old homecoming week, with snacks, beers and drinks being exchanged along with introductions, inquiries and well wishes. Janine, Shannon and especially Capt'n Pete did not know everyone, but that soon changed in the spirit of celebration and conspicuous consumption.

Jack's cell phone once again interrupted the conversation, and after an incoming one way communication, followed by an OK, hung up and said, "That was Courtland in Miami. He's about to board a plane for Nassau. He'll be there in about an hour." He turned a full circle, made his choice and addressed the owner of the Riva. "Jesse, first part of your official duties starts now. Could you go to Nassau to pick him up and bring him back here? You know the way through the reef, don't you?"

"Sure, Jack. I have it on the GPS. How will I recognize him?" Jesse replied.

"Take Janine with you, I think she still remembers what he looks like."

Janine threw Jack a pout, and grabbing Jesse by the arm, said, "Ignore him, Jesse, the big man just likes to give orders. I'll ride with you and Diane any day. Besides, the sooner I see my man, the better." Jesse and his wife, Diane, were old friends of Janine's from the regatta days. With oohs and aahs ringing in their ears, they were soon aboard the Riva and underway.

"All right, since we have already started, let's party today. Then after dinner tonight, and with everyone present, I'll explain our plan of action. That OK with everyone?" Jack waited for the whoops and yells of agreement, and was not disappointed.

It was late afternoon when the Riva returned bearing Courtland and his better half, Janine, as well as Jesse and Diane. They were talking animatedly to each other and seemed to have bonded during the short time they had spent together. Jack noted with interest that all the people in the flotilla, with a couple of exceptions, had the same reasonably lean, whipcord physique that seems to be prevalent amongst sailors. It was a testimonial to the benefits of being on a constantly moving boat, where you got your exercise using all the muscle groups whether you wanted it or not.

Dinner was a Chinese fire drill, and Capt'n Pete, despite being helped by no less than six women, was hard pressed to keep up with the constant demand for more food. People would load up their plate, retire to their own boat, and when they were finished, come back for more. Fifteen mouthes to feed was a lot more that he was used to handling. He finally sat down with *his* plate, telling everyone that if they wanted more they could cook it themselves.

Finally finished with feeding their faces, everyone convened on the flybridge, the only place on the boat that could accommodate that many people at one time. They sat on any horizontal surface they could find, leaned on the vertical surfaces, or merely stood in place looking at Jack expectantly.

"You are probably wondering why I called this meeting tonight," Jack began, to quiet snickers and mild laughter. "We are gathered here, in the sight of God, to find a treasure." Laughter, this time profound, broke out and Jack held up his hands and shrugged his shoulders. A sense of companionship and good will settled on the crowd as Jack turned serious. "I have known each and every one of you for a long time, and trust you all completely, but I must swear you all to secrecy, at least for now, about what I'm going to tell you."

He looked around and held each person's eyes before continuing. From everyone he got an acknowledgment of some kind, a slight nod, a wink or a half-hidden smile. "I know that Sean got you over here with the promise of a treasure hunt, and while that's true, it is not the kind of treasure hunt you are probably thinking about. He also asked you to bring scuba gear, but I don't think you'll be needing it."

Carl immediately jumped up and said, "Well, if you only got us over here to work for you, I think me and Max will go back to Valentine's, find some ladies and enjoy ourselves over there."

Jack smiled, and noticed Shannon nodding enthusiastically, "Okay, not a problem. If you let Sean know how much I owe you, I will arrange to have you paid when we get back."

Sean and several others went down to the main deck to help Carl and Max extract their 50 foot Baia from the raft up, easing the outside boat away as the Baia slipped forward and away from the hull of 'Final Option'. Once they were seen leaving the bay through the break in the reef, Sean and the others returned to the flybridge.

"All gone and good riddance," Sean said as he came up the stairs. "Never should have invited them in the first place, but if I hadn't, they would have been wondering why they had been excluded from a club event."

Jack had paused while the Baia was being sent off, but now continued, "The truth is this. Resting below us on the ocean floor, but hidden from view, there lies a Nazi submarine from WWII and we are going to attempt to salvage it. There is another group also attempting to salvage this sub, and they are not particular about the tactics they employ. They have already beaten and tried to drown Capt'n Pete, kidnapped Shannon, but we were able to get her back and, at various times, they have attempted to use strong-arm methods on us. What you are really here for is to provide us with security and witness accounts if anything should go wrong. You will all be paid handsomely for your time and trouble, but if anyone wants to back out, I'll understand, I'll compensate you for your expenditures so far, and we will still be friends. But you have got to let me know now, before you become too deeply embroiled and are unable to get out of it."

Shocked looks were exchanged between all the newcomers to the group, and the questions were forthcoming from one and all.

"How did you find it?" and "What would be worth salvaging on a rusty WWII wreck?" seemed to be the gist of most of the questions.

Jack held up his hands for silence. "So, is everyone in?"

Nods of agreement followed his question, so he gave the assembled crowd a brief description of the adventure up to the present time, including the fact that the sub carried gold bullion aboard and that was what they would be salvaging. Each of the newcomers would also be asked to help to carry and stow this gold aboard 'Final Option' as it came up from the ocean floor. He also explained to everyone the role of each member of the crew of 'Final Option' and where he or she fit into the puzzle. He deliberately left out any mention of the galleon, because they would need to come back to deal with that end of things later. Seeing everyone's excitement mounting, he started handing out assignments, finally finishing with, "We start first thing in the morning, so get a good night's sleep."

Very early the next morning, before dawn in fact, Jack and Courtland were up and preparing to take the generator and crash pump down to the submarine. As soon as the sun had risen high enough to light the way to the cave entrance, they set out, towing the waterproof carriers behind them.

It took only a short time to set up the machinery and hoses, and soon they started pumping the water out of the sub. Fortunately, Sean had had the foresight to include high efficiency mufflers on the generator, so the noise the motor made was substantially subdued. The huge cathedral-like cavern was big enough to disperse the carbon monoxide fumes from the generator, so they didn't need to take any extra precautions in that regard. They did, however, take the precaution to triple-strain the water coming out of the sub in order to prevent the pollution of the water inside the cave, but as it turned out, the water was already surprisingly clean. As the morning passed, they only had to stop the pump and change the filters twice, and they were not overly surprised when early in the afternoon the water stopped flowing from the submarine.

"Seems that we have a dry hole," said Jack as he reached down and switched off the generator. "Guess I had better go and see if there is anything in there worth salvaging."

Courtland followed Jack over to the stairs they had built up to the sub's deck and took a position by the slide as Jack mounted the steps. As he gained the deck, he switched on the flashlight he had brought and peered into the now drained but still damp steel tube leading into the guts of the sub. He noted, with relief, the welded hand and foot holds that still looked substantial even after all this time underwater. Swinging one leg onto the upper foothold, and testing his weight on it, he committed his other leg one rung lower. Moving with great care, he slowly eased his body down the tube until he finally stood on the inside deck facing what used to be the main control room.

Jack made a complete circle of the room with the flashlight, finishing where he had started, the torn up, empty space where the twin periscopes should have been. They were gone, of course. Ripped out of the deck when the conning tower had separated from the hull of the sub. The other dials, gauges and the wheels that controlled the dive planes were all intact, and although everything was strewn about in a haphazard fashion, all the navigation instruments, the valves for controlling the ballast tanks and the other controls seemed almost in a ready to go condition.

Spotting several skeletons jumbled together in one corner of the room, Jack made a mental note not to let the women into the sub. They didn't need any more stress than they already had.

"I am in the control room, with several deceased members of the sub's crew." Jack shouted up to Courtland. "I am going to go forward to see if I can find the Captain's cabin and the safe."

"OK, Jack. Just be careful in there, because there are bound to be displaced objects and sharp corners. Try not to get hurt, I don't know if I can fit through the tube to come and get you." Courtland replied.

Jack stepped forward, aiming the flashlight up and down to illuminate the path of least resistance and, almost immediately, came upon the hatch leading forward. He had to bend almost double and squeeze his way through, for there were indeed some objects blocking part of the opening. Once into the tiny passageway, the first cabin he came to, if such a small space could truly be called a cabin, was indeed the captain's cabin. And there on the wall was the built-in safe, apparently intact.

He partially unzipped the front of his full wet-suit, silently thanking the manufacturer for including the full, thick soled booties that were part of the suit. The thought of stepping down on a piece of sharp, rusty steel was not something he had any particularly desire to do. From inside the suit he withdrew a ziplock baggie which contained the combination to the safe, which he had obtained from the Senator.

Holding the flashlight in his teeth, he reached out and turned the dial on the front of the safe. It moved with only a slight amount of resistance, and by the third number, no resistance at all. After the last number was dialed in he grasped the handle in one hand and pulled down. Nothing happened.

'Must have rusted shut over the years,' he thought to himself. 'Not surprising.'

He reached once again into his wet-suit and came up with a small can of penetrating oil in an aerosol can, which he sprayed liberally onto the lock, the handle and the hinges of the safe. After exhausting the spray, he went in search of a piece of pipe or rod, or a tool he might use to pry open a stubborn safe.

Once again making his way slowly forward down the passageway toward the bow of the sub, the beam of his flashlight suddenly picked up a brilliant glimmer from the deck in front of him amongst the black and dark gray interior of the sub. He bent down to examine the object, and found a crushed, broken wooden box within which was the prize they were searching for. Gold!

He carefully removed the broken wooden slats of the box and eased the gold bar from its hiding place, lifting it up to light. He knew that gold was heavy, but the weight of the bar still surprised him. He had to use both hands to transport the bar back to the control room, so he once again had to chew on the base of the flashlight, a not very appetizing meal. He noticed that some of the objects partially blocking the hatch to the control room were the same type of boxes as the shattered one and, sure enough, another broken one showed the same golden glimmer as the bar he held in his hands.

He entered the control room and lay the gold bar on what had been the chart table. Playing the light obliquely over the surface of the bar, he could see the words, U.S. Department of the Treasury, 400 Troy Ounces, .999 Pure, as well as a serial number. He felt a little light headed knowing that he had held in his hands, and was now laying on the table before him, about $750,000 in pure gold at today's prices. But it could also have been the low level of oxygen inside the hull of the sub. Since he now felt that he had accomplished even more than was originally planned, he decided to leave the sub and get some fresh air.

"Courtland, I'm on my way out." Jack shouted.

"Bout time, I was beginning to get worried."

Jack took one more look around and, once again chewing on the base of the flashlight, climbed the footholds to the outside deck of the sub and descended the stairs, grinning from ear to ear.

"Can I take a guess? That maniacal look on your face means you found something good?" Courtland inquired, as Jack made it back to the sand.

"Actually, yes. GOLD!!!!!" Jack started dancing around in little circles, surprising himself as well as Courtland. "A few minutes ago, I was holding in my hands about three quarters of a million dollars in pure gold, and it felt so good. I've only seen a couple of bars so far, in busted up boxes, but there are many intact boxes in there."

"How about the safe?"

"I've sprayed the whole thing with penetrating oil, but it still refuses to budge. Assuming the combination is the correct one, we will just have to wait until the oil does its job. In the meantime, we have a small problem. There is no way to climb that inside ladder while holding a bar of gold with both hands. We'll have to rig up a heavy box on a stout line and you will have to lift it out of the sub. And I need a length of pipe or a tool to get some leverage on the safe handle."

"It's almost time time to leave, in any case. The tide will be turning soon. Let's call it a day and bring back what we need tomorrow."

"Sounds good. Tomorrow Sean can join us and hopefully we can at least get the gold out of the sub and onto the beach. He and I can alternate between the beach and the inside of the sub, while you life the bars from the sub and send them down the slide. I also want to see how the jury rigging on the winch is going. And...... I want a beer!"

"Sounds like a plan to me."

Chapter 19

Jack, having stayed to secure the generator and the pump, surfaced a few minutes after Courtland, who was tying his Hydrospeeder to the aft swim platform. The Bahamian sun shone down from the sky at the oblique angle of late afternoon, and glinted harshly off the water.

Jack climbed the swim ladder onto the platform, having been lent a hand by Courtland who practically yanked him up bodily, tied off his Hydrospeeder and together they removed their scuba gear and wet suits and hung them up to dry. Several faces peered down at them from the aft deck, clearly expecting answers to their unasked questions.

They looked out over the bay at the setting sun, which was warming their cold bodies quite nicely, before joining the others on the aft deck, where Shannon handed them both an ice cold beer. They sat at the dining table surrounded by a gathering crowd.

"Well?" said Capt'n Pete.

"The generator and the pump worked well and they had cleared all the water out of the sub by mid afternoon. I went down into the sub but didn't have much time to really explore before we had to return." Courtland was giving him a strange look of disbelief, and Jack hoped that he had the sense to play along with the brief description of events that Jack had supplied. "I did find skeletons in there, though, which is why I don't want any of the women inside the sub. Sean and I will be doing the work in there because

Courtland is just too damn big to fit down the hatch. We will obviously find out more tomorrow."

Sean, sensing that Jack was holding back, said to Capt'n Pete and Shannon, "Why don't you start dinner, while I show Jack what we have accomplished in his absence. Then we can all get a good night's sleep, 'cause I think tomorrow is going to be a ball-buster."

Sean led Jack up the stairs to the flybridge, turned and indicated the aft boat deck where the Novurania RIB normally sat. The space was empty, for the RIB was now tied to the side of the big boat away from the raft up. Instead of the normal wire used to winch the RIB from the water to the deck, Jack observed a large reel of polypropylene line which had been mounted onto the ship's davit. "Wow, there must be a couple of miles of line on that reel," he said.

"Three miles, in fact. It should be more than enough to reach all the way to the end of the cave. We have tested it and it takes very little power to pull it out and 've pulled the Cary back here from over a mile away with no strain at all." Sean was quite proud of his work, and could tell that Jack was impressed. "As we got the Cary closer, we were able to swing the davit around so that the line came straight to the aft swim platform. That should make for easier unloading once we start bringing up the gold." He looked Jack straight in the eyes and raised one eyebrow, "You *did* find the gold, didn't you?"

Jack smiled, grinned actually, and said, "Yes, I did." The two of them threw a high-five, grinning at each other.

"So what's the plan for tomorrow?" Sean asked.

"Like I said, you and I are going to be in the sub, retrieving the gold from the various places it was stored and bringing it to the control room, loading it into the box for the trip up to where Courtland will be stationed on top of the sub hauling it up and sliding it down to the beach. We will need to rig up a strong box and a stout line for the hauling. From the bottom of the slide, Shannon, Katie and Janine will carry the gold to the carriers and load them. From the size, shape and weight of the ingots, I figure we should be able to take eight to ten ingots per trip to the surface. Once they finish loading, one of the girls can ride the carrier to the boat, where it will be unloaded and stowed properly by the people on board. Once unloaded, she can ride the empty carrier back to the cave, being pulled by the line rigged to the generator, and also bringing back the surface line, so they just need to switch both lines to the next carrier, which should be already be loaded by the time she gets back. It might be a good idea for them to take turns going up, since it will still leave two of them loading the next carrier, and it will insure that they don't get nitrogen narcosis. Capt'n Pete will be on board the boat organizing the men as to where to stow the gold to maintain the equilibrium of the boat, low down and as close to center as possible. Have I missed anything?"

"The safe."

"Oh, yes. I'll need a piece of pipe for leverage and another can of penetrating oil, and assuming I have the right combination, it should come open. If not, who knows. It would probably be a good idea to bring a hammer and a crowbar, too, in case the wood boxes holding the gold bars prove reluctant to give up their contents, despite being underwater for so long. How about the Speeders?"

"You've got two, I've got two, Dave on his Donzi has one and I think Jesse has one on his Riva, so we should have one for everybody. And with that, let's go eat. We can fill the others in on our plans when everyone else goes back to their boats for the night."

"Sounds good."

"Another perfect day in paradise." This sentiment was voiced by Katie over breakfast with everyone nodding agreement. The whole crew seemed content and ready to work, and work hard. The night before they had all listened, with rising excitement, to the plans laid out by Jack and Sean. Sean still sensed that Jack was holding something back, but was content to let his friend reveal it in his own good time.

Slowly and carefully, all the members of the diving team donned their gear, wearing full wet suits and looking for all the world like a Navy SEAL team readying for an underwater assault. They followed Jack, who was towing a waterproof satchel containing the tools they would need, and Sean was carefully pulling out the line from the surface that they would need in order to tow the carriers back to the boat. After a short stop at the entrance to the tunnel to allow all the Speeders to enter the GPS coordinates into their respective machines, Jack led them through the tunnel into the cavern.

The silence within the cave was broken by Sean, who had been scanning the cave and suddenly spotted the golden throne. "I don't believe this. Now that is what I call a toilet," he announced jokingly, "although it could use the addition of a book holder."

"Be careful what you say around Janine's great grandfather. Or you may be in a world of hurt."

"My apologies, my lady. It caught me by surprise, that's all."

Sean was joined by Katie, who, whether through fear, surprise or intestinal fortitude, had not uttered a sound at the sight of the skeleton. Together they walked over to examine the splendid artifact more closely as the rest of the team unpacked and set up all the equipment. Jack retrieved his underwater digital camera and started recording the various scenes, both 12 mega-pixel still pictures and 1080i HD video, as the others worked, hoping to create a visual record of the position and condition of all the remaining articles from both the sub and the galleon before they were moved and brought to the surface. Jack, Courtland and Sean left their wet suits on for the protection they offered from the rusty, sharp objects on and inside the sub, but the three women shrugged out of theirs and wore only swimsuits. The one piece black Lycra racing suit Shannon had worn in the Keys and tiny, string bikinis for Janine and Katie. Jack made sure that they were included in the pictures and video, too.

"Jack, Sean. I think we are ready to start," announced Courtland, who had been manhandling the heavier items and supervising the distribution of all the equipment. "If you two want to start unloading the gold from the sub, I'll haul it up and slide it down to the ladies."

They all took up their assigned positions and without hesitation, the unloading started. Jack led the way into the sub and pointed out the things he had found on his previous visit, and while Sean searched the sub, retrieved the gold bars and brought them to the control room, Jack took the pipe and penetrating oil to the captain's cabin to make a second attempt to open the safe. As soon as Sean had loaded the first box into the sling that Jack had created the night before, Courtland lifted it from the inside of the sub, and slid it down the ramp to the waiting hands of Shannon, who, with the aid of the hammer and crowbar, broke open the wooden boxes to reveal the gold within. They had decided, because of the extra weight of the thick wooden boxes, to extract the gold and leave the wooden boxes behind in the cave. The first few boxes brought oohs and aahs at the glittering sight that had been revealed but the fascination soon wore off and the hard work devolved into a steady routine. Janine and Katie brought the bars to the first carrier, and as soon as they had 10 bars loaded, called out to Courtland who relayed the message to Sean and Jack.

"I'll take the first load up," volunteered Shannon, "someone else can break open boxes for a while. I'm sorry, but I need a break."

Jack, who had come out of the sub with Sean, agreed quickly, adding, "Capt'n Pete will be happy to see you and you can give him an update of our progress."

Jack gave Shannon a quick synopsis of the situation in the sub, including the fact that the safe still resisted his attempts to get it open. He then, with the others paying close attention, went over the extraction procedures and safety measures once again to be sure everyone was clear on their role.

Shannon donned her dive gear, and with everyone helping, got the 275 odd pound carrier into the water, hooked up to the tow line and properly floated, not too buoyant but not sinking, either. When she was ready and properly positioned, she switched the signal devise from stop to pull, and everyone held their breath.

It seemed to take forever, but was in reality only seconds, until the carrier with Shannon holding on behind it, began to move slowly across the water toward the tunnel. She waited until she was well away from the beach, then purged some air from the carrier's buoyancy tank, and like a submarine, it sank below the water's surface. She found it easy to stabilize the carrier's depth, using her knowledge gleaned from hundreds of previous dives, and she found that she could keep it exactly halfway between the roof and the bottom of the tunnel without much difficulty.

With the steady pull from the tow line, it wasn't long before she was clear of the tunnel. She added air to the buoyancy tank and was soon floating serenely alongside the swim platform. The boat's davit easily lifted the carrier onto the swim platform and many hands steadied it as it came to rest. Shannon was given a standing ovation, hugs and slaps on the back as she emerged from the water.

Capt'n Pete gave her a hug and a peck on the cheek, and helped her off with her gear, then stood in anticipation by the carrier.

"If you will do the honors, my dear, we will get this lot below decks," he said, indicating the carrier. "I have been looking forward to this for quite a long time."

Shannon walked to the carrier, bent down and undid the catches. As she straightened up, bringing the lid of the carrier with her, she announced, "Ladies and gentlemen. Behold, seven and a half million dollars worth of gold bullion."

There was a collective gasp, and time stood still as the gold, seeing the sun possibly for the first time, glistened and glittered for all it was worth.

"But, wait a minute, this is U.S. gold, I thought you said this was a Nazi submarine?" Jesse asked, being particularly observant.

"Long story, my friend. I'll tell you over dinner tonight." Capt'n Pete said. "In the meantime, let's get this first lot stowed away where I showed you. OK?"

Shannon, in preparation for her return journey, had a bottle of water, a granola bar and a trip to the head while the gold was being distributed into various places in the boat. However, before she left, she took the time to address all the people aboard. "I just wanted to say that Jack and I and the others on this boat cannot thank you enough for your hard work and for helping us out. You all probably know Jack better than I do, and you know that he is as honest as the day is long. You will all be compensated handsomely for all your efforts and loyalty. Count on it."

Final preparations were made and, with Shannon and the carrier once again a team, the uneventful return passage through the tunnel was accomplished, with the generator in the cave pulling as strongly as the boat's davit. When she surfaced inside the cave, she saw that the next carrier had already been loaded with the gold Jack had salvaged, while Sean had tried his hand at opening the safe, again without success.

Katie was pulling her wet suit on over her bikini. "My turn next. Any advice or difficulties?"

"Not really. You have as much diving experience as I do, so if you just keep it centered in the tunnel, you won't have any problems. After that, it's a snap. Basically just float to the surface, you don't even have to kick your legs. The davit will pull you right to the swim platform. Just enjoy the ride."

The day passed quickly, with only a lunch break when Shannon brought down sandwiches and refreshments on her second round trip of the day. By 5 pm they had made 9 round trips and Shannon was preparing for her fourth ascent while everyone else was packing up and getting their Speeders ready.

"We will need to leave one of the Speeders down here and Shannon will ride the carrier down in the morning. Good job, everyone. I don't know about you, but I for one am going to sleep like a log tonight. I am wiped out." Jack said, and everyone nodded in agreement. "OK. One last time for today, Shannon. We will follow you up."

After another uneventful transit, Shannon surfaced behind the swim platform, followed by the whole crew on their Speeders. The boat gang swung into action removing the gold bars from the carrier as the Speeders were lifted onto the swim platform and tied down for the night.

Capt'n Pete produced beers from the galley and they all sat on the aft deck watching the sun set in the west beyond the island which was, by now, a very familiar sight. Nobody spoke for a long time, each savoring their own thoughts of their accomplishment so far.

"Seventy five million dollars represents our efforts today," Jack reflected, "I think we can all be proud of ourselves."

"Remember, pride goes before a fall." Shannon, acting the pessimist, added.

Dinner was nothing short of a celebration. Everyone talking at once about their upcoming plans, their unexpected ticket to adventure and their new found ability to actually make those plans without having to worry about where the money was coming from. Capt'n Pete produced an amazing Spanish paelle, chicken, shrimp, clams and lobster, choriso sausage, tomato in saffron rice with tons of Greek and Mediterranean salad and everyone ate with gusto.

Over after dinner drinks, Capt'n Pete told his amazing story once again, explaining to the latest arrivals, how American gold bullion had come to be carried upon a Nazi submarine, and the adventures they had had to go through to get to this point. Although he knew about the Spanish galleon, he judiciously left those details out of the story, for which Jack was immensely grateful. The visitors all returned to their respective boats to get a good night's rest for they had all worked hard.

The second and third day of the Gold Lift, as their process had been dubbed, went as smoothly as the first. On the second day, using their combined strength, Jack and Sean had finally been able to force the handle of the safe past all the rust accumulated in the mechanism. The contents of the waterproof, fireproof safe proved to be dry and intact, and with great care, Jack sealed them in a waterproof pouch to be taken to the surface. They did not, on a rather rudimentary inspection, appear to be that important, but Jack knew by the determination the Senator had displayed all along that they must hold impressive information.

The third day, however, held the biggest surprise. After thoroughly scouring every inch of the sub, they were astounded to discover that they had, not the 297 bars of gold that they were expecting as noted in the Ernst-Jurgen's diary, but 312. The extra fifteen gold bars, in similar but not identical wooden boxes, were marked Deutsche

Reichsbank, 10 Kilo (22.05 lbs.) Feingold 999.9, a serial number and an eagle carrying a swastika in oak leaves.

"Looks to me like someone on that U-boat was doing a little smuggling of their own." Jack speculated, doing a rough calculation in his head coming up with a little under six and a half million dollars at today's prices.

"No prizes for guessing who that someone might have been." Shannon was thinking of Horst's SS relative aboard the sub when she voiced her hypothesis. "It had to be Kessler."

"I think that we had better leave this gold here with the golden throne to be picked up and negotiated later. Let's just deal with the Senator and the U.S. Treasury first."

After the last run of the final day, Jack and Sean took the polypropylene line back into the cavern, left all the equipment secured around the golden throne, to be dealt with at a later date. Jack sat down, with congratulatory drinks for everyone, on the aft deck surrounded by all of the people still involved with the end game of the project.

"Just to bring all of you up to speed now that we have all 297 bars of gold aboard. I have arranged to transfer this gold to a U.S. Coast Guard vessel in the Gulf Stream before we get back to Florida. I have made the arrangements with an old friend, C. Bryant Palmer, who is currently the Secretary of the U.S. Department of the Treasury. I am sure that you can understand why I would trust him a little more than I would the Senator. He has already promised us a substantial reward for the return of this gold to the States."

"We are going to leave early tomorrow morning, and will try to maintain 30 knots for the entire crossing. Mine will, of course, be the slowest boat, so the rest of you will just have to form up on me and keep kind of an arrowhead formation in the open waters and line astern when we are in a channel. The Senator's boat can only do 18 knots so he can't catch us, but he does have the Donzis and the helicopter."

"What did Charlie find out about Smiley and Sanchez?" Sean wanted to know. "Are we certain that the Senator's offer was bogus?"

"Turns out that they *are* both Treasury agents. But, they are both under suspicion of wrong doing in another incident involving the Senator which occurred a few years back. Seems they were investigated by Internal Affairs for bribery in a scheme benefiting the Senator, but due to lack of evidence and the Senator's influence with certain other members of Congress, no charges were ever filed. According to Charlie, they are as crooked as the Senator himself. I very much doubt if we can trust them any further than I can throw an elephant." Jack was very happy to get that information out to the people who mattered. "Now I suggest that everyone return to their boats and get a good night's sleep. We leave at sun-up tomorrow."

As they were all trooping out of the salon, a phone started ringing. They all looked at one another, until Jack suddenly realized that it was the throwaway phone left behind by the Senator.

He reluctantly picked it up off the coffee table and forced himself to answer. "Jack here, Senator. What can I do for you?"

"Just calling for a progress report, Jack. It's been almost a week since our agreement and you *did* promise regular reports in return for my crew leaving you alone. How are you coming along on our project?"

"I haven't contacted you yet, because there simply isn't anything to report. We have found the sub but it is laying upside down with the conning tower broken off. We have been trying unsuccessfully to find a way inside, but we may have to get an underwater cutting torch to cut our way through the pressure hull." Jack was improvising, thinking quickly to try to forestall the Senator's suspicions that he might be stalling.

"Well, Jack, I can see where you might have a problem with that. I have a cutting torch on my boat which you can use just as long as you chose to cut in the middle of the boat instead of at the ends. There are still live torpedoes in there, you do realize, don't you?"

"Well, thank you, Senator. I was hoping that I would not have to go to Nassau to get what I needed. I am going down again in the morning to assess the situation, but I'll come by during the afternoon tomorrow to pick up the torch. I'll also bring you digital photos and video to show you why we have taken so long to get back to you. Would that be alright with you?"

"I could send Horst over in the Donzi, if you like."

"As I said before, Senator, I would prefer that Horst and your other crew members stay far, far away from this boat. I have my own method of getting there and back, thanks all the same. I'll see you tomorrow afternoon, all right?"

Before the Senator could answer, Jack quickly hung up, effectively silencing any objections the Senator might have had. The smile on his face told the others how pleased he was that he had managed to come up with a story on the spur of the moment which would basically freeze the Senator in place, awaiting Jack's arrival at a destination where he would never turn up.

And with that, they all retired, full of anticipation for the coming day.

Chapter 20

At 4 am the next morning, way before the sun poked its head above the horizon, all the crews were up and checking over their boats for the run back to Ft. Lauderdale. Jack called for a captain's meeting in the main salon of 'Final Option' and everyone sat down with coffee and toasted muffins.

"I need to get a status report from all the boats. Are there any issues with any of the boats and does everybody have enough fuel to get back to Ft. Lauderdale?"

Only Jesse from the Riva spoke up, all the others nodding their heads and mumbling assent. "I will have to stop in Nassau to refuel. I used a lot of fuel when I went to pick up Courtland."

"OK. You will leave first and make your best speed to Nassau, and we will pick you up when we get there. Everyone else stick together and we will travel as a group."

Jack pulled out a chart of the Bahamas, laid it out on the dining table and indicated each waypoint as he spoke. "We will exit the bay at first light, turn south and round the South East Point of Eleuthera, past Davis Harbor and cross the Exuma Sound from Cape Eleuthera to Ship Channel Cay, across the Middle Ground and enter Nassau Harbor from the east. There we will meet Jesse in the Riva, and proceed on to Chub Cay. We will stay there for the night and then, in the morning, move on to the North West Channel buoy, before crossing the flats to Bimini. We need good light to spot the coral heads on the flats, so I don't want to push on to Bimini until tomorrow. Hopefully the Senator won't realize that we are gone before nightfall, and he may suspect, but he won't know for certain, that we are heading for Ft. Lauderdale. With the numerous directions we could have taken, logically he won't even know where to look. From Bimini, I have the coordinates to meet up with the U.S Coast Guard cutter 'Redoubt' in the middle of the Gulf Stream, where we will transfer the gold and the documents to the cutter. Then we sail for home, sweet home. Any questions?"

"Customs?" someone wanted to know. They were all concerned with their ability to return to Bahamian waters in the future without running afoul of the law.

"We'll clear out at Chub Cay. We have to wait for the sun to get high enough to see the coral heads, anyway. There shouldn't be a problem, I know all the customs people and the harbor master. There may just have to be a little, how do I phrase this, monetary incentive passing hands. Purely a donation to Bahamas Air Sea Rescue Association, you understand. How can they help us wayward sailors if they don't have state-of   -the-art equipment? No big deal." Jack said, with a grin. "Anything else? No? Then, back to your boats, start 'em up and lets break up this raft and be on our way."

Before leaving, Jack placed a call to Moses and Birdman in Briland, as he had each day since the salvage operation had begun, advising them of their progress and finding out any changes to the status of the 'Shillelagh'. They were overjoyed to find out that the flotilla was leaving momentarily so that they could finally get out of their hotel room and attempt to get rid of their cabin fever. Jack advised them of the plan and told them to stick it out for another 24 to 48 hours. They grumbled a little but acquiesced.

As the sun clawed its way out of the ocean to the east, Jesse's Riva was the first to exit the bay through the reef. At soon as they were in open water, the roar of supercharged engines announced their intention to make it to Nassau sooner rather than later. The boat soon disappeared from sight headed south. They were followed closely through the reef, in a more leisurely fashion, by 'Final Option' and 'Leprechaun', both of whom accelerated to around 30 knots. The Skater cat and the Cigarette Top Gun took up station behind the Cary and matched Jack's speed with ease, although every once in a while one of them would duck out of line for a high speed run around the formation. Jack smiled at this exuberance, knowing he had a bunch of good friends around him.

They cleared South East Point at around eight a.m. and set off for Davis Harbor and Cape Eleuthera, the sun bright, the sky cloudless and the waves less than a foot. In other words, thought Jack, a typical Bahamas day. Even at the leisurely pace of 30 knots they were eating up the distance to their destination at a great rate. Jack spotted Cape Eleuthera and had just changed course to cross Exuma Sound, when the throwaway phone the Senator had left with them started ringing insistently.

"Oh, God, not the Senator." Jack had been hoping not to hear from him at least until late afternoon. He picked up the phone and barked, "Jack!"

"So, Jack, where are you?"

"Preparing to dive on the sub, as we discussed yesterday."

"Now, Jack. I know you are lying to me. I am in my helicopter and flying over the bay at this moment, and I don't see your boat or your friends' boats anywhere in the bay. Really, Jack, I *am* disappointed, I thought we had an agreement." The Senator sounded equal parts miffed, pissed off, condescending and threatening all at the same time. But, as we all know, most politicians have those traits, especially the bent ones.

"Well, now, Senator. I reckon that makes us even now, since you lied to me. You see, I did some checking of my own, especially on your friends Smiley and Sanchez, and I found that while they still nominally work for the Treasury, they are so firmly in your pocket that dynamite couldn't shift them. Therefore it would seem logical that the agreement I signed last week is worth about as much as your word is, Senator, and that is exactly nothing."

The Senator sounded amused, "Well, Jack, it seems that you are more resourceful than I gave you credit for. However, the fact remains that I still want those documents."

"And what makes you think I would give them to you, even if I had them?"

"Oh, I know that you not only have the documents, but the gold as well. You see, Otto, our friend with the Mercedes, has been keeping a close eye on you from the cliff top and reporting your every move to me since you left my company. He has been telling me of your recoveries the past few days, and by my calculations, you should have recovered all the gold in that allotted time. He also told me about your early departure this morning, and the direction you were heading. It didn't take much effort to figure out that you were heading for Nassau, and if you look east, you will see that I have already found you."

Involuntarily, Jack glanced over his right shoulder, eastwards into the rising sun. Sure enough, there was the Senator's bright yellow Bell Jet Ranger helicopter heading toward them at a height of less than a hundred feet. At that moment, Jack's own cell phone started ringing and was quickly answered by Shannon, who mouthed Jesse to him before heading down the stairs to the aft deck. "I see you, Senator, but what difference does it make? There is no way you can stop me going where I want to with just that helicopter."

"Unfortunately, you are right, Jack. Which is why I have already called Horst and he is on his way here with the two Donzis. With their superior speed, they should catch you before you get to Nassau. All I have to do is keep you in sight, and I don't think that that will be too difficult at all, do you?"

"Senator, it has been most unpleasant speaking with you, don't bother calling again." With that remark, Jack hung up the phone and threw it into the glove box beside the helm.

Shannon, hearing Jack's final comment to the Senator, came back up the stairs, holding Jack's phone out to him. He took it from her, and said. "Jesse, change of plans. As soon as you are done refueling, leave Nassau and go straight to Chub Cay. Arrange slips for everyone except me, and stay there until I contact you. Have you got that?"

"Sure, Jack. What's happening?"

"The Senator is on to us, and I'm trying to think of a way to outfox him."

"Remember the hidey hole we found last year on Allen's Cay on our way back from Staniel Cay? Could you use that again?"

"Unfortunately not, because he is shadowing us in his helicopter. We can't hide from that and he is directing his two Donzis toward us. I don't even know how much time we have before they catch us. I'll call you back when we have a plan."

As he hung up the phone, Jack noticed with pleasure that they were approaching Ship Channel Cay, the entry into the Middle Ground and halfway from Eleuthera to Nassau. They passed between Bluff Cay and the Dog Rocks and entered Ship Channel without any sign of the Donzis behind them. Jack signaled line astern to the other boats. Once past Beacon Cay, with its light tower and ruined house, it was a clear shot straight to Nassau Harbor, and with the westing sun clearly showing the scattered coral heads, they made a safe passage in through the back door of the harbor.

As they cruised slowly down the center of Nassau Harbor and under the twin bridges leading to Paradise Island, Jack was surprised and pleased to see the Senator's helicopter, their constant companion for the trip across the Middle Ground, suddenly veer away and head for the Nassau International Airport. He realized that the chopper must be very low on fuel by now and quickly sent Sean out of the harbor to reconnoiter for the Donzis. The rest continued slowly down the fairway past the cruise ship docks until some ten minutes later when Sean sent the all clear, and all the boats sped out of the harbor and set a course for Chub Cay at their best possible speed. Jack hoped that they could get far enough away from Nassau before the Senator returned that he would have to waste precious time searching for them in Nassau, on the assumption that it was their destination for the night.

Thirty minutes after Jack's flotilla of boats had left Nassau Harbor, the two Donzis and the helicopter arrived simultaneously at the main entrance. The Senator immediately dispatched one of the Donzis to the eastern end of the harbor, the back door where Jack had entered earlier, while the second Donzi, with Horst in command, and the chopper searched the harbor from one end to the other, obviously without success. With dusk descending and with 'Shillelagh" being only twenty miles away, the Senator was forced to give up the search and fly the chopper to its landing pad on the boat for the night. The two Donzis were going to spend the night at Atlantis Marina, with the crews staying at the Atlantis Resort, definitely not a hardship by anyone's standards, although the crew knew from past experience that they had better lay off the sauce since this was not a pleasure cruise. Nobody wanted to get in the firing line of Horst or the Senator. Horst himself spent most of his time ashore on the phone, calling all the marinas in the area trying to locate 'Final Option'. He met with no success at all; the boat, for all intents and purposes, having disappeared off everyone's radar.

Horst picked up his cell phone and called the Senator. "I haven't been able to locate the boat anywhere within conceivable cruising range, but I do have a plan which has at least a chance of working."

"Do tell," the Senator asked drolly, rolling his eyes. "And this had better be good."

Horst flinched a little. "The two Donzis are going to spend the night here at Atlantis, while 'Shillelagh' goes around the top of the Berry Islands, past Great Stirrup and Great Isaac lights and then anchors off Bimini. You should be able to get there before dawn. We will bring the two

Donzis across The Flats in the morning and meet up with you at Bimini."

"That's all very well. But how does that help us catch Elliott and his crew?"

"Well, if he has gone the way you are going, we are not going to catch him anyway. He could cross the Gulf Stream to any of several ports on the east coast of Florida before we could find him. However, I don't think that's what he has done. I think he is hiding somewhere in the Berry Islands and intends to cross The Flats to Bimini in the morning. That would put you in front of him and me behind him. I think it's the only realistic shot we have of catching him."

"I don't like it much, but as you say, it seems to be our only play. Our Final Option, as it were."

"I'm sorry, sir, but did you just make a joke?"

"I didn't mean to, but yes, I guess I did. Never mind. Call me in the morning, we are leaving for Bimini right now. And make sure you and your men are wide awake and sober tomorrow."

As dawn broke the following morning, the crew of 'Final Option' were hauling the anchor up and preparing to get underway. As hypothesized by Horst, Jack had indeed gone to an anchorage in a bay just south of Little Whale Cay, which was known to only a few people, most of them locals. He had chosen not to join the others in Chub Cay Marina because it was only too easy to get information on his whereabouts from the ever helpful dockmasters scattered around the islands.

They cleared the white stone beacon at the entrance to the bay, leaving it to port to follow the channel outbound, and immediately afterward they turned first south and then west as their course led them past Whale Cay and Bird Cay on their way to just south of Chub Cay. A quick phone call to Sean ensured that the others would rendezvous with them out of sight of the harbor.

Once all together again, they came up to speed and headed for the North West Channel Beacon, where they entered The Flats, headed for Mackie Shoal Beacon and finally to North Bimini, coming out at North Rock. With the high, bright sunlight and flat calm water, they easily spotted and avoided the numerous coral heads along their route, and made good time to North Rock.

"Damn it all!!!" Jack yelled as they cleared the Rock, pointing south to where 'Shillelagh' was anchored just offshore of the island of Bimini. Jack hoped that they could slip by unnoticed, but of course five boats in line astern emerging from behind a prominent navigation landmark was difficult to miss.

Already the big boat was in the process of retrieving its anchor and getting underway. But just then a bigger surprise came with a radio call from Sean, who was bringing up the rear of the convoy. "Don't look now, but we've got company. The Senator's two Donzis are right behind us."

Someone shouted over the radio, "Tally Ho!!", and it was on for young and old.

The Senator's two Donzis, just clearing the Rock, suddenly found themselves surrounded by four roaring, snorting, fire-breathing powerboats who were larger, faster and infinitely more aggressive than they were. They broke away from each other and attempted an escape from the onslaught of so many aggravated crewmen, who were behaving like the berserkers of old Norse legends. What followed could only be described as an old fashioned dogfight of WW2, with boats charging in all directions and barely missing each other. For a time at least, it seemed that the smaller, but more maneuverable Donzis could match the larger, faster boats but, inevitably something had to give. It happened when one of the Donzis turned the wrong way and crossed the deep wake of Sean's 50 foot Cary. The hole left in the ocean by the 70 mile per hour passage of the Cary was just too deep and too steep at the particular angle of attack that the Donzi pilot had chosen. The boat went airborne, clipped the top of the wake, turned turtle and came crashing down nose first onto the other side of the deep, wide wake and stopped dead in the water. It was already sinking by the time the three crewmen, all of whom had been ejected from the boat before the sudden stop, came to the surface, dazed and spitting water.

The other Donzi, seeing the fate of its companion, made a beeline for the 'Shillelagh' and was almost there by the time the four larger vessels had assessed the situation. Sean conned his boat over to the men in the water, and allowed them to haul themselves onto the swim platform. He extracted from them the promise of no trouble, reinforced by the presence of a 12 gauge riot gun, in return for a trip back to their big boat.

Accompanied by the other three boats, Sean came within 50 yards of 'Shillelagh' before advising the men to swim for it. None of them seemed to be in any physical distress and Sean did not want to get any closer because of the potential of more trouble.

Jack, in the meantime, had hauled ass in 'Final Option', and was almost on the horizon when the four boats turned away from their adversary and hurried to catch up. They all turned their heads in dismay as they heard the jet engines of the helicopter start their banshee whine. A short while later, they cursed as the chopper passed overhead on its way to Jack's boat, while they were still only halfway there. Grinning like a hungry hyena, they saw Horst in the back seat preparing what looked like a hunting rifle. The fact that the starboard side door of the helicopter had been removed gave them a clear view of what he was doing. The Senator was seated in front beside the pilot. A tense radio call informed Jack of his predicament, but all they could do was watch as the chopper dove like an eagle toward its prey. Jack had his own worries, for the steadily increasing northeast wind had kicked up the waves here at the beginning edges of the Gulf Stream, and Jack had already been forced to slow down slightly, as the bow of the boat slammed into another wave and caused the bow to migrate skyward. All too soon, it would be too rough for the crossing, let alone the rendezvous with the Coast Guard cutter, 'Redoubt'.

Selecting the low power setting on the VHF radio, for he did not want to be overheard, the Senator called Jack, "Please stop now and allow Horst to board your boat. You know what I want, Jack, and I am determined to get it. Once I have it you can go on your merry way."

As Colonel Potter on M.A.S.H. was fond of saying, Jack simply replied, "Horse hockey."

Once more, Horst allowed his temper to get the better of him. Despite the pilot's protests, he ordered him to fly in front of Jack's boat, descend to wavetop level and turn sideways so he could get a good shot at Jack and the others gathered on the flybridge. Since the permanent Bimini top on Jack's boat was solid and the people on the flybridge were visible only through the clear plastic side and front panels, Horst had little choice but to shoot from a very low angle.

The Senator warned Jack over the radio, "Stop now, or we will fill your boat so full of holes it'll look like Swiss cheese."

The pilot complied reluctantly with Horst's orders and turned the right side of the helicopter, the one with the door removed, towards Jack's boat. Horst readied the rifle, one of his favorite weapons, and started droning to the pilot. "Steady, steady, down a little, steady, hold it still!"

For Jack, time seemed to stand still. One second he was scanning the horizon for any sign of the Coast Guard cutter, the next his vision was blocked by the bright yellow helicopter. His attention was drawn immediately to the large black square where Horst sat holding the largest rifle Jack had ever seen. The bore of the barrel down which Jack was looking seemed to be about a foot wide. "DOWN!!!!!" he yelled as he dove for the deck. Everyone followed his example.

Aiming carefully, Horst fired. Unfortunately for him, at that exact moment, Nature took a hand in the conflict as the boat dropped into the trough of a wave and the 450 grain bullet passed over the top of the Bimini top on the boat at supersonic speed, missing everything and spinning off into the water hundreds of yards behind the intended target.

Horst cursed out loud, operated the bolt on the rifle and steadied himself for another shot. His view was immediately blocked when the boat, moving at thirty knots, hit the face of the next wave and rose like a broaching whale directly toward the helicopter. The pilot, his view from the left hand seat partially obscured by the Senator's bulk, was a split second too late in reacting to the impending doom coming his way. His immediate reaction was to haul up on the collective with all his strength and twist the throttle open to its furthest extent, the second being to roll the aircraft away from the bow of the boat.

The first move worked perfectly, the second not so much. As the helicopter started to rise, the right hand skid of the helicopter was snagged by the bow rail of the boat and simply tore the rail right out of its mountings and jammed it in the helicopter's skid. This action, of course, caused a massive imbalance in the delicate envelope in which all helicopters operate, and it tipped suddenly to the right toward that part of the ocean's surface currently occupied by Jack's boat.

One of the rotor blades struck the forward part of the superstructure and immediately tore out of the rotor hub and went sailing off toward the horizon all on its own. A micro-second later, the other carbon-fiber rotor blade struck the side of the house and shattered into a million razor sharp fragments, smashing the side windows and fiberglass along the way. The rotor hub, suddenly relieved of the weight of both blades to push against, screamed its way into over-speed, still accelerated by the twin jet engines at full throttle. The body of the helicopter, having slammed once into the superstructure of the boat, turned turtle, ejecting Horst, the only one not wearing a seat belt, but still bearing its other hapless occupants, before hitting the concrete hard water five feet behind the boat with a tremendous eruption of parts and water. Leaving the scene of the crash at thirty knots, the boat suffered no more damage as the helicopter disintegrated just below the

268

surface, the twin jet engines literally tearing themselves to pieces due to the ingestion of incompressible salt water into their delicately machined compressor blades. The superheated blades fractured as the ocean water cooled them so rapidly that they lost structural integrity and inertia hurled them through the engine casing and through the aluminum skin of the helicopter. Anything in their way was simply sliced to small pieces upon their exit from the aircraft. Seconds later, the still turning tail rotor disappeared into the bright blue water and the ocean returned once again to its normal state, unseeing and unfeeling about the loss of life which had just occurred.

Up on the flybridge, everyone was sitting on the deck in a daze, unsure of exactly what had happened. Jack, standing up in time to see the tail of the helicopter disappearing into the ocean depths, was immediately on the VHF radio. "Mayday, mayday, mayday. This is 'Final Option' to any station. Mayday, mayday, mayday! Over."

"Final Option, this is the Coast Guard cutter 'Redoubt'. What is the nature of your emergency and your present location? Over."

"Redoubt, we are approximately 25 miles due east of your position and we have been damaged in a helicopter crash. Over."

"Are there any casualties? And are you in danger of sinking? Over."

Having asked and received shakes of the head from everyone, Jack replied, "No casualties on the boat, but I doubt if anyone in the chopper survived. It exploded on impact with the water. We do not, repeat, not appear to be taking on water and essential systems seem to be working. Over."

"Final Option. Please stay in the area and assist if you can. We have you and several other boats on radar and we are already on our way, and we will be there in less than one hour. Over."

Sean in the Cary, who had been listening to this radio exchange, arrived at the spot the helicopter went down. He and Katie had witnessed the tragic events from less than a quarter mile away, having almost caught up with Jack's boat. He thumbed the transmit button on his radio. "Redoubt, this is 'Leprechaun'. I am at the spot the chopper went down, and apart from a couple of seat cushions and some debris, there does not appear to be any survivors. Over."

"Leprechaun, please collect what debris you can and await our arrival. Over."

Having weighed anchor and immediately, under orders from Horst, set sail towards the west, 'Shillelagh' arrived at the scene thirty minutes later, under the command of the first mate. Over the radio, its crew were informed of the situation with their boss, captain and pilot and were told to stand by for the arrival of the Coast Guard cutter. With no more fight left in them, they complied.

Less than an hour later, the U.S. Coast Guard cutter 'Redoubt', all 170 feet of her, arrived at the crash site. After performing a perfunctory survey of the area, the efficient crew of the cutter quickly rafted 'Final Option' alongside on the lee side of the larger vessel in order to facilitate the transfer of the gold. Two figures crossed the gap between the vessels, a man and a uniformed woman, and Jack smiled with recognition at one of his new guests.

"Charlie, it's good to see you again after so long." he said, approaching the man with an outstretched hand, all the while taking in the slight figure of the woman accompanying him.

"Jack, it's good to see you again and I'm glad you made it. Allow me to introduce Commander Lisa Barron, Captain of the Redoubt."

Jack shook her hand and introduced all the crew members aboard.

Surveying the damage to 'Final Option', Charlie said, "Christ, Jack, what the hell happened to your boat? It looks like Godzilla attacked you with a giant can opener and took out his revenge on you."

"It's a long, long story."

Commander Barron interjected, "If you have as much gold aboard as we think you do, we will have lots of time to tell it. It will help me put the helicopter crash in perspective and I'd just like to hear the whole story, too."

"I don't suppose it matters a whole lot now, but I also have documentation about how American gold came to be on a Nazi submarine in the first place. And now I suggest a drink, a place to sit and I'll tell you all about it." All agreed, with the exception of the Commander, who said, "Still on duty, you know."

After three hours of labor, the sailors of the cutter had finally transferred the full load of gold onto their ship, much to the relief of Jack and his crew, who were just happy to be rid of the cause of all their troubles. The weather, having finally settled down somewhat, eased enough to allow the four other boats to proceed to their home ports with a promise to rendezvous later at the Downtowner Bar and Saloon, on the New River, next to the city jail. Only in Ft. Lauderdale would the city jail occupy a piece of prime real estate, right on the river. Go figure. A quick call to Max, a City of Ft. Lauderdale dockmaster, ensured that 'Final Option' had secured a berth on the south side of the New River, one slip down from the Downtowner, and for as long as necessary. Max was surprised to hear from Jack so soon after learning that Jack had given up his slip at Pier 66, to disappear into the vast, blue ocean, on his way to Europe. But as always, he was happy to help.

As they proceeded west up the river, they could see that some people in the houses and parks lining the banks would stop to admire this yacht coming in from the ocean, only to gape uncomprehendingly when they saw the damage to the starboard side. Normally the boats coming up this river, unlike the Miami River further south, were pristine and perfect, without a blemish. They cleared the Third Avenue Bridge just as dusk was falling, and made their way slowly toward the Downtowner. Bobby, the manager of the Downtowner, was standing at the seating area above the free floating dock the city had put in for the use of the many small runabouts that traveled the waterways of Ft. Lauderdale every day, but especially on weekends. He smiled broadly at the sight of Jack's familiar vessel coming to pay him another visit, and waved enthusiastically at Jack, up on the flybridge guiding the boat up the river. However, his jaw dropped to the floor when Jack executed a perfect 180 degree turn that brought the badly damaged side of the boat into view as he lined up for the dock. The fenders had already been placed for the height of the dock and, as Jack used the bow and stern thrusters to push the boat the last few feet into their assigned space, Shannon, Janine and Courtland stepped ashore with the lines and soon had the boat secured.

Bobby arrived just as they were finishing their tasks and preparing to attach the power cords and water lines to the boat. Courtland headed below to bring up the boarding ladder. Jack finished shutting down the electronics, the main engines and, lastly, the generator as the shore power came online.

Bobby waited until all the necessary tasks had been completed, and then asked, "What the hell happened out there, Jack?"

"Long, long story, my friend. I'll tell you over a drink or three, I'm parched."

After locking up the boat, Jack and Shannon, Courtland and Janine, and Bobby walked the couple of dozen yards to the Downtowner. They entered through the courtyard to the right of the building, savoring the familiarity of the establishment where they had so many good memories. Bobby turned on his charm and authority and actually cleared a space in the corner where Jack preferred to sit. David, the bartender that night, also known affectionately as Dickhead to his friends and those who could stand to hear his sometimes lame jokes for the third time, rushed over to take their orders, which was unusual since most times he preferred to, quote, pace you, unquote, even when it was your first drink of the day. "Skipper, what'll you have? Rum Runner. Dark and Stormy?"

"Yes, in that order." Jack replied, catching sight of a news report on one of the many large flat screen TVs in the place, "But first, turn up the sound on that TV."

Dickhead grabbed the remote and turned up the sound so all could hear the report. Normally, he would have ignored the news reports, but for some reason, he watched this one along with everyone else.

"This is Channel Seven with breaking news. We have just learned from a report issued by the Coast Guard that the Republican Senator from Massachusetts, Senator Shamus O'Malley, has been killed in a helicopter crash 25 miles from Bimini in the Bahamas. According to the report, the helicopter, normally sitting on the aft deck of the Senator's yacht, and which was carrying the Senator, the Captain of his yacht, and a pilot was traveling back to the States when it developed a mechanical problem and was forced to attempt an emergency landing at sea. Unfortunately, the helicopter became uncontrollable and hit a private yacht before crashing into the sea and exploding. There were no survivors from the helicopter, but fortunately there were no casualties on the yacht. Channel Seven News has obtained this exclusive footage (they cut to footage showing a bruised and battered 'Final Option' entering the fairway into Port Everglades) of the as yet unidentified private yacht involved in the incident returning to Port Everglades just before dusk this evening. You can clearly see the damage sustained by the yacht in its collision with the helicopter. It's reported that the occupants of the yacht called the Coast Guard and attempted to save the Senator and his fellow passengers. Unfortunately, they were unable to do so. Stay tuned for further developments in this story."

Jack turned to the group watching the news, "And that, Bobby, is what happened to my boat. I don't know about anyone else, but after that, I definitely need a drink."

One by one, the rest of the adventurers drifted into the Downtowner, Sean and Katie among the first to arrive. Noticeable by his absence was Capt'n Pete, who had been ferried over to the 'Shillelagh' by Sean, after learning that the first mate under Horst Keller was an inexperienced sailor who had never docked a boat of that size before. After assurances by the crew that no harm would come to those who helped, Capt'n Pete agreed to return to his former command and bring it and its crew safely back to Florida.

The food arrived, and as always, there was plenty of it and it was delicious. As the evening wore on, more drinks were poured and many toasts were made, and an intoxicated stupor enveloped the gathering. The whole group was well aware that, because of a special request made by Charlie, the subject of their salvage operation was not to be discussed in public, especially any mention of gold bullion. The bar slowly cleared of the Friday evening crowd, leaving only the original crew to close the establishment. Around midnight, Capt'n Pete arrived and, first thing, ordered a Jameson's, for he had brought 'Shillelagh' back to Pier 66, and she was safely in her slip. David, aka Dickhead, whose shift had ended hours before, stayed late to ensure that everyone had an enjoyable homecoming, despite the fact that they weren't Patriots fans. If he, or anyone else for that matter, had been able to see into the future, they would have known that this celebration was going to be the last for a long time to come. But for the moment, they remained blissfully unaware.

Around 3 a.m., a shadowy figure slowly emerged from the lazarette on the stern of 'Shillelagh'. He looked around surreptitiously and carefully made his way to the bridge deck, keeping to the shadows on the outside of the boat away from the pier. After checking for any night watch which might have been present, he used his own key to let himself into the bridge, and then into the captain's cabin directly behind the bridge. He quickly gathered all his belongings, emptied the ship's safe of its contents, including an unregistered and unidentifiable Glock 9 mm automatic, and left it unlocked but closed, and then retraced his steps back to the aft deck. He waited a long time back there in the shadows, watching the routine of the private guards and timing their movements, until just before dawn. With a few early risers on other boats to give him cover, he left the boat and made his way through the lush landscaping, climbed the steep embankment up to the roadway, walked at a comfortable pace across the 17th Street Causeway bridge...and, whistling quietly to himself, the big man disappeared.

Epilogue

It has been three months now since the destruction of the Senator's helicopter ended the threat to the crew of 'Final Option'. The boat has been repaired to our immense satisfaction by the talented craftsmen at Bradford Marine on the New River and we have moved back aboard this morning. It was an emotional homecoming, since I had endured this period of time living in a house. Just so there aren't any misunderstandings, this house was not substandard by any stretch of the imagination, but in my opinion, any house, no matter how comfortable or expensive, is simply a boat so firmly aground that no-one in their right mind would ever think of moving it. I could not imagine myself ever wanting to own or live in one again unless I had no other choice. The idea of not being able to move away from noisy neighbors, waking up each and every morning to the same view and being unable to escape the hustle and bustle of the city when it suits me seems to me to be immensely less than desirable.

The gold which we recovered was returned to the Treasury, transported to Fort Knox under armed guard, and Charlie made good on his promise, actually getting us a fifteen percent salvage fee, plus they also paid for the time and use of the boat, including paying for the cost of repairing the boat to my satisfaction. The government seemed quite happy to receive their gold back, hence their generosity. Of course, it is not every day that a private citizen returns over two hundred and twenty million dollars to the government. Everyone who assisted us in any way shared in what turned out to be a sizable bonanza. The original story of the Senator's demise held up quite well under scrutiny, and the official account of the recovery of the gold was separated from the Senator's story, since none of the opposition's participants were around to tell their side of the story. Having been left behind on Harbor Island, Otto disavowed any knowledge of the plan to kidnap Shannon, and was allowed to return to his pineapple plantation. Due to lack of evidence, the crew of 'Shillelagh' were released but fired from their jobs. Smiley and Sanchez were fired from the Treasury Department and told that if they contradicted the Government's story, they would be prosecuted.

Capt'n Pete, of course, had returned from Bimini with the 'Shillelagh' in fine shape, despite the loss of one of their boats and their helicopter, and docked it on the outer pier at Pier 66. Last I heard, he was living aboard her and negotiating the purchase of the yacht from the Senator's estate and operating it as a charter yacht, with a new crew, of course. Shannon and I will miss him being on our boat, of course, since he had become such a fixture. Even though we will continue our journeys without him, we wish him well in his future endeavors.

The only jarring note to come out of all this is the still unexplained robbery on 'Shillelagh' the night she returned from Bimini. Some surmised that Horst Keller had somehow survived the helicopter crash and, in the confusion afterward, managed to swim over unseen and slip onto 'Shillelagh' and secrete himself away on board until the boat got to Pier 66. According to the police report, all his personal belongings were missing, as well as an alleged amount of $200,000 out of the ship's safe, which was the Senator's emergency money. The strangest thing was that there had been no break in, either to the boat or to the safe. An investigation was conducted, but no sign of Horst or the money has ever been found. The only thing that raises some suspicion in my mind is a report of a stolen 38 foot Cigarette in Palm Beach the next night. It still remains missing to this day.

Courtland and Janine recently announced their engagement, which came as no surprise to anyone who had seen them together. With their share of the salvage fee, neither will have to work for a living ever again, unless they choose to, which is a great feeling to have. Courtland went home, quit his position with his law firm, sold his house and moved with all his possessions to be with Janine in South Florida. I heard that they are planning an outdoor January wedding, taking advantage of the slightly cooler Florida weather at that time of the year.

Sean and Katie went back to their old jobs, but with considerably less enthusiasm than before. When their share of the salvage fee arrived, they both quit their jobs and became people of leisure. Sean retained ownership of his watering hole but put a competent manager in charge so he could spend more time with Katie. In fact, they seemed to have become inseparable. Everywhere Sean went, Katie was there, too. And lately I have noticed a very large rock on Katie's left hand ring finger. This was pointed out to me, not in the least way subtly, by Shannon, who kept glancing at her own ringless finger. We expect an announcement of their engagement sooner rather than later.

Sean's boating buddies, who came over and helped us out with their enthusiasm and hard work, were quite content to return to their preferred way of life, but all of them turned up with newer, bigger and faster boats once the rewards were distributed.

Birdman and Moses had formed the unlikeliest of friendships during their time together in the room at Valentine's. They basically had nothing in common, but enthusiastically learned from one another. After a quick stopover in Nassau to pick up a passport for Moses, they had flown the chopper over to Birdman's home base at Executive Airport in Ft. Lauderdale, and started hanging out at the local bars and restaurants. Their shares of the reward money ensured an enjoyable life for them both. Janine, of course, was overjoyed to have her father so close, and invited him to everything the whole group was doing, which he always gratefully accepted.

I have never learned of the government's position or course of action on the sub's documents that I handed over to Charlie, after making two copies, one for me and one for Capt'n Pete. Perhaps they have decided to let an embarrassing situation lie, without further action, or maybe they will, for some reason, bring it up in the future. Perhaps it's better not to know. I don't know what Capt'n Pete has done with his copy, but I do know where my copy is. It rests in the strongest safe deposit box I could find in South Florida, along with the journal and jewels we salvaged from behind the golden throne. The throne itself and the fifteen bars of Nazi gold still rest in the cavern waiting to see the light of day. Someday, we will have to decide what we are going to do about that. But not today.

As for Shannon and I, we are planning a trip to the Caribbean on our newly refurbished boat, just as soon as all our friends are married off. They are welcome to come, of course, but I expect we will be on own. And who knows, maybe Shannon's finger won't be ringless for much longer.

If you enjoyed this first novel in the trilogy, and I sincerely hope you did, below is a selection from the second book in the series.

Enjoy.

DOUBLE TROUBLE

{Book 2 of the Final Option Trilogy}

A
CARIBBEAN
MURDER/MYSTERY

Present Day

It was the smell that finally woke him. On impulse, he opened his eyes and was met by a blinding, stabbing pain that caused him to close them again immediately. He lay still for a long while in the not-quite darkness of his closed eyelids before tentatively easing just one open to a slit. The pain was not quite as bad this time but it was augmented by the little elves with the big sledgehammers making small rocks out of big rocks in his brain. With that one eye open just a smidgeon he was able to see the cause of the smell which had awoken him. He was lying in a puddle of vomit. It was his own, he presumed, if for no other reason than the chorus of anvils going off in his head.

'Oh, no,' he thought. *'Not again.'* Presumably, he had tried once again, unsuccessfully, to drink someone under the table the previous night as he had tried in Key West, only to be suffering similar consequences this morning.

He rolled over to his right, away from the source of the smell, but his stomach rebelled. The final remnants remaining in his stomach of what must have been his last meal were forcibly ejected from his body to form another puddle in the sand.

'God, I hope it tasted better going down than it did coming up.'

He slowly struggled into an upright seated position, trying to ignore the merry-go-round racing through his skull. He managed to pull his feet closer to his butt, rested his forearms on his knees and gratefully lowered his throbbing head onto the back of his arms. He sat like that for a long time, eyes closed, rocking gently, letting the salt-tinted ocean breeze try its best to sober him up. When he finally sensed some semblance of equilibrium, he lifted his head and cautiously opened his eyes.

He was seated on a small crescent of beach a few yards above the high water mark, between two puddles of what used to be the contents of his stomach. He slid, on his butt, a couple of yards toward the water to try to escape the smell of his own making. He noticed for the first time that the smell was not receding because it was plastered all over the front of his once-white T-shirt. With some difficulty, he managed to pull the T-shirt over his pounding head and then he threw it forcefully toward the water.

He felt better. Well enough, in fact, to try to regain his feet. It proved to be a struggle, but when he finally managed to straighten out, he turned a full circle trying to ascertain his whereabouts. Apart from the ocean, he seemed to be completely encircled by house-sized granite boulders that appeared to be tumbling down upon the narrow strip of sand, even into the water at each end of the beach.

'The Baths,' he thought. *'On Virgin Gorda. This must be the beach at Devil's Bay. Now, how the hell did I get here?'*

Slowly, for he did not wish to disturb the tranquil waters within his brain that might start swirling again with the slightest provocation, he looked down at himself. He saw a fairly muscular upper body with a flat stomach, a pair of tan six pocket boating shorts, no belt and no shoes. The latter didn't bother him much since he had spent years of his life walking around barefoot.

'Now how did I know that?' he thought.

Inside the waistband of the shorts, he felt underwear, slightly damp with seawater, as the salty taste on his fingertips told him. His pockets were also a little damp, as was the side of the shorts upon which he had been lying. There was, unfortunately, no wallet, no ID, no credit cards, no folding money, and not even any change.

He suddenly heard distant voices growing steadily louder, so he turned slowly and spied in the shallow water his discarded T-shirt. Feeling semi-dressed, despite the fact that he was on a beach, he was determined to reclaim his only other piece of clothing.

With infinite care and holding his head with both hands to stop it from jostling, he made his way to the waterline. He waded the few feet into the water to the sodden scrap of material, and gingerly, keeping his back straight and bending his knees, picked it up.

He was gratified to discover that the immersion into the salt water had washed most of the vomit off the front of the T-shirt. He also noticed the outline of a motor yacht printed in the upper left corner of the material right above the words 'Final Option'.

'Now why does that seem familiar?' he wondered.

Turning slowly, he walked back up the beach, feeling a little steadier now. He sought out, and found, a small shaded spot amongst the jumbled boulders. Placing his T-shirt on a piece of sunlit rock to dry, he lay down on the beach to finish the recuperation process.

As the voices were quite loud now, children's as well as adult's voices, he silently wished for a magic knob to turn down the ever increasing volume. His hands involuntarily covered his ears, and his eyes screwed shut as the shrieks from half a dozen young children discovered the beach that the boulders had, until now, hidden from view.

He curled himself into a fetal position and, hidden from the thirty or so people on the beach behind his granite boulder, tried to shake off the hangover he was fighting. Surprisingly, he fell into a deep sleep quite quickly, since the water in which the children were now playing was muffling the noise of their exuberance.

He awoke in the middle of the afternoon, opening his eyes to a tiny, blond girl who was squatting in the sand not two feet from his face, her right arm extended and one finger poking him on the nose. She was staring at him intently. Such a suddenly unexpected sight caused him to move his head backward and as he did, he cracked it on the rock behind him. He saw stars and, once again, the elves with their big sledgehammers inside his head started up their pounding.

"Are you OK, Mister?" the little imp wanted to know. "I didn't mean to startle you."

"Yes, sweetie, I'm OK. I just didn't know you were there." He reached his hand to the back of his head, and felt a sizable knot had formed there, far out of proportion to the slight blow he had just taken.

"AMY!!" The anxious call of a searching father came from behind the boulder.

"I'm here, Daddy." the little blond called back.

The man who hurried around the boulder was in his mid-to-late twenties, tall and obviously very fit. He snatched up the child with one arm and demanded, "What are you doing with my little girl?"

"Nothing, sir. I've been asleep right here since before all of you arrived. Your little girl came up to me while I was asleep."

"*Really?*"

"Daddy, I saw him from the water and he wasn't moving. I just wanted to make sure he was OK. Please put me down, you're hurting me." The little girl was squirming in his arms.

The father looked as if he wanted to kill, but he released his daughter, who muttered, "Sorry, Mister, I'm glad you're OK," before scurrying off back down to the water.

"*Are* you OK?" The father wanted to know.

"Sure, just bumped my head when your daughter startled me. I'll be all right."

The father turned and followed his daughter after the warning, "Just stay the hell away from us!"

A short while later, he collected his now dry T-shirt and put it on. He made his way out onto the beach and found the trail leading to the intricate passages and grottos in amongst the huge granite boulders, stacked one upon another, which made up the National Park known as The Baths. Squeezing his way through the small triangular openings between boulders, he slid down a slippery sand-covered slope barely aided by a rope set on pitons in the side of the rock. He waded through the knee deep pools of seawater between forty foot boulders, and agonizingly traversed the narrow uphill climb, and he finally made it to the restaurant at the top of the hill. This was where the buses from the pier dropped off the tourists who had come across the Sir Francis Drake Passage on the ferry from the cruise ships berthed in Roadtown, Tortola.

'Now what,' he thought. *'No money or ID, how am I going to get to Roadtown?'*

Just then, he heard a shout behind him. "Hello, wait up."

He turned and saw hurrying toward him the father from the beach, a beautiful woman whom he assumed to be the man's wife, and between them, holding their hands, was the little imp, resplendent in her bright patterned sundress.

"I'm glad I caught you," the man said. "I just wanted to apologize to you for earlier on. I came on way too strong, and I'm sorry to have given you any grief. I am just so worried these days about my little girl."

He extended his hand, "I'm Bill, this is my wife, Caroline, and you know Amy."

"Bill, Caroline, and Amy. Pleased to meet you under better circumstances. I'm Jack." He didn't know where the name had come from and he hoped that it was correct. It just seemed to him that it was the way he had always introduced himself. He extended his hand to Bill and Caroline, and then Amy tore herself loose from her mother's grip and solemnly shook his hand, too.

"Hello, Mister Jack," she said. "I'm glad to see you feeling better. Where are your shoes?"

In that charming way that children have, changing subjects in the middle of a single statement, Amy had put her finger directly on the problem facing Jack in his immediate future. He put on his brightest smile, and knelt down to her level.

"Hi again, Amy. Well, you see, I don't know where my shoes are, or my wallet," he glanced quickly in Bill's direction. "I think someone must have taken them while I was asleep."

"It wasn't me!" she cried, a little fear in her eyes.

"Of course it wasn't. It happened long before you came to the beach, and besides, take a look at how much bigger my feet are than yours. You could never fit in those shoes. You would look like one of those circus clowns with the big floppy shoes if you tried to wear them." Jack was pleased to see the fear disappear right out of her eyes, to be replaced a split second later by a huge grin as her imagination supplied her with the image of herself in clown shoes.

"Your wallet is gone?" Bill seemed concerned. "I've heard that sometimes things have a tendency to disappear from places where tourists go, wallets, money, even cameras and cell phones, but shoes? That's a new one."

"I'm not really concerned about the wallet or the money in it, but my ID and credit cards and my ferry ticket were in it, and now I have no way to get back to Roadtown. Unless I get lucky and can hitch a ride with someone going back for free." Jack feigned helplessness.

"Don't worry about it. Just hang around with us; you can be Amy's Uncle Jack. They don't check the tickets that closely on the way back, but if they do catch you, just explain the situation to them. What can they do? Put you off at the next port of call?" Bill smiled hugely at his own witticism, turned to Caroline for approval, which was granted by a nod of the head, and finished with, "but if necessary I'll buy you a ticket."

"Thank you. I mean that sincerely. I haven't been thinking too clearly all day." Jack was being totally honest, and was quite surprised by the man's generosity toward a stranger, especially considering that a few hours before he had almost accused Jack of child molestation. Jack suspected that the reversal had something to do with Caroline, who did not seem surprised or put off by Jack's easy going manner with Amy.

It was only a short ten minute wait for the bus which would take them to the ferry terminal. The time was spent pleasantly with Jack quizzing Amy about her vacation and her schoolwork.

Together they boarded the bus as a family group and it was only when they were on their way that Bill asked, "So, Jack, are you going back to your boat?"

Caught off guard, Jack stammered, "Yes. Yes, of course. How did you know?"

"Your T-shirt, 'Final Option'. We saw her at the marina in Roadtown when our cruise ship docked. You know, she is a really beautiful boat, even Caroline commented on that, and she is not into boats as much as I am. Someday I hope to have a boat like that to live on, but I don't think I could ever afford one that size. What is she, around seventy feet?"

"Yes."

"What brand?"

"Neptunus." Once more the answer sprang to his lips before he had a chance to think about it.

"I don't suppose there is a chance of taking a look at her when we dock?" Bill asked hopefully. Caroline and Amy had been listening to the conversation and both looked on with anticipation.

Jack, always the impulsive type, jumped in with both feet. "Sure, as soon as we dock, we can walk over and take a look. Sure hope I left it in decent shape; I wouldn't want to disappoint you."

The trip from Virgin Gorda to Roadtown took about forty five minutes and before they knew it, the ferry was sliding into the dock next to the huge cruise ship that was Bill's, Caroline's and Amy's temporary home and transportation. Full of anticipation, Jack's three guests followed him past the cruise ship to the marina on the opposite side of the harbor. Jack made a show of walking up to the locked security gate, and rattling it.

"Something must be up," he said. "This gate is usually open. Obviously, since my wallet is gone, I don't have my swipe card anymore, so I'll have to walk to the office to get a new one. Why don't you guys wait here on the bench and I'll be back shortly. OK, Amy?"

"OK, Uncle Jack."

It took Jack only two minutes to get to the dockmaster's office and as he walked in, he was greeted with, "Good afternoon, Mr. Elliott, how can I help you today?"

Jack took a chance. "Unfortunately, I was mugged today and all my ID, credit cards, and money were taken, including the swipe card for the gate. Can I get a new one?"

"Of course, sir. It'll just take a second." With that he grabbed a blank card from the drawer, swiped it through the register and with a flourish, handed it to Jack. "Anything else I can do for you?"

"I've forgotten. Did I leave a spare key to my boat here in the office?"

"Yes, you must have, since it's a requirement. We might have to get into your boat while you are gone, in case of fire or sinking, you know what I mean? Or in a situation like this, since I presume they stole your keys, too, right?"

"Yes, exactly for a situation like this."

"OK, let's see. Jack Elliott, 'Final Option', that's Slip A44, aha, there you go, sir, your key and alarm fob. Anything else I can help you with?"

"No, I think you've done enough for now, and I thank you."

As he exited the building, Jack did not notice the dockmaster pick up the phone and dial a local number. A few seconds later, he said, "He's here."

Jack retraced his steps to the locked gate where his new-found friends waited for him. He waved the new swipe card as he approached and they joined him at the gate as Jack swiped them all inside. Jack walked confidently up to 'A' dock and led them to Slip 44. He could see their anticipation building the closer they got to the big yacht.

As he walked past the yacht toward the boarding ladder, all the details of the boat came flooding back. He knew the boat intimately, all the cabins, what was in the galley, and where every instrument and light switch was located. He led them onto the boat, back to the aft deck, disabled the alarm system, which appeared to already be disengaged, and opened the aft main salon door.

As they entered, he switched on the lights and the beauty and simplicity of the salon shone brightly. Jack remembered the time and effort that had gone into the new design of this cabin and was justifiably proud of it, and from the dropped jaws and instant smiles on the faces of his guests, he felt that he had hit the ball out of the park. The three of them walked around, touching and admiring; even Amy seemed overwhelmed.

Jack spent almost an hour with his new friends showing them the wonders of his floating home, finishing the tour with drinks for the adults and apple juice for Amy. Sooner than anyone wished, it was time for them to rejoin their cruise ship for their journey home. Bill handed Jack his business card before he left, which had a Wellington, Palm Beach address and phone number on it, and asked him to come see them when Jack returned to the States. Jack promised that he would.

Looking forward to a hot shower and a change of clothes, Jack waved to his guests as they proceeded down the dock toward the shore. Just before they reached the end, they stepped aside to allow a well-dressed gentleman to pass. Jack was about to turn away, but something about the man made him stay and watch as he walked determinately toward him. The man was tall, easily as tall as Jack, but rail thin and pasty white. His suit was immaculate, but the bow tie was somewhat incongruous. It was the look of utter seriousness on his face that made Jack wait as he approached.

"Mr. Jack Elliott?" The accent was pure English, straight out of Downton Abbey.

"That is correct."

"Please allow me to introduce myself. I am Chief Inspector Ian Cavendish of the British Virgin Islands Police Force. If I may have a moment of your time, I wish to speak to you on a matter of some urgency."

"Can this wait till I have had a shower and changed into something more comfortable? As you can see, I am somewhat filthy at the moment."

The man considered this for a few seconds, then said, "As long as I can wait comfortably inside, I don't see where that would be a problem."

"Then, welcome aboard. Make yourself at home in the salon. Help yourself to a drink, if you wish. I won't be but a few minutes."

Jack went below into the main cabin, quickly undressed and showered and changed into tan Chinos and a light blue, short sleeved shirt and slipped into a pair of well worn boat shoes. He felt a whole lot better, but wondered what the Chief Inspector would want with him.

As he climbed the stairs, Jack called out, "OK, sir, I am now clean and at your disposal. How can I help you?"

The Chief Inspector actually smiled as Jack entered the salon. "Have a seat, Mr. Elliott. We have a matter to discuss."

Jack sat in a chair across from the sofa upon which the Chief Inspector had seated himself.

"First, can you tell me where you took this boat last night when you left the marina around ten thirty, and when did you return?"

Jack was stunned. He had no idea that the boat had been out the previous night. "I don't know, Inspector, I don't remember anything about last night. All I can remember is that this morning, I woke up with a terrible hangover on the beach at Devil's Bay on Virgin Gorda, and it has taken me all day to get back here."

"Chief Inspector, if you please. Can you tell me where your wallet and ID are?"

"I have no idea. All I know is that they are missing, along with my shoes. I have to assume that sometime last night I was mugged."

"And you have no idea where or by whom?"

"No. I have no recollection of anything that happened last night. I must have been so drunk that I passed out."

"Is there anyone who can verify that you were on Virgin Gorda this morning?"

"Yes, the couple and their child who passed you when you were on the dock were the ones who found me on the beach and helped me back here to the boat."

"Do you have their names and address?"

"Sure, that is his business card there on the table. After I finished showing them my boat, he asked me to come see them when I get back to the States."

"And where are they staying here in Tortola?"

"They are not. They are on that cruise ship just leaving now." Jack pointed out the salon window.

"Well, that *is* regrettable. It means that I will have to do what I came to do originally, at least until we can establish an alibi for you."

"Alibi? Why would I need an alibi. What did you come here to do?"

"Mr. Elliott, I have come here to arrest you for murder. You have the right to remain silent......"

"Murder? You have got to be kidding me! Who am I supposed to have murdered?"

"Why, your fiancée, Shannon O'Loughlin, Mr. Elliott. Your wallet was found right under her strangled body this morning."

51247232R00165

Made in the USA
San Bernardino, CA
17 July 2017